THE HONEYMOON

By dhtreichler

Dedication:

To everyone who has experienced fear in their lives
and risen above it.

Published by Reelization Global Media

CHAPTER ONE:

ANNIE THOMPSON

The pictures of Lake Victoria, from the Kisumu Safari Camp in Kenya, do not do it justice. I hold Charles, my husband of four days, as we gaze out on the massive lake. Ribbons of red and gold filling the sky from the sun setting on the distant shore. Images of the incredible animals we saw these last two days parade through my memory. Seeing them in a zoo and seeing them here… where they were meant to live, has changed my thoughts about captivity. Animals deserve to be free… to be able to roam and find their own way in the world.

I squeeze Charles a little tighter, still not believing we are finally married, and that we are here in this magnificent place… together. So many things seemed to make both the marriage and this trip impossible… and yet… here we are.

"The herds we will see in the Serengeti will just dwarf what we've seen so far…" Charles leans down to kiss the top of my head, but I am not content with that. I take his face in my right hand and pull him down to give me a proper kiss that I can share with him and not just receive.

"I don't know when you found the time…" I start to respond, but he cuts me off.

"This is likely the most time we will have together until I finish my residency, so there was no way I wasn't going to see everything there is to see." Charles smiles that sheepish smile, the one where the dimple stands out, that I have seen before when he is not telling me the whole truth. "Besides, Jill, my father's assistant, kind of pulled it all together for me."

"The truth, the whole truth and nothing but the truth…" I poke him in the side, glad he did not try to mislead me about how much effort he made. We talked a lot about how important it was for us to be completely honest with each other, given the baggage we both brought to this relationship. At least we are off to a good start. And the red sky this evening should mean no rain overnight. That is a good omen for the long trek, starting at daylight, to Tanzania and our new camp. I cannot wait for our first day in the game preserve of the Serengeti. That is why we decided to come here in the first place. The big herds. Thousands of the animals we only see in the zoo and in internet photos and films. Taking pictures from the ground and as we fly over in a helicopter.

The sun finally sinks below the horizon. The sky begins to darken. I have been just amazed at how dark the night is here. How many stars fill the sky when I look up. I have never been anywhere that I could see so many stars. Even the star belt of the Milky Way. All the images from somewhere else that informed my childhood are here, before me, with the man I have chosen to spend the rest of my life with. I still cannot believe he also chose me.

"We going to keep up our perfect record, or do you need to rest tonight?" Charles asks with that sparkle in his eye he has displayed every day, about this time, since the wedding back in Richmond. We both know that record will come to a screeching end when he has to go back into the hospital. But four days in a row, with multiple orgasms, has taken a toll on me.

"How about we ease into it tonight?" I suggest. Maybe a good glass of Pinotage will help me get into the right frame of mind. As if we had not already had a bottle with dinner. I did not know much about South African wines before coming here, but I am beginning to like them.

"Stud service at your beck and call…" Charles grins as we turn to enter our tent. But this is no typical tent. It is on a permanent foundation with hot and cold running water, a heater for the colder nights, and a nook where we eat breakfast every morning. Although M'bane, our guide, told us at dinner that we would not be eating here in the morning. They have a box breakfast for us on our transit Range Rover. We can eat when we get hungry along the way. Thoughtful, since we are getting up in the middle of the night to leave. I am still not used to this time zone. Seven hours earlier than Rochester, Minnesota, where Charles is completing his residency at the Mayo Clinic in Neurosurgery. And even though we are married now, I'm not leaving Washington DC until he sets up his practice, hopefully somewhere a whole lot warmer. But not quite as warm as Kenya.

Charles pulls the tent flap closed behind us. He turns to look at me. I can feel his eyes. I engage him with my Mona Lisa smile… if you can figure out what I am thinking, you get the prize. Apparently, concluding as to what that smile is telling him, he goes to the bar and pours two glasses of red wine. He brings them to me. We clink glasses one more time, "To the perfect marriage. You and me. Your family and mine."

I know where he is going and have to protest, "You know I don't harbor any of those ambitions. We want to appear to have a quiet family life. Anonymous."

"You'll never be anonymous now that you're married to what will soon be the preeminent neurosurgeon in the world," he laughs.

"Who I'll never see as you cater to the rich and famous… or the poor and downtrodden," we've had his conversation before, too.

He takes a sip to formulate his response. I have seen him puzzling over something since yesterday. An embryonic thought, which I expect will not arrive fully formed. "Doctors without borders…"

"You have to prepare yourself that they don't do neurosurgery… There may be one hospital in this whole country that could support what you do." I point out.

"But together we could do so much good…" Charles is still evolving his thinking.

"Do you really think you could just immunize, set broken bones, and try to avoid one or another bad bug? I'm the one promoting we should do something more than just make money. But maybe you could give back by perfecting new techniques that can be used throughout the world, and I can do the pro-bono legal work that will let us both feel better about our lot in life."

"Not the same… but maybe you're right. Maybe it shouldn't be only about what I do, but what we do together. Now that we are together… for the rest of our lives…"

"I hope it is the rest of our lives… don't think I could go through all this again." I let him know how tough it was for me to get here.

"I certainly don't want to… you're perfect, we're perfect… what more could either of us want?"

"More of your time and attention, when we get back from this alternate reality…" I lay out there for him because we have had this discussion before as well. Another sip of the wine and I start to undress him. He does the same for me. We crawl up into the big king size brass bed with a mosquito net all about.

"This will work, because we both want it to…" Charles tells me as he snuggles up next to me.

I do not know how long we have been asleep. Not long is my impression. I hear a vehicle drive into the camp. It wakes me. The motor shuts off and I hear doors close. "Charles…" I poke him, "I think the transport just arrived."

Charles opens his eyes, but it is clear he is still sleep.

"Charles… we need to get dressed…" I pull the covers back and step out into the slippers we have to wear here as we never know what might have crawled in during the night. Charles does not react, so I lean over the bed and poke him again, which seems to be the only thing that works.

"What?" he starts to rouse as I hear someone pulling back the flap to our tent. No one has done that the whole time we have been here. In the dark I count four shapes enter the tent and come right up to me.

"We're not ready yet…" I protest as something comes down over my head. Rough hands begin to pull me away from the bed. "Let me go!"

"What's going on here?" Charles must be getting the same treatment. "Where's M'bane?"

"M'bane… not here… you come." I hear the voice, but do not recognize it. British accent, but not British. Someone who attended a British school, but speaks a different language.

A hushed discussion in a language I do not recognize. Two or three voices and they stop talking, start moving me towards the flap to the tent. "Where is Charles?"

"I'm here," he responds. He is very close, but behind me.

"Who are you?" I demand to know. "If you're taking us to Mwanza Camp, let us get dressed."

Through the bag over my head, a hand covers my mouth. Rough hands hold me tighter, pull my hands behind my back. I feel something tying my wrists together. I am being pushed hard thought the tent entrance and stumble as we descend the three steps down to the ground. I hear Charles stumble as well. A muffled attempt to shout. They must have a hand over his mouth as well.

We cross a short distance. They stop us. I am pushed onto my back into what must be a vehicle of some kind. Not a Range Rover as we have been touring in and are supposed to go to Mwanza.

CHAPTER TWO:
ANGELICA MYERS

As I work in our home office, I hear a tone that indicates Mom has sent me a text. I glance at the phone and see her note, <Where is Annie today?>

I have to think for a moment. I call to Howard, my tall patrician looking husband. Silver just beginning to creep into the sides of his hair, that make him seem even more distinguished. “Where are the kids today?”

Howard is working in the kitchen, since I took the office on this Saturday afternoon. He does not respond, but in a moment, I hear him walking towards me. When he gets to the office door he leans against the jamb and looks at me as if he is trying to remember something. “Day seven, isn’t it?”

Now I am the one who has to think. “Yes… they left on Sunday. Nairobi on Tuesday. The first camp Wednesday and Thursday, down to the Tanzania camp yesterday, so they must be in the Serengeti today.”

“Would explain why we’ve seen no pictures since they left Nairobi.” Howard muses.

“They have other things on their mind than sharing pictures…” I suggest the obvious.

Howard rolls his eyes at me, like he always does when I say something that is not worth mentioning.

But then the note from Mom nags at me, just the way she always nagged at me when I was growing up. “Wild animals can be unpredictable…” I point out.

"She's with a doctor…" Howard dismisses the concern I am revealing in my comment.

"A resident… he's not a real doc just yet… and not likely he's going to have to deal with a head injury."

"Unless a lion were to bite her head off like you bite mine off, from time to time." Howard needles me, even though I do not bite his head off. Maybe I am a little sharp once in a while…

"Touché…" he clearly got me and is reminding me to relax… I cannot fix the world by myself and I need to stop thinking I can.

Howard must see that I am not finished with this discussion. He comes in and sits down across the oak desk from me. His favorite chair when he is not sitting on this side. "What's really bothering you?"

We simply should have said no…" I let it out.

"She's an adult, even though you wish that were not true…" Howard reminds me. "Harvard undergrad. Harvard Law. Supreme Court clerk for two years and likely two more, until Charles finishes up at the Mayo. She's not a lightweight."

"She's still my daughter…" I remind him

"Yes, mama bear…" Howard gives me that ironic smile. He loves to use that on me.

"What's wrong with me being worried?" Now I am revealing more than I want to.

"Nothing… but you worry about so many things…" Howard begins.

"That's my job… to worry about all those things," I shut that down immediately. Not going to have the discussion again.

"She's going to be thirty in two years. What were you doing when you were thirty?" Howard reminds me that I was long gone from my family at Annie's age.

"Annie was coming up on her first birthday." I recall with a nostalgic smile.

"So… give her some space. I know your mother didn't. You bitterly complained about how she smothered you and Annie to the point you had to tell her to stop coming to visit so often."

"And as I got busier with my career, I had to go back and ask her to be more involved with Annie because I didn't have the time." I admit, but Howard knows all this having lived it with me.

"My first term as a state representative… I couldn't stay home with her, even though I wanted to. And if I had…, where would we be?" Howard has regrets, but would not change a thing. Of that I am certain.

"It all worked out," I decide I need to get back to the recommendations I am reviewing before a full-blown discussion of it on Monday. I am not a hundred percent on board yet, but need to know what I do not know to either say no or move it forward. "As you said… she's not a lightweight."

"But she is fragile…" Howard reminds me. I shake my head not wanting to think about her periodic rebellions and the ensuing shouting matches and finger pointing and declarations that our careers are more important than she is. I can see how she would feel that way, although we both did our best to be there for the important things in her life… just not the everyday things.

"Did you know she's taking a self-defense class the court offers for its employees?" I try to give Howard a little comfort around his feelings of guilt.

"Do the justices take it too?" Howard is not serious in this question.

"Actually, they do, when they first join the bench." I let him know our daughter is rubbing shoulders with the new justices as well as the one she is assigned to. Sometimes the informal relationships end up being more important than the formal supervisory relationships. I have seen that in my own career. Someone who does not have to deal with you all day, sees what you bring to a job and will stand up for you when an opportunity appears. Sometimes even when your supervisor will not, because she or he does not want to lose you from their team. That is how I got where I am.

"Think she will give me lessons when she gets home?" Howard is not serious.

"I am sure she could give us both lessons," I try to wrap this up.

"How long has it been?" Howard asks me and I have to consider his question since I am not sure what he is really asking.

"Since?"

"We last heard from them?" I now see that Howard is actually as uncomfortable about this trip as I am, but he did not want me to freak out about it.

"Three days… when they left Nairobi."

"Not many cell towers in the bush…" Howard seeks my confirmation.

"There are settlements near the camps where they are staying… would expect them to have cellular coverage, but just don't know if they are too far to pick up from the camps down by the lake…" I have thought about this too. "Would you feel better if someone checked in on them?"

"They would be mortified…" Howard reminds me. "Just as you were when your mother checked up on us on our honeymoon."

"That was different…" I try to leave a space to maybe convince him.

"Because we were in Cape Cod instead of Kenya?" Howard is not going to end his comparison there. I am sure. "When we got married there were a lot of strange people in Provincetown. It wasn't the safest place to be."

"Hop across the bay and you're in Boston," I point out. "For the kids, hop across the lake and you're in freaking Sudan… armpit of the world, with an active civil war and people dying from all kinds of nasty things."

"I get your point… but they are there with professional guides who live there and won't stay in business if anything happens to the tourists who come to visit. The kids are not the only Americans who have made this trip in the last month. I just don't see why you should get all worked up about it."

"What am I supposed to tell Mom?" I finally ask the easy question that might get me back to my work.

"Today is the Serengeti." Howard responds simply, but he looks at me more carefully, as if he is seeing something he is not particularly happy about.

"I can do that, but you know my mother… some kind of alien radar that picks up trouble even before it happens."

"This the first text you got from her since the wedding?" Howard is testing my intuition.

"About them? Yes. But no. She's having fits about my father not paying attention to her."

"Your father never paid attention to her… that's why she micromanaged you… and us." Howard remembers all too well how involved she has been with every decision we have made.

"But she has great political instincts that have served you well…" I push back.

"Had… I'm not so sure she really has the pulse of the people anymore. Too much time watching Fox News with your father and not nearly enough time on CNBC or CNN to balance things out."

"I don't expect to hear from the kids until they get back to Nairobi. At that point Mom will have so many pictures to wade through that we won't hear from her until they return next week."

CHAPTER THREE:

CHARLES THOMPSON

This nightmare just continues… why can't I wake up? Why does the night just go on and on interminably? I think my eyes are open, but I can't see a thing. I can't move my arms or hands, which are behind me. Can't pull them apart? What kind of dream is this?

I feel Annie next to me, want to ask her if she is having the same dream, but something in my mouth keeps me from being able to talk. This is all just so real… but it can't possibly be.

The bump tosses me up like we are in a vehicle going over a rough road. Swaying back and forth. All part of this insane dream. Then I hear voices, but they aren't speaking English. Don't recognize the language. Not one I have heard before. The voices are quiet, as if they are afraid I might understand them. Or maybe they want me to hear them, know they are there, but not allow us to even guess what they may be talking about. Who is in this nightmare? How would I be able to invent a language I don't understand in my dream? Have I heard it before somewhere and my mind is recreating it for me now to make this seem more real? Does the mind really do that? Maybe I should have taken a psychiatry residency rather than neurosurgery. No, I always wanted to be a surgeon because Mom never got the chance when that was all she really wanted to be.

Another bump. An angry word spoken, as if someone just told the driver to be more careful. But the spoken word was meaningless to me, even though the tone told me everything. Can I figure out what they are talking about by listening to the tone of voice? Never tried. But as long as this nightmare continues, I need something to keep my mind off of feeling restricted like this. I don't like not being able to see, not being able to move around, use my hands, understand what is going on.

Does this dream have anything to do with marrying Annie? Is this my mind telling me I'm no longer free to do the things I want? That I have restrictions I'm not used to? That I can't see what is going to happen next? That I need to get used to making decisions without certainty like I used to? When I finally wake up, I will have a lot of questions for my psychiatry colleagues back at the hospital.

I feel Annie trying to move closer to me, but she also seems unable to move freely or talk to me. Is that my mind telling me that she is probably feeling the same about our marriage? That I am now restricting her in ways she is not used to? Why can't I wake up? I want to, but no matter how hard I try, I am stuck in this bad dream.

Another bump. I try to roll over to get into a more comfortable position, but feel what seems like a stick poke me. Why would someone poke me with a stick? Who would do that? How much longer am I going to be trapped in this dream?

But then again… what if this isn't a nightmare. Not a dream? What if this is real? I need to consider that. When did this dream start? We were in bed at the Kisumu camp, having just made love and fallen asleep. Were we asleep an hour or a minute? I don't know. Is this the dream I am having at Kisumu? If it is, someone will be waking me up soon to leave for Tanzania and the Mwanza camp. I thought that was who came into our tent. The driver and guide for the next leg of our honeymoon trip. I am so confused. I felt Annie get out of bed. She said something to someone and then I felt the rough hands on me, pulling me out of the bed and putting a bag over my head. They bound my wrists with something… behind my back. That is what this feels like. They gagged me and dropped me on my back. I heard the doors close and the vehicle move. Annie was next to me. But that is the dream, isn't it?

And if it isn't a dream, who is doing this to us? Why would they? No one even knew where we are except our parents. They certainly wouldn't do… what is this? A kidnapping? None of this makes sense. I try rolling again, and this time, rather than a stick poking me, I feel rough hands, pulling me back over and pushing me down, as if trying to let me know that rolling over is not permitted. *Why the hell not?* And while I think Annie is next to me, maybe it's not. Maybe Annie is doing this to me and maybe that's a bag of clothes I feel. *But why would she do this?* There is nothing I know about her that would suggest she might play a joke like this on me. Sure, she has a great sense of humor… even laughs at my poor jokes and observations of absurdity… sometimes. But this would be just so over the top. I can't begin to think she might do this to me. Or even to us. Would she do that? Hire someone to fake a kidnapping, just to make me think it was real? This all makes me realize I don't know Annie as well as I thought I did. What is she capable of? That thought never entered my mind.

Another bump in the road… another reminder this is either one hell of a dream, or one hell of a nightmare. The more bumps and the longer this keeps going…

Suddenly I find myself rolling as if I am in a vehicle of some sort and it took a sharp turn at speed. The other person next to me was also thrown in the same direction at the same time. I feel the doubt that this is a dream creeping into my thoughts. I have no idea how long this has been going on. That is the problem with not being able to see. I have no idea if the sun is out or it is still the middle of the night. No idea if it has been minutes, hours or days, although it sure seems like it has been a whole bunch of hours. Maybe even a day or more. But let's be practical about this. If we had been driving that long, I would have thought the vehicle would have stopped so they could change drivers. Get gas. I don't remember a long stop, although the rocking and road noise, if that is what it is, has not been constant. We might have stopped for a minute and I did not notice. I am half in a fog anyway, not having had much sleep on this whole trip. And now this.

I hear what sounds like someone hitting the brakes and am thrown forward. If we are in a vehicle… and I am becoming more convinced that is the case… we have now come to a stop, although I hear the motor running. We have not parked; we have merely stopped. Does that mean we are in a more urban area that has cross streets and traffic control? Or does that mean we are merely stopped and waiting for someone. Maybe a new vehicle, if for some reason this one may have been seen. More likely whoever is involved here is just being cautious.

Waiting to see if we are being followed. See if anyone is watching us somehow. But why would anyone be watching, since hardly anyone even knows we are here?

The voices start back up… low… almost a whisper. Still in that language I don't understand. If we are waiting for someone, I could guess they are wondering where that person is. Does that mean we arrived early or late? Too early for whoever was to meet us here, or too late and that person has already departed? My mind is just running wild with speculation, since I have absolutely no idea what is actually happening, and am still half wondering if I am dreaming this whole thing.

Then I hear a word I do recognize: Mogadishu. What country is that? Somalia, I think. Could be wrong about that. Geography was never my strongest subject in school. Now I am listening closer but do not pick out any other words from the stream of sounds. Mogadishu. What do I know about it? For some reason I think it is the capital of Somalia, which is one of the worst countries in the world for warlords, and lawlessness. In fact, I think in that movie… the one with Tom Hanks, where he was the captain of a container ship… Captain something, I think. Seems to me the pirates that tried to take over his ship were from Somalia. Pirates… and not even Captain Jack Sparrow from Pirates of the Caribbean. Piracy just seems so out of place in the modern world… but I guess there are places where it still exists. And going after container ships… that is just so unbelievable to me. I even told Annie that. But we aren't on a ship… so we shouldn't need to worry about pirates. Unless, whoever has us, intends to sell us to pirates, who would then ransom us. I guess anything is possible in this part of the world.

Then I hear another word that catches my attention. Addis Ababa. The way the voice said it makes me wonder if we are either in Mogadishu, on our way to Mogadishu or someone from Mogadishu is looking for us. But the reference to Addis Ababa, which is the capital of Ethiopia, gives me hope that maybe we will not be cast off into the ocean off Mogadishu. Maybe we will end up in Addis Ababa, which is a more modern city, even if Ethiopia is generally regarded as another

African basket case, because the people there can barely avoid starvation most years.

It has been a long time since I thought or read about any of this. High school, most likely. And that would have been a decade ago, or more. Is any of this relevant to what we are experiencing right now? Am I even remembering correctly about these things? A decade is a long time to not think about something and then try to remember what is pertinent and what is not.

The vehicle lurches as we start moving again. Okay, I can now eliminate one possibility from my list. We are not changing vehicles here. But the road must be unpaved as we are going slower and yet the vehicle we are in, is rocking a whole lot more. As if we are trying to pass over an unpaved and not maintained roadway. The rocking gets much more extreme. This can't be a dream. And if it is not… I have to acknowledge we have been kidnapped by someone unknown, and taken somewhere, also unknown, although we now have two possible locations where we might be headed. But as I think about what I know of the geography of Africa… which isn't much…we are or were a hell of a long way from either of the destinations our captors have mentioned in the last few minutes. With the kind of roads we have and are now on, we must be days away from either. I'm not aware of any trains or anything that might get us there faster. Clearly would not take us on an airplane as we would not be cooperative.

It seems to me we must have been just in the wrong place at the wrong time. Someone wanted to kidnap westerners, preferably Americans, but not necessarily. And even though no one knows who we are, any Americans will do. How do I explain this one to the hospital? They weren't keen on me taking my honeymoon here in the first place. Neither were Annie's parents… but she has a way of getting what she wants, although I don't think she really wanted to come here either. It was all me. And here we are, because I wanted to see big animals in the wild. Take pictures with the big lens Mom and Dad gave me for my birthday. That was dumb.

CHAPTER FOUR:
LILA THOMPSON

"Where are the kids today?" I ask Beau, my husband of twenty-nine years, who I swear on some days, has completely forgotten he has a wife. He gets into his work. Deep into his work, and I am not sure if he even knows what day it is. But then he will do something completely unexpected and sweet. What am I supposed to say then? Somehow, I suspect it is his assistant, Jill, who reminds him he needs to do something or I won't be warm and loving when he gets home. I like Jill, and hope that Beau does not feel the same way about her. From what I have read, it seems that men like Beau are more susceptible to office romances than most men, because they are just so detached from the rest of the world. I know I should not worry about him, but I do, from time to time.

I see him rise to his full six foot four inches, rub a hand through the sandy brown longish mop on the top of his head. That same puzzled smile I have seen so often and come to love about him, appears. "The kids?" Should have known he is not thinking about them at all.

"Charles and Annie… you know? His wife?"

I see a blink of confusion for a moment, "Charles… has a wife?"

"Last week… you were there. At the church?" I begin to wonder if he has really forgotten or he is just playing with me and his reputation for not remembering things.

"Last week?" Beau glances around, "Was that where we danced together?"

"Much to your chagrin, I am sure… but yes. Charles got married and went off on his honeymoon. To Africa."

"Oh, that's right… Charles wanted to shoot an elephant with that giant telephoto lens we got him for his birthday last year."

"I still think that lens was a mistake," I repeat a comment I have made, I do not know how many times. "Had his nose down all through med school. Gets a great start on his residency… but he still has a long way to go. We should have put our foot down when he said he wanted to get married. Should have insisted he could live with Annie if that works for them, but he needed to keep his head down. Now, he is thinking he can do it all… finish his residency and have a wife… maybe a kid… and go big game hunting with his camera."

"We got married before you finished your residency…" Beau reminds me and now I know he has just been playing with me.

"We did… and I gave up my surgery track," I point out once again. This has been one of his favorite refrains when I push on Charles to not let up like I did. Beau can do anything he sets his mind to. Charles and I are not so lucky. We have to work every minute of every day to just stay ahead of the profession. So much is changing every day. And Beau is one of the people who leads the charge on all those changes with the work he is doing for the military.

"Charles is on top of it… cut the kid some slack…" Beau strongly suggests, and when he strongly suggests there is no arguing with him. But that does not mean I am going to do what he wants me to do. In fact, I seldom follow his suggestions. But, just as seldom do I advise him I have not.

"Is it just my phone, or has Charles gone radio silent?" I watch as Beau checks his phone and shrugs.

"Last message was when they were leaving Nairobi." He looks up at me to see if that is the answer I was looking for.

"There must be coverage at the camps… "I begin, but Beau cuts me off.

"I would be surprised if they had anything other than Satcom at the camps."

"Meaning no cellular coverage…" I try to clarify.

"Charles said he wanted to be off the grid for a week… no patient calls, no hospital calls, no Mom and Dad calls…"

"He didn't really say that… did he?" I wonder as I do not remember that comment.

"He did…" Beau gets a twinkle in his eye. "Not exactly those words… but that was what he would have said if he thought he could avoid a Mom torrent. You being hurt that you're not there in bed with them, giving Charles pointers on how to impregnate Annie on the first try."

"That's not fair…" I push back. "I don't want her to get pregnant on the first try…"

"You just said you thought they should have waited even getting married until he finishes the residency…"

Beau is using my words against me… again. "Best time to have a child is early on. We saw that with Charles. The longer we have been married, the less and less I see of you… completely tied up in your work. And Charles is just like you. He wants to be the absolute best at what he does. He will stay up all night studying film to make sure he knows exactly what he is going to do in the surgical suite."

"I'm glad he's that way… but this week… he should enjoy being off the grid. Give him a chance to really get to know Annie, to work some things out… we both know how challenging it is to be married these days."

"What are you saying? You making a comment about us?" I wonder if Jill is more of a distraction than I was thinking.

"Starting out… making the adjustments to a life of two rather than a table for one. That's all I'm saying. Nothing about us… we seem to be in a groove. Don't you agree?" Beau seems to be realizing what I just said.

"I wish you were around more… a lot more." I confess, although this is not the first time he has heard this from me.

"I'm here most of the time… just busy. And being busy is a whole lot better than not being busy." Beau makes the same point he always does. If he were not busy, we would have no money to put a son through Med school and honeymoon in Africa.

"Why did we let him go to Africa?" I change away from a losing argument.

"Because he wanted to go," he reminds me. "And just like his mother… when he makes up his mind…"

"I know, I know." I abandon that line of reasoning with him. "Think I'll text Angelica, see if they've heard from Annie."

"My guess is they haven't either…" Beau goes back to the report he was reading on his laptop.

I send a note to Angelica Myers, <Hey Angelica. Hate to bother you, but have you heard anything from Annie?>

It does not take more than a few seconds for the response to come across, <Assume you have not heard from Charles either>

<Crickets> I respond.

<Probably means they're out with the animals. Giraffes don't carry cell phones, so no need for towers> Angelica responds to make her point.

<Where are they today?>

A little longer wait before a response. Means she probably had to ask Howard. <Serengeti>

<You have any concerns? About the lack of communications?>

<Tough part of the world for modern conveniences>

<If you hear from them, would you let us know?> I do not want to sound too worried.

<Sure. You do the same>

“Am I right or am I right?” Beau asks, although I know he is not trying to be snarky, although he is.

“Said giraffes don’t carry cell phones in the Serengeti,” I know will get a response from him.

“And neither do people… It’s all satcom out there. Probably should have given Charles my sat-phone so he could alleviate his mother’s apprehensions.” Beau is trying to get me to chill.

“Yeah, I wish you had,” I suddenly wonder why we did not think of this before. “Should we ship it to him today?”

“Likely would get held up in customs. Not much chance they would get it before they return,” Beau is only half listening to me now. I know that trailing voice. He is fully back on his work.

“Beau…” I try to get his attention again.

“Yes…” trailing off.

“Could you…” I begin, but wait until he turns to look at me before continuing, “look at satellite imagery of their camp… see if you see any signs of them?”

“Maybe they’ll wave…” Beau clearly thinks this is an invasion of privacy, but he will do it.

CHAPTER FIVE:

ANNIE THOMPSON

I try not to get my hopes up when the vehicle we are evidently in comes to a stop once more. Too many hours since this all began. Too many bumps in the road, swerves and turns that tossed me, and I assume Charles, about the back of this vehicle where we lie on the floor. Must be a van of some sort as we are not on seats. We are being hauled around like sacks of flower or something much worse. What has been running through my mind all this time is why me? Why us? I would have thought the tour company would have made sure this was a safe itinerary. No indication of any safety concerns. We are just another couple on a safari. And yet, we have become the hunted rather than the hunters.

The engine is on, but we are no longer moving. Waiting for traffic maybe? Waiting for someone to meet us here, wherever here might be? Generally, when we have stopped and left the motor running, I have heard two voices talking. Low. Not wanting us to be able to figure out what they are talking about. And with this bag over my head, I cannot see anything. Cannot see who they are. Where we are going, although even if I could see out the windshield, likely I would have no idea where we are, let alone where we might be going.

Charles is moving again, at least I think it is Charles. Someone on the floor of this probable van, next to me all this time. Not moving much, not saying a word. But then with the gag in my mouth, even if I wanted to say something, no one would be able to understand me. And I have so many questions, but no answers. I am not even sure that whoever is with us speaks English. Even if I could talk, it is likely they would not know what I want to have them tell me. Like, who are they? Why have they done this to us? Where are we? Where are we going? What do they want from us? I hope it is just money. A ransom, but I do not have any insight into what is going on. That is only a guess. I hear what sounds like another vehicle approaching. It seems to me it has pulled up next to us. I hear the low voices, as if someone in this vehicle is talking to someone in the other. Police maybe? Come to rescue us?

I only have to listen a moment to know there is no indication in the voices of anything other than a conversation. Nothing about step out of the van. Open up the back. Let me see what you have back there. None of that. Just a conversation about the weather… at least that is what the sound of the voices suggest to me.

A door opens and is slammed shut. Makes me think someone got out of the other vehicle. Do not think it was this one as I would have expected a vibration here and not just the sound. Footsteps. Coming along side of this vehicle. Around to the back. I hear and now feel the door open at my feet.

Someone grabs my legs and pulls me toward them. I try to kick, but this person has strong hands and holds my ankles together. Pulling me until my legs are out the back and then I am stood up. Hands still bound behind my back. Gag in and hood over my head. It sounds like they are doing the same to Charles, although he struggles more effectively than I. Apparently kicks one or more of the men who are taking us from this van. Are we going to the other? Just changing vehicles? Going on somewhere else? Or are we somewhere? Is this where they have been taking us all along? I will likely know these answers in just a few moments.

A hand in my back… roughly pushing me forward. But I cannot see. Do not know where to put my bare feet, whether I am going to step on something sharp or uneven. I step gingerly and decide we must be on a dirt road. It is not stone or paved, but uneven. Ruts like tire tracks that have driven over this place a million times. Another rough push in the middle of my back. Someone must be directly behind me; unhappy I am not walking fast enough. Or maybe, just reminding me that I am completely in their power. I listen for Charles. Where is he? Behind me? In front of me? Is he still back at the vehicle that brought us here? I cannot hear him. Cannot tell how many of us are walking now. Are they separating us? Am I completely alone now? At the mercy of someone I have not even seen, except as a shadow in a dark tent before the bag went over my head.

What did I see? Shadows. I think there were four of them. May have been black men as they seemed to be hard to see in the dark. But one of them. The one who grabbed me before the bag went over my head. There was something about him. A reflection of light in the dark. Like a gold chain around his neck, maybe. A long chain as it was down and not just around his throat. That was all I saw before the bag over my head put me into this sensory deprived state. Now I have to interpret sounds, as there have been no conversations in English I could listen to. I have to interpret how I have been tossed about in the back of the van or vehicle that brought me here. Sharp turns. Sudden stops. Long idle times where these men were waiting. For what I do not know. But waiting they were. And then for no reason, we would be off in another direction. Were they trying to be unpredictable? Not follow a direct path, wherever it is we have been going? Or is it simply that they have been taking an indirect route because there is no direct route in Africa, other than across plains dotted with immense animals who are seldom friendly. The guides do not seem to want us to get out of our vehicle and pet them. More likely, the animals would like us to get out of our vehicles so they could feast on us.

Charles had a romantic image in his mind about this trip. That is what he tried to explain to me when he suggested coming here. A safari. We would see things that are unimaginable. We would bring home pictures we could frame and hang in our apartment, wherever we finally land, to remind us of this time we have together. Getting to know each other in a way we have not been able to until now. Deepen our understanding of the other. Solidify our love. That was what Charles thought. That is what he expected… not this.

What did I expect since Africa was never on my short list of places to visit? I would have been happy with a hotel room in Branson, Missouri and tickets to country western shows, even though I am not much for country music. But I am up to try to understand what I do not. To listen to others and try to understand why they enjoy country music so much. I have to admit I went to an Alan Jackson concert once, with friends. They chose the event, not me. What I learned was Alan Jackson sang some songs I had heard before. And a whole lot I had not. But they were not just the twangy heartbreak that seemed to define country for me. What was the old joke about country music? If you play it backwards you would get back all the things you had lost? Your trailer, your horse, your dog, your spouse… Branson Missouri would have been fine with me, if that was what Charles had wanted. But it never came up. I just wanted to spend this week with him before he disappears back into St. Mary's Hospital in Rochester, Minnesota, which is attached to the Mayo Clinic there. Time is what I wanted, and now we may be finding that time is the one thing we will never have.

The rough hand grabs my hands behind my back and brings me to an abrupt stop. I hear a door slide, as if it were a barn door on an overhead track. Then the rough push forward. I feel I am now on a dirt floor. The ruts are gone, but it is not smooth like a concrete flooring. Uneven, but not rutted, which tells me I am inside. Ruts result from rain and mud being driven through. No wet ground in here, wherever here is.

Hands on my shoulders pushing me down, but down to the ground as I feel no chair to sit on. I come down hard and it hurts, but with the gag in I cannot protest this rough treatment. Cannot even comment on it.

Unexpectedly the bag over my head comes up and my eyes open. He's here! Charles is here with me! I am so relieved. He is tied with his hands behind his back, gag in and a black man standing over him holding the bag that had been over his head. Charles nods to me in recognition. We are still in our bedclothes, bare feet and nothing else. I look up to see the men. Yes, there are four of them. Not sure if they are the same four as took us from the Kenyan camp. They wear the same clothes as nearly every person I have seen here wears. Bush pants with cargo pockets and lightweight plaid long sleeve shirts. Western sneakers on their feet and a scarf over their faces. I am sure that is to keep us from being able to identify any of them. Four men, who look just like anyone else you would meet in this part of the world, with the exception all of them are holding an AK-47. That is to be expected since I have been told way too many times that Russia has been arming the insurgents in this part of the world.

I glance around. This is a warehouse. Pallets of boxes stacked so they can easily be accessed by a fork lift. And now I see it sitting in a corner. It is plugged in so must be electric. That means it is relatively new as most used to be propane in this part of the world. Another fact I have mother to thank for me knowing. The pallets have writing on them, but it is not in English. Not surprising, but that means whatever is being stored here did not come directly from the US. I look at the writing, but the words are not ones I recognize. My guess is Arabic as the characters are written right to left. And this close to that part of the world, probably makes sense. But I wonder what country? Saudi Arabia, Iran, or United Arab Emirates would be my guess. They are the countries in this part of the world that have the most advanced manufacturing capability. And even that is nothing special or particularly advanced. But then the AK-47 has been around forever and is made in nearly every non-western country of the world. Damn you mother… why did you decide I needed to know any of this? Pique my interest in observing things that others ignore.

Glancing over my shoulder, as much as I can, still bound, I realize this warehouse is actually pretty full. If these are arms… that will not be good. But I can hope this is food or building materials or something that will support people and not oppress them. But this is Africa. And there are a whole bunch of countries that are not exactly bastions of freedom or even economic security. Why is it Africa has always been like this? Unable to modernize other than in a few major cities? The average person here has a subsistence living. They fish to catch their food. Hunt and grow crops to supplement the catch of the day. No big farms that produce grains or vegetables that are processed and sold in stores. Most of what is found in the city stores is imported from Eastern Europe and Central Asia. Should have taken Mom's advice about studying non-romance languages when in school… but they were so much harder to learn and just never interested me that much, until now.

CHAPTER SIX:
HOWARD MYERS

"Lulumon," I call my assistant, who sits just outside the door to my office. A door I seldom close even for confidential meetings, because I want Lulumon to be aware of everything that goes on in here. Need that independent person in case anyone wants to disagree with a decision I make.

"Yes, Governor Myers," she responds as she comes in and stands just inside my door. She is wearing that electric blue blazer over gray slacks and black high neck blouse. She looks good with her long black hair falling past her shoulders.

"Would you contact the travel agency we used to book Annie's trip to Africa?"

"That in your private file, sir?" Lulumon reminds me she did not book it since it was not state business.

"Yes, sorry. Thanks for reminding me."

"What would you like me to ask them?" Lulumon holds her tablet to take a note.

"Just ask if there have been any reported issues in the area where Annie and Charles are," I try to state this delicately so Lulumon does not ask the wrong question.

"Issues, sir?"

"No one seems to have heard from them since they left Nairobi," I try to sound like this is likely not an issue. "Probably just the lack of towers in the game preserves, but I know Angelica will be a lot happier if she knows there is nothing to be concerned about."

"Angelica?" Lulumon challenges me.

"I'll feel better, too," I admit.

"No worries, sir. I'll be discrete," and Lulumon returns to her desk to find the number and make the call.

I text Angelica, <Checking for issues in central Africa>

She must not be in a meeting as she responds almost instantly. <Kenyan Ambassador is doing the same>

I am surprised she made that ask. Normally she does not seek favors for herself or our family. She must be more worried than she has let on.

While reading the text from Angelica, Frank Ibrahim, my head of security comes into my office, "Governor."

"Frank, have a seat," I respond trying to shift my thoughts away from Angelica's response.

"All is quiet in the great state of Virginia, today, Governor." Frank often gives me this same report. For some reason, it seems to me that when he does, something breaks loose within a day or two. Something that ends up with me on television news trying to explain our response.

"I have something a little further afield for you. And you can say you don't want to take it on and I won't be upset or concerned." I wonder if I really want to ask this of him.

"If I can learn something by doing it, I'll be all in." Frank responds with a broad grin.

"Can you informally talk to some of your old buddies at the CIA?"

"I informally talk to them all the time. They keep telling me it's time to come back home. Keep telling me that with all the middle eastern languages I know, how I could be doing something important, rather than herding cops to do their job." Frank is telling me I need to find a way to keep him engaged or I am likely to lose him. And I would hate to see that since he is so good.

"I think I mentioned that Annie is in Africa..."

"You did," Frank now is seeing that my request may not be something he wants to take on. "And now you are wondering about them... out in the preserves, getting jostled about in Range Rovers, chased down by wild animals and living amongst insects and snakes and all those creepy crawlers."

"If there was a problem, I would expect someone would get in contact with us..." I begin.

"They would," Frank is definite about that.

"And likely there is no threat we need to be concerned with..." I continue.

"Governor... if Annie were my daughter... and she married some guy who is crazy enough to go to that part of the world... well, yeah... I'd be concerned... maybe even a little more uneasy about it all than you have been so far... I know some guys who have been working in South Sudan... not so far away. They're pretty wired into what's going on in that part of the world. It's always good to catch up with them. 'Bout time for me to check in."

"I would greatly appreciate it, Frank," I respond, but motion for him to stay a bit longer as he tried to get up from his chair. "How are you doing?"

"Me, sir?" Frank clearly was not expecting this question.

"How is the job? Is it what you want? Or do you need a bigger challenge?"

Frank shifts uncomfortably in his chair, probably trying to

understand if this is a trick question, or if I am the one disappointed in his performance in the job.

"Ten years as a seal, fifteen years doing field work for CIA. I'm still alive, got a pension waiting for me over there, and a start on another over here. This is such a nice change… nobody waiting to kill me because one of my brothers took out a family member, or disrupted their plans of violence. I'm doing fine, sir."

"But is this job enough for you?" I push him still thinking about his comment about the CIA trying to bring him back.

"Enough, sir?" It seems Frank Ibrahim has not considered this question until now.

"Would it make sense for me to move additional responsibilities under you?" I suggest as a way to keep his interest.

"Could you give me a for instance?" Frank is not sure what I am asking.

"Cyber security… is managed by our Chief Information Officer. Should we be thinking about combining both under you? Scan for threats and react to them all in the same tribe… if you will. Rather than having to climb a wall to go talk to someone who has a piece of the puzzle you do not."

Frank sits back in his chair and I see he is thinking this through before responding. That is a good thing. He looks back at me, "I need to talk to some folks about that. I know a few organizations that are moving in that direction. Not sure if they have made the whole move. But clearly… everyone wants everyone playing together better in the sandbox."

"What got me thinking about it is Annie's trip…" I change direction on Frank and watch his eyes narrow as he wonders where I am taking him now.

"How so, sir?" Frank does not look directly at me, listening to my words and tone of voice to see what I reveal there.

"Lots of different organizations have a piece of the information I would like to have, but no one has all of it in one place. Can't one-stop shop it, if I might use that as a simile. Angelica is working channels she can access, Lulumon is checking in with the travel agents, and here I am asking you for in-country assets who will have a whole different perspective on what is going on over there."

"You're thinking we need a one-stop shop for cyber and physical security issues in the state," Frank summarizes.

"Tell me what you think, and if you conclude that would be an improvement and needed change, I'd like you to lead that effort," I let him know exactly what I am thinking.

"Would certainly be an interesting set of comparison data," Frank nods to himself.

"Any insights your buddies might have would be greatly appreciated." I conclude and Frank hears the dismissal tone, rises.

"I'll think about cyber and physical, sir," and Frank retreats from my office. He is barely gone when Lulumon appears and steps further into my office than usual, speaks softer than usual.

"Governor, Myers… I was able to talk to Wilson at the travel agency," she stops and waits for me to acknowledge, which I do. "He was able to confirm that another party has the Kisumu Camp this week, but there were a couple days between Annie's stay and the next family coming in. He had that information in his file because he talked with Annie about staying the extra two days at Kisumu before going on to Mwana Lake Camp in Tanzania for the Serengeti part of the trip."

"They didn't extend…" I try to remember what I knew about this part of the trip.

"No. As far as Wilson knows, they are in the Serengeti game preserve today. He confirmed that is a really remote area and cell coverage is non-existent. He also looked at his bulletin wire. Nothing that would raise a concern about Annie and Charles."

"Would you ask him to contact the tour operator? Any hick-ups we should know about?"

CHAPTER SEVEN:
CHARLES THOMPSON

The hood comes off. I have to blink several times to adjust to the low light in this place, although I have no idea where we are. Another industrial building of some sort. Warehouse, maybe, but there does not seem to be anyone working here. I try to understand what people do in this place. Looks like they store tires and truck parts. That would mean that someone is going to come looking for something here at some point. And my guess is we are only here for a short time before the four men who took us from the Kenyan camp move us again.

Annie is behind me, I suddenly realize. Hearing her cough since we still have gags in, making it impossible to talk. I shift around so I can see her better and she is looking at me as if she is wondering what I am going to do about our predicament. I hear footsteps and glance back over my shoulder to see one of the men, still wearing a mask up over his nose so I cannot really see his face, come up behind me and remove the gag. Another comes over and places a dish of something, unrecognizable, in front of me. The first one cuts the zip tie that has bound my wrists and then repeats the ungagging and untying of Annie. She too gets a dish of something to contemplate. Apparently, they are feeding us.

Picking up the bowl, I realize it contains a mash of cooked vegetables and a roll that kind of looks like toilet paper, only it is brown and more like a mesh. Breaking off a piece, and tasting it, I decide it must be a kind of bread, although unlike any I have had before. There are no utensils, which makes me believe the way they expect you to eat this is to break off a piece of the bread and scoop up the vegetables. Annie is looking at the dish the same way I am, apparently wondering if it is safe to eat this.

"Eggplant… I think," I answer the question I see in Annie's eyes.

One of the men comes back and takes the bowls from us, keeps one and hands the other to another of the men. They lift their masks minimally and eagerly eat the mash, scooping it into their mouths with their fingers. Guess I was wrong about the toilet paper looking bread. Both men unroll the bread and fold it before stuffing sections into their mouths, chewing quickly and watching us watching them.

"So much for that," Annie has to clear her throat twice before she is able to get that short statement out. "Any idea…"

I shake my head and call to the men who have now finished the meal originally offered to us, "Any of you speak English?"

One of the men in the back answers, "No food… tomorrow." I can barely see him, but notice, as I look closer, that he wears a gold chain around his neck. Not a short chain, but a longer chain. None of the others have such a chain.

"I think he is telling us we won't get fed again until tomorrow," I inform Annie.

"I'm not hungry…" Annie responds and rubs her wrists where the zip tie had been chafing them.

"Why?" I call out to the gold chain wearing man in the back. I decide to keep the question simple and open ended, hoping that will be easier for the man to respond to.

But he does not.

"I don't know who you think we are… but we aren't."

Again, my question is greeted with silence. Watching the reactions, it seems to me that only the one speaks any English, and with his single response, it does not seem like he understands all that much.

"Ransom?" I ask to see if the one man will give us any insight.

The gold chain man steps forward, motions toward a back corner and instructs us, “Piss.”

I glance at the other men to get a sense of how they are likely to react, and judge they are not going to. I rise, wobbly, since I haven’t been on my feet much in the last day or whatever it’s been. I reach for Annie and help her up. Together we gingerly walk back in the direction gold chain man had pointed. We find a sort of bathroom. It consists of a small room with a hole in the floor, and a tank with water, I presume, and a chain. I guess we do our business and flush it away by pulling the chain.

Annie just looks at the hole in the floor like she has no idea what she is supposed to do with that.

“You squat over it…” I explain.

“There’s no toilet paper… how do you…” Annie looks at me unsure what she needs to do here, but I assume she needs to do something since we have been travelling a long time.

Looking around, but finding nothing, I decide to rip my t-shirt and hand her a small piece of the cloth. That apparently satisfies her as she drops her pajama pants and does her business. She wipes and drops the cloth into a basket net to her.

My turn. As I squat, I realize that since we have not eaten for at least a day or more and will not until at least tomorrow, we should not need to make many pit stops like this. I tear another small patch of my t-shirt, clean up and also drop the cloth into the basket before rising.

“You holding up okay?” I ask Annie. She nods, but the fact that she will not answer tells me she is struggling. “They will release us when they get what they want.”

Annie shakes her head, “You don’t know that… we don’t have any idea what they are planning.”

One of the men appears at the door and glares at us.

“I think they want us…” I nod towards the man so Annie will

know what I mean.

"Don't tell them anything…" Annie whispers as she passes in front of me.

This man does not point his weapon at us, but he is holding it in such a manner that it is clear he could fire at us before we could ever get to him. And I have no doubt that he would shoot us without a second thought. He follows us back to where we had been sitting. Once we get there, the one who had cut us free approaches with zip ties and motions for us to turn around. He pulls my hands behind my back and I feel him cinch up the tie. He goes to Annie and ties her hands in the same way. No hood or gag this time, but he pushes us towards a door I had not noticed earlier. The door slides open and a white van… old… beaten up. I briefly wonder if it even works… waits for us.

We gingerly step out onto the stone drive between the building and the van, still in bare feet. Probably intend to keep us this way to ensure we do not get any ideas about trying to escape. Where would we possibly go without shoes? The distance is not far, but my tender feet slow the crossing. I see in the eyes of the man who is waiting for me that he is enjoying my discomfort. Cannot see much more than his eyes with the mask, but his eyes tell me a lot. I glance around. We are in the middle of nowhere. No buildings close by. A stone and dirt road. No wonder they were willing to let us return to the van without gagging us. No one could hear us anyway. I look for any sign of where we are. Turn and glance back at the building where we have been. No signs. Just a cinderblock building with a tin roof and a sliding door that does not appear to even have a lock. I guess that when you are in the middle of nowhere you do not need to worry about locks.

When I get to the van, the man turns me around to sit on the floor, I pick up my feet and scoot back inside. Annie does the same; and in a moment, we are sitting next to each other along the left side. Two of the men, get in back with us and squat down, watching us with their rifles across their laps. They are taking no chances with us, but I have to believe the last thing they want to do is to kill us. If we were to die, they would have no hostages. Our deaths would also likely trigger a massive man-hunt for them as the US State Department would be all over our deaths. I have to believe they are all over our disappearance. By now, they must know something happened to us. That would explain why they keep moving us from one location to another.

The man with the gold chain gets in the passenger side, and the fourth man, the driver side. Then, we are on the road again.

"Thank you," I call out to the gold chain man. I see a slight nod, which tells me he understood what I said. Probably understands a lot more than he has indicated so far, and probably speaks better English than he has let on.

"Why did you thank him?" Annie whispers.

I shake my head to let her know I do not intend to answer her question. While it would appear that only the one man understands what we are saying, I am not staking my life or Annie's on it. And since we do not even know if we are who they intended to take captive, we have to assume the worst, hope for the best. At least the fact that we have not seen any faces, gives me hope that we might walk out of this alive. But how do I communicate all this to Annie?

"Is this really happening to us?" Annie asks as if she knows the answer but is hoping there is another explanation.

"I've been trying to wake up since this all began…" I respond. "But I can't figure out how to."

"Just make sure that if you do wake up, that you don't leave me behind." Annie looks up at the gold chain man in the front seat. It looks like he has fallen asleep. Probably means he has not slept since we were taken, and neither have we. When will exhaustion overcome us? It is bound to happen. Likely better if we try to sleep on our terms than when our bodies simply give out.

"Try to take a nap… we will need to be wide awake when we get wherever they are taking us."

CHAPTER EIGHT:

BEAU THOMPSON

"Beau?" Jill, my assistant pokes her head into my office. "Joe just sent you the link to the imagery you requested."

I nod in appreciation and look for Joe's email. Finding it I click on the link and bring up satellite imagery of the Kisumu Safari Camp in Kenya on Lake Victoria. I check the date stamp. About an hour old. The first thing that strikes me is the camp almost seems like it is abandoned. No vehicles present, no people walking about. That might not be unusual since it would be late afternoon there. Could be the kids are still out on their safari and simply have not yet returned. The camp employees could be inside preparing the evening meal. This image certainly does not establish anything. But then again, they are not even supposed to be here now. Should be at the other camp in Tanzania. Out in the Serengeti today.

Best way to establish where they are is to do a cellphone ping. Geolocate on the ping. I initiate the procedure and wait for the map showing the location of Charles' phone. It comes up at the Kisumu camp. Then they are still there. I ping Annie's phone as well. Comes up in the same building as Charles' phone.

I send a text to Angelica, <Appears the kids are still in Kisumu>

<What has confirmed their location?> Angelica responds almost immediately.

<Cellphone ping> I send back knowing she will understand what I have just found.

<In camp?>

<If they are out on safari likely would not have registered if they took them with them>

<Called Annie early morning for them. No answer>

<Probably slept through it> I know Charles… he does not do mornings.

<Will call this evening. Dinner time> Angelica informs me so I do not have to try making the call as well.

<Might explain why we aren't getting pictures>

<They left the phones in camp?> Angelica tries to decipher what I am suggesting. If they decided they could not send pictures from the bush with their phones, they decided to leave them behind so as not to lose them. Take pictures with their expensive new camera lens and show us the pictures when they get back.

<Probably worrying about nothing… did our parents do this to us?> Angelica almost sounds like she thinks we should just let it go. But I think I know her well enough to know she does not let anything go.

<Of course>

<Did you say Kisumu?> comes up almost immediately.

<Yes> I thought I was clear about where I found the phones.

<They aren't supposed to be there, left for the Tanzania camp a day or two ago>

<Unless they left their phones behind, they are still in Kisumu>

<Annie's phone is permanently attached> Angelica informs me, probably remembering more when she was in high school than now, but I understand what she is saying.

<The only time Charles does not have his is when he is in surgery> I confirm that Charles is unlikely to leave his phone

anywhere. But the safari guide could have told them to leave them in the camp so as not to lose them in the bush where they would not work anyway.

<Think we need some on the ground verification> Angelica is not comfortable.

<Agree>

<Howard has reached out to the tour company>

<They should be able to confirm if the kids extended at Kisumu> I realize the tour company will not talk to anyone at the camp.

<Also asked that they get in touch with someone at the camp. To verify> She is a step ahead of me.

<Getting imagery from Mwanza Lake Camp, just in case phone got left behind> I inform her, although I am seriously doubtful they would have left both phones behind.

<□>

“Jill?” I call to my assistant who sits just across from my door.

“Beau?” she responds immediately.

“See if you can locate Harry Boyer at Innovation Partners. I think he is in Kenya on a business trip.”

While waiting for Jill to find Harry, I bring up the imagery of the Mwanza Lake Camp where the kids are supposed to be. Check the date stamp. These pictures are a few hours older. The contrast to the Kisumu camp catches me instantly. I count at least ten people I can see, multiple vehicles, some bush trucks and some delivery vans apparently bringing in food and supplies, maybe more tourists coming in for the next day treks. I wonder if I should send a note to Angelica, but decide against it. This is just an impression. But I cannot help but wonder why the Kisumu camp looks deserted.

Returning to the Kisumu photos I realize that deserted is exactly what it looks like and yet that is where their phones are registering. The more I study the pictures, the more uneasy I get about it.

“Beau… I have Harry Boyer for you,” Jill calls. That did not take as long as I expected since it is getting late in Kenya.

I pick up the phone, “Harry… everything good in Kenya?”

“Who died, Beau? You never call me when I’m on a trip…”

I visualize the short balding ex-boxer who would burrow into a fighter and just pound away at the other guy’s mid-section, because he had trouble reaching their jaw, giving up height and arm reach in almost every fight. But Harry never gave up. And his strategy made it hard for anyone to really connect with him.

“I have a favor to ask…” I try to be as direct with Harry as he is with me. Do not waste his time.

“Had to be or we wouldn’t be having this conversation.” Harry responds.

“Charles is somewhere close to you on Safari for his honeymoon…” I begin.

“That’s right. You mentioned that at their wedding… great affair by the way. I got lucky with Alison that night. Gonna see her again when I get back.”

“Alison is a great person… I let Harry know I have an interest in protecting Lila’s sister from Harry if he is not going to be serious about her.

“Oh… right. No, I only have honorable intentions, bro.”

I can tell that Harry is reconsidering Alison, but that’s not why I called. “Anyway… Charles was supposed to move on to a camp in Tanzania to do the Serengeti, but that was two days ago and I’m getting pings that their phones, at least, are still in Kenya.”

"And since I'm right here, I might as well swing by and say hello and tell ET to phone home so Mommy and Daddy can get some sleep?" Harry is not subtle.

"That something you could work into your schedule?" I come right out and ask, knowing it might not work.

"What's today? Wednesday? I'm in Nairobi, would have to take a chopper over… where are they staying?"

"Phones are showing at Kisumu Safari Camp on Lake Victoria."

"Will probably be an all-day trip by air, and will set back the rest of my meetings unless I send Taylor. He would be the better choice since he was Charles' best man. Would make more sense for him to show up than me… if you know what I mean."

"Didn't realize Taylor is with you." I admit but instantly see it would be the best solution. Avoid awkwardness.

"Teaching him the business… he actually has a better sense of business than I do, even though I built this up from the ground. He just sees so much more opportunity than I ever did, and has a better grasp of how to realize it. Some point I'll just step back and let him go with it."

"You know where to send the bill…"

"The interest will be a case of wine… I'll let you pick the bottles since you know you'll end up drinking it when you come over for dinner. I have such lousy taste in wine and generally women, but I'm trying on both fronts."

"How is Taylor's Mom? That was Jenny, wasn't it?"

"Hard to keep track, I know… but yeah. Taylor says she's happy with the new guy. He's got more money than God, and takes her anywhere she wants to go. But not Africa. I'm still surprised you let Charles come here for a honeymoon. But I'm sure everything is good with them…"

CHAPTER NINE:
ANNIE THOMPSON

This house is tiny. One room that includes the kitchen and bath with no separating walls. No cabinets to keep food. No refrigerator, no stove top to cook anything. No heat, no air conditioning. Just a fetid smelling room with a chamber pot and cooler like we used to take to the beach to keep sandwiches and sodas cold with a bag of ice. Who lives here? I assume it is one of the men who are holding us as captives, but I have no idea which one. I cannot imagine this as my life. I should feel sorry for these men if this is what it is like to live here. But I have to believe that if life is so bad here that they could simply move to South Africa where they could get a job in a factory. No one is powerless to make a different choice. I am just glad that I chose my parents wisely.

Charles has his head down like he is thinking about something. He has been really uncommunicative. I am not quite sure why. His reluctance to talk has made me even more wary about these men. Although only one is in here with us. I assume the others are right outside, guarding the place and making sure we do not somehow get away. But with my hands zip tied behind me and barefoot, I really do not see me making a run for it. Particularly when I have absolutely no idea where in the world I am. All I know for sure is I am no longer at Kisumu and this certainly does not look like the pictures of Mwamza. No safari jeeps. No elephants, lions, giraffe or rhinos. None of the animals we came here to photograph. I really wish now that Beau had not given Charles that lens. Amazing how simple things cause a spiral effect on your life. Spiral out of control that is.

I whisper to Charles, “What country do you think we’re in?”

Charles shakes his head, which tells me either he does not want to say anything the guard might overhear or he really does not have any idea. Normally Charles has a guess about such things. He spends a lot of time trying to figure things out when he does not have all the information he needs. Makes him a great doctor, I suppose. But I would just like to get an opinion from him about whether we are in shit or deep shit, because as I remember some of the countries not so far to the north from Kisumu are in the middle of a civil war. Not a place I would want to find myself. Like South Sudan. But the Horn of Africa countries are not exactly warm and welcoming places for Americans, either.

I start coughing, and find it hard to stop. I call to the guard, "I would like a bottle of water." He just laughs at me and shakes his head. I cannot see the smile, but I certainly can hear that annoying laugh. I have no idea if he knows what I asked. Probably not. But it apparently does not matter what I asked, the answer is automatically, no.

Charles looks up at me, apparently responding to my asking for water.

"How long can we go without water?" I ask the doctor inside Charles' head.

"We are not there yet," is the only answer he will give me, and it is not an answer. Apparently, he is also concerned that we may die of dehydration before this is all over. At least I do not need to pee.

Charles looks up as I do. A distant sound approaching. It sounds like… no it is… a helicopter. I would recognize that whomp, whomp, whomp sound of the rotating blade anywhere. It sounds like it is coming directly towards us. I hold my breath… waiting to see if it is going to land here, pick us up, and take us back home. I no longer care about going to the Serengeti. I am done with Africa and with our honeymoon. I will be so glad to wake up in my bed in the District and return to my downtown office near the White House. Drink my latte in the morning while I am waiting to wake up.

The whomp, whomp, whomp, passes directly over this house, but does not stop to hover. Charles looks at me, crestfallen, as we both realize the helicopter is flying on to some other place. It has not come to rescue us. No latte in the morning. No walks past the White House on my way to work.

"That is the first aircraft I've heard," I whisper to Charles.

He nods in agreement, but continues to refrain from answering me with words. He must think the guards understand more than they are letting on. If that is the case, then he is likely getting annoyed I keep asking him questions. He would probably like it better if they put the gags back in.

Suddenly I realize that the guard who is watching us, did not react to the helicopter flying over. That would mean to me it is a common event. He was not worried that someone was coming to rescue us. He did not approach us threateningly. He barely flinched. But where are we? It was dark when we got here. No lights on, but there were city noises I heard. I do not think we are out in the middle of nowhere like the last place. Would make sense. Go from country to city and back. Make it harder to track us down. Keep anyone looking for us guessing. I am not convinced anyone is looking for us. We were supposed to be out in the Serengeti. No cell towers out there. And if I remember correctly, the Mwanza camp did not have cellular communications, just sat-phone. Charles and I talked about that. We decided that for two days in the bush, we did not need a sat-phone since our guides have one in the Range Rovers, they take us around in. Anything happens, the guides can get us air evacuated out. Was that what we heard? A helicopter evacuating someone out of the bush? Likely.

Charles scootches around and rolls over to put his head in my lap. I would love to push that stray hair back into place as I have so many times. But my hands are tied… literally. What is he doing? I look at him hoping he will say something. "Nap time," and he closes his eyes. I am supposed to believe that he wants to take a nap with his head in my lap. He has done this to me before, but usually in bed in either his or my apartment. Being a resident, he has learned how to take brief power naps. Fifteen to twenty minutes and he is back up and running at full speed. Is that what he is doing now? Brief nap to get himself powered up for a long haul, trying to figure out how to outwit these men. Although I do not see how we can possibly do that. But Charles is resourceful. This little maneuver makes me believe he has come to some conclusion. It could be as simple as deciding if he is more rested than these four men, that they will make a mistake, and we will be able to capitalize on it. Charles likely has three different plans in mind and is just waiting for something to happen he can exploit.

Charles' breathing slows and I know he is asleep. How can he sleep? I still cannot, even though he has been trying to convince me I must. I lean forward to kiss him on the head. He does not wake, but when I do that and he is taking one of his naps, he never does wake. I glance up at the one guard who is in with us. He seems sleepy, but is keeping me fully in his sight. Is that what Charles spotted? That this guard is getting really tired? That might be it. Will just have to keep my wits about me and be prepared to react when Charles does.

I close my eyes and feel the full weight of my exhaustion, weighing me down, causing my head to drop closer to Charles. I let the eyelids stay closed longer and longer, but I know I am not asleep. I am not about to let go and not be prepared for whatever these men are planning. When is this going to end? Have they made their demands? Is someone on their way to negotiate for us? Bring us home? Is this simply a ransom demand? Rich Americans who let their guard down for a moment and were carried away? It is entirely possible… but the likelihood just leaves me suspicious there is more going on here than we can possibly understand with the limited information these men have given us.

Charles stirs… was that fifteen minutes? Couldn't have been. I just closed my eyes. But I see his bright brown eyes looking at me, trying to make sense of my expression, which I am certain is more one of exhaustion than anything else. Maybe fear is in there somewhere. I am afraid of what is going to happen. Not knowing leaves you open to so many possibilities, and generally most of them are not good outcomes. But the not good outcomes are the most likely, from my experience. Does that make me a pessimist? That I expect the not good outcomes to be more likely than the good ones? Probably. But I have concluded that if I expect the worst, I am never disappointed, only surprised.

Charles tries to sit up. I push on him with my legs, but without his hands he is having trouble. He tries a couple more times to get back up into a sitting position, but cannot manage it. He lies back down, head in my lap and looks up at me as if this were just another Sunday afternoon… time that we can share because neither of us is running off. Why are Sunday afternoons always the best time? I think every moment of every day should be the best time, but that would mean that Charles and I were always available to the other, and that will never be the case.

The door to the house opens, and light comes through that blinds us both momentarily, until the door closes and we are able to see the man who has entered. He is not wearing a mask, but does not seem concerned about it. He does not look at us, but crosses the tiny room and talks very quietly with the one guard. I instantly see that the guard is not happy with whatever news he has been given. The guard stands up and comes toward us, grabbing Charles by the arm and bringing him up to his feet. A moment later he is doing the same to me. No words are said. We are pushed towards the door where the new man had entered. The new man watches us, but does not move. He is apparently not coming with us. Maybe he is the person who lives here. He has given these men permission to hide us here until someone finds out, and likely now, someone has found out.

I am the first through the door. Bright light. I can barely see anything. The road is sharp stones on my bare feet. I step gingerly and find myself pushed harder from behind. My eyes are adjusting. We are in a city. People are around, but they seem not the least interested in us. No one has stopped to watch. Apparently, the reason they did not gag and hood us is that might have caused more reaction that just letting us walk out this way. If I call for help, no one will have any idea what I am saying. A man on a motorcycle watches us briefly, turns away and rides in the opposite direction the van faces. Will he tell someone what he saw, or was he simply trying to get away from any possible bad outcomes from us being here? Or is this really a dream? But as Charles said, we have both been trying to wake up, and so far, it has not happened.

CHAPTER TEN:
ANGELICA MYERS

I am in my office at the Pentagon, the eleven displays on the far wall connect me with the commanding generals of each major command, including the seven regional commanders. This is the morning stand-up briefing. Each commander has five minutes to inform me of anything I need to know about events they are responding to, or anticipating. Eleven commanders, fifty-five minutes, and five minutes of discussion. The stand-up hour that begins every day, even though it is the middle of the night for some of those I am watching and listening to at the moment.

General Woods of TransCom is providing his briefing. Known to be the most terse of all the commanders, he seldom uses all of his allotted time. "We set a new record for most material in pre-placement."

"I assume that means we are better positioned to respond to any event than in any non-conflict situation."

"Correct, Madam Secretary."

"Besides the usual dirty dozen… what else do you need help from me on?" I respond knowing he is giving me several minutes to use as I please for a change. Normally I am the one who asks one question and finds that the entire five minutes has been consumed with that answer.

"At the Moment I am good, Ma'am."

"I hope you all learn the power of brevity…" I smile at the faces watching me. Being the first woman Secretary of Defense has been a learning curve for both those on the monitors and myself. Keep it short but do not neglect to inform me about something I absolutely need to know. I cannot help them with Congress or the President if they do not keep me informed.

"Madam Secretary..." General Hatfield, Commander of Special Operations Command is next to speak. "The daily list must be updated with a quick-turn operation in the Middle East."

"Which country?" I absolutely must have this answer and he knows it.

"We are not sure... The mission is on the border between Afghanistan and Pakistan. As of an hour ago the missionaries we are trying to extract were on the Afghan side of that border. But the Taliban appear to be moving them into Pakistan. By the time we arrive they may be across the border."

"The Taliban have them..." I seek confirmation.

"They do, Ma'am."

"So, this will be a hostile extraction. I would feel a lot better if they were in American hands and we were just trying to get them out." I realize our five minutes is quickly evaporating.

"There will be an encounter unless the missionaries somehow get free, but we are not expecting that to occur." General Hatfield sounds resigned to an incident.

"Why aren't we waiting for the Taliban to hand these missionaries over to the Pakistanis and then negotiating for their return?" I demand to know.

"Our sources on the ground have informed us the Pakistanis intend to imprison the entire group on suspicion of being spies for the US." General Hatfield fills in a blank for me.

"Are they?" I know better than to assume anything.

"Yes, Ma'am. They have been delivering intelligence on the Pakistani intelligence forces that have been supplying the Taliban for a decade."

"Why us rather than letting CIA handle this themselves?" I do not like the idea of an international incident because CIA could not take care of their own.

"CIA requested the mission because events overcame their planned extraction." General Hatfield explains what I assumed.

"So, they were trying to get them out, but simply started too late." I seek confirmation.

"CIA does not like to extract productive resources, even if compromised." General Hatfield confirms what I have concluded.

"How many are there?" I decide I will need to brief the President and I will need this fact.

"Six. Two families including two children under twelve."

"Get them out on the Afghan side if at all possible. The President will not want to explain to the Pakistani Prime Minister why we took action in his country… again. There is still a huge lack of trust on both sides because of Osama being protected in Abbottabad and the US going in, killing him, and bringing his body out." I close out this discussion within the allowed five minutes.

"Understood, Ma'am."

"General Maxwell," I call on the commander of SouthCom, which is responsible for Mexico, Central and South America.

"We have increased the training for Mexican, Peruvian and Colombian Navy special forces on interdicting drug shipments coming to the US," General Maxwell has a tendency to never quantify a report. I am never quite sure what he is doing or whether it is within budget. And for me the budget is paramount, since it gets so much scrutiny.

"Numbers, General." I chide him.

"It amounts to a ten percent increase in trained sailors and special forces." General Maxwell was expecting my question and no matter how I phrase it he always seems to find a way not to give me the specificity he knows I am looking for.

"Is that ten sailors and special forces or ten thousand?" I am not kind in my tone of voice.

"By the end of the year we will have enabled our partner countries to man an additional two-hundred and twelve air and sea craft, which we are also supplying as part of our military aid packages."

"And that is the ten percent increase in interdiction missions?" I suggest to push him to further clarity.

"Yes, Ma'am."

"So over two thousand air and sea-based teams, picking up shipments every day." I get a little more granular.

"Two-thousand-one-hundred and twenty when all are in service, so on a typical day figure two thousand." General Maxwell had the information but simply chose not to share it with me. And somehow, he thinks he should be the next Chairman of the Joint Chiefs of Staff. Not going to happen.

"General Tsetse, what is the latest from AfriCom?"

"Piracy is increasing at the horn," is his blunt assessment.

"Who do we think is behind it?" I push to see if anything has changed.

"Russia, China and Iran are all putting money into the pirates. It has almost become a competition between them to see who can disrupt shipping more, and at the same time, garner increased influence with the coastal nations that are all turning a blind eye."

"Who seems to be winning this little competition?" I ask since it seems there is a new lead dog every time this subject comes up.

"The fast boats are Iranian; the weapons are Russian and the intel seems to be coming from China. Although the Russian weapons are really old… seems they had stockpiled 1970s era equipment they apparently thought they'd never need before the whole Ukrainian invasion. Apparently, thought the Wagner Group would be able to manage it for them. But Wagner has lost so many men in Ukraine it seems the stockpiles have been left unguarded. The pirates have simply been helping themselves."

"The Russians aren't pouring new money and men into the situation, but they have enabled it by pulling the Wagner forces out to fight in Ukraine."

"Exactly."

"How do we reverse this trend?" I put it directly to General Maxwell.

"Step up naval patrols, more armed drone surveillance, be willing to take out the fast boats before they commandeer ships. Basically, assert ourselves," comes as his rehearsed response.

"Do we care about Russian oil shipments to China and India through this area?"

"The Chinese have bought off the pirates who are not commandeering their shipments."

I nod, now knowing the situation, but then I have to ask, "Are there any covert operations going on in Africa right now?"

"Yes, Ma'am."

"Are any likely to blow up?"

"It is possible…"

"My daughter and her new husband are in Kenya on safari. Should I be worried?"

CHAPTER ELEVEN:
FBI AGENT DAKOTA PLAINSMAN

The white federal style governor's mansion in Richmond is old. As I approach the front door, I see a plaque indicating this building has been continuously occupied by the governors of Virginia since 1813. That's like right after the war of 1812 with the British, when they burned down the White House. Like I said, old. Before I even ring the bell, the door opens and a guy who could easily be one of us, ear piece, sunglasses, even though he is inside, non-descript gray suit, and very plain tie and a shoulder holster, probably with a forty-five-caliber sidearm. Why do these local security teams always think a bigger caliber is better? Intimidation probably. In the kind of close encounters he is likely to find himself, that bigger bullet is not going to make any difference in the outcome.

"Agent Plainsman?" the guard asks. "May I see your credentials?"

I am expecting this request and have my badge and ID card ready. The security guard makes a big deal of reading every word on my ID card, then talks into a microphone in his left hand. "Seven zebra twenty-nine seventeen." He is reading off my badge number to make sure it matches the FBI employee data base. I see him nod to the message through his earpiece and he hands my credentials back to me. He then steps aside to let me in, "The Governor and Secretary Myers are waiting for you along with Mr. and Doctor Thompson in the family room, which is right here." He points to a door just behind him. Of course, he would position himself between me and those I might wish to harm if I were not really an agent. I nod to him and make my way across the marble floor, glancing up at the old paintings and wood stairwell that dominates this reception area.

The family room is decorated in the same style as was evident in the reception area. Old paintings on dark wood walls. The colorful curtains on the windows are very heavy fabrics and those colors repeat in upholstery and throw pillows around the room. Someone spent some time decorating. Likely was not the governor or his wife given their job responsibilities.

"Agent Plainsman, I'm Howard Myers," the tall and thin graying governor steps forward from clearly having been talking with the other couple. "This is my wife, Angelica, and this is Dr. Lila Thompson, and her husband, Beau Thompson."

I shake hands around and nod to each. The secretary appears more athletic than her husband, even though her face is lined and her hair coloring too perfect. The slender doctor is shorter than the others, hair pulled back in a pony-tail and too-white teeth. Beau Thompson makes me curious. His physique is more like the guy at the door. He was a star athlete in college, playing both football and baseball, but he went right on to grad school and completed a doctorate in particle physics before starting his own company, with the help of family money. His team mates ended up in key government positions, which helped him win large contracts. And now, his family has married into the family of the Secretary of Defense.

"What can you tell us about our children?" the governor has decided to be their spokesperson.

"This may take more than a few minutes, so you might wish to sit to discuss." I respond noting the facing couches and a chair at one end. I move toward the chair so the couples may sit together, but note the governor is also moving in that direction. I defer and elect to stand between that chair and the couch where his wife now sits. "To start with," I begin, now that I clearly have their attention. "The FBI has classified this case as a missing persons."

Beau Thompson interrupts me, "Their phones… did you find their phones at Kisumu?"

"Yes, thanks to your initiative, Taylor Boyer filed a report with us of his visit. He also found what appears to be all of their luggage." I provide the extra detail I know they will ask if I do not up front.

“That’s why you think they are simply missing?” The secretary asks.

“We have people in country who are working with the Kenyan authorities. They have experts on site and have been investigating thoroughly. At this point there are no indications that lead us to any conclusions.” I try to select my words carefully given this audience.

“Conclusions…” Beau Thompson wants more clarification.

“The camp was scheduled to be without visitors for the three days after Dr. and Mrs. Thompson planned to leave. From what we can determine, the camp staff was not expecting them to show up for breakfast as they had an early morning departure scheduled.”

“And since the camp wasn’t going to be in use for three days, the staff did not clean their room that day.” Dr. Thompson seeks to confirm what she thinks I am telling them.

“That is what they told the Kenyan officials who asked that direct question.”

“This is more than a missing person, Agent Plainsman…” the governor informs me. “My daughter would not leave her phone behind. It is practically a permanent attachment.”

“Charles is the same way… his whole life is in that device,” Dr. Thompson adds.

I nod, “That was our expectation. However, the Kenyan officials informed us that phones are often forgotten when visitors leave the camps. Seems that the camps ask that the visitors not carry them when out amongst the animals because they often get lost in the bush. Safer to leave them in the camp. And after several days of not using them, people tend to forget them.”

“But that doesn’t explain their luggage remaining behind,” the secretary drills me.

"No, it does not, and that is the reason we are treating this as a missing persons investigation."

"Why not a kidnapping?" the governor is expressing his opinion about what happened in not so many words.

"It has been three days since they were scheduled to leave and apparently did. If they were kidnapped, generally a ransom demand is made within twenty-four hours. I assume you still have not heard from anyone purporting to have them."

"We have not," the secretary confirms for me.

"If it were a political kidnapping…" I begin.

"It would have been all over the news by now…" the secretary is letting me know she has already examined this aspect and come to the same conclusion.

"I have to ask, who knew their schedule?" I put out there.

"The four of us and the agency that booked the travel," Dr. Thompson answers for all of them.

"What agency was that?" I look to Dr. Thompson, but Governor Myers answers.

"James River Adventures, here in Richmond. They book all the travel for our family."

I make a note of that in my phone, "They were just married, like a couple weeks ago? Is that correct?"

"Just one… week ago," Beau Thompson responds.

"Did they say anything to their guests about their honeymoon trip?" I push as I doubt those aware was as small a group as they indicated.

"Their official story was they were delaying the honeymoon until Charles finished his residency," Dr. Thompson informs me.

"Is that what was in the announcement?" I ask as I bring up the article that was in the Richmond Times Dispatch. No one responds as I quickly read. "Says here they will honeymoon in an undisclosed exotic location."

"Not enough to alert anyone who might have wanted to take them hostage," Dr. Thompson voices her opinion.

"In my mind, it was likely an inside job…" Beau Thompson voices his. "Someone at the camp or maybe the transport service found out who they really are and gave them up for a big reward."

"The Kenyan authorities are looking into that," I anticipated we would get here at some point. "If someone has them, that is likely the way we will locate them."

"You continue to sound skeptical that someone has taken them from the camp," the secretary is clearly unhappy with me. "Why is that?"

"Lack of evidence… lack of contact with a demand… lack of any indication that someone discovered who they are, rather than the assumed identities they were using."

"You may be making some bad assumptions…" the secretary informs me. "We are watched extremely closely by a whole bunch of not so nice people."

"You're referring to the Russians and the Chinese…" I know where she is going, but hoped I would not need to get into this.

"Principally… but there are others who would have facial recognition equipment that could pick my daughter out of a crowd. And with all the media coverage of the wedding, they likely have Charles in their databases as well."

"I would remind you, Madam Secretary, that this is an FBI investigation, and if you were to engage Pentagon assets, it would likely be an abuse of your position, and an obstruction to the investigation that could easily delay our discovery of their whereabouts and complicate any attempt to bring them home."

CHAPTER TWELVE:
CHARLES THOMPSON

The motor is running, but the van is not moving. Does that mean we are waiting for someone else? Are we going to change vehicles one more time? With the hood on and gag in, I cannot communicate with Annie or them. Cannot see them to know if it is even the same four men who took us from the camp. Have we been handed over to someone else? The Iranians maybe? They would love to get their hands on us to blackmail our government and Annie's mother. I did not want to think that was what is going on, but the longer this is taking for some resolution… I just do not know anymore.

My left foot touches someone. Is it Annie? If it is, she did not move in response. Maybe she is afraid it is not me, but one of the four men. Maybe she is afraid they will rape her if she gives them any opportunity. The longer this goes on, the more likely, in my mind, that they will kill us and dump our bodies somewhere they will never be found. Out in one of the game preserves, where the animals will likely tear us apart for dinner? Not something I would have ever thought of at home… but this is clearly a different part of the world, with different expectations and different possible outcomes.

I am sure now that it is Annie I am touching. Her breathing is labored. She must have the gag in as well and I wonder if she is choking. The longer I listen, the more convinced I am that Annie needs help. Needs to get that gag out so she can breathe easier. The voices are to my left. I roll over in that direction and try to make noise, pounding my feet on the floor of the van.

Someone I cannot see, roughly grabs me and rolls me over onto my stomach. My feet are pulled back, looped together and a rope comes around my neck, now holding my feet against my buttocks and my head pulled back by the rope. I do not know how long I am going to be left like this, but I am feeling like a beached whale… unable to move in any direction.

One of the men sits on my back, to make sure I do not try anything. I try to say he needs to untie Annie, but the man on my back slaps the back of my head. The message is clear. No help for Annie and they are clearly willing to restrain me even more if necessary.

The motor turns off and it becomes very quiet. Is this why they restrained me, to make sure I could not make any noise now? And if that is the case, where are we and what is about to happen?

The back doors unlatch and swing open. A voice I do not recognize barks at someone angrily, as if unhappy about something. Hopefully the way they have me tied up, but who knows? The man sitting on me gets up and rough hands begin to untie the rope around my neck and feet. Oh… I try to relax from the cramped position I had been in, luckily for not that long. But I cannot relax because something is about to happen and I do not have any idea what it is going to be.

Same rough hands slide me towards the back door and looking down I see that it is dark out. They are unloading us at a time when it will be difficult for anyone to see what is happening. They stand me up on the dirt road and make me wait while they apparently do the same to Annie. When we are both out of the van, the door closes and the vehicle pulls away. We are pushed in a direction, but again without shoes we walk tentatively, slowly and that makes those we cannot see unhappy with us. They push harder to get us to go faster, but I still carefully pick out where to place my feet. Last thing I want to do is break an ankle or something by stepping on something I cannot see.

We come to what must be steps as they stop us and then tap our legs as if to get us to step up. I do and find five steps in front of me, leading into another building, but I have no idea what it looks like with the hood still obscuring my vision. The space we have come into does not have any lights on. I am not sure how our captors know where they are going in the dark. But then I am pushed down into a sitting position. I assume, but do not know for sure, if Annie is also next to me. I hope she is.

The hood comes off and the gag is untied while my eyes try to adjust to the dark, but the hood goes back over my head before I can make out anything other than three indistinct shapes. One of them is sitting right next to me. I hope it is Annie, but did not see enough to be sure. Makes sense they would be keeping us together, but I am not completely sure they are doing anything that makes sense to me.

"That you, Annie?" I whisper hopefully loud enough she will hear, but not the others.

"Charles?" sounds frightened now. More so than earlier. She must be getting pessimistic that we will ever get out of this endless nightmare.

"Remember the breathing exercises we are doing before going to bed?" I remind her to get her mind off the situation. "Try doing them now. It will calm you and that's important."

"Are you doing them too?" she apparently wants to make sure I am not just asking her to do something I am not.

"I am," I respond quietly, but firmly so she will hopefully do as I ask.

Her breathing changes and I follow. Slow deep breath. Blow it out a little at a time until it is all out. Then breath in slowly, filling my lungs and holding it… full lungs… for about five seconds. Doing this relaxes the muscles in my diaphragm. Brings them under conscious control rather than unconscious fear driven tension. How long can I keep her going on this before the panic overtakes her… overtakes me… again?

"Where do you think we are?" Annie whispers and I can barely hear her question.

"No way of knowing… but probably not in Kenya anymore. People there must be looking for us by now, so my guess is they took us somewhere else."

"Why are they doing this to us… moving us all the time? Sometimes with hood and gag, others neither. Sometimes they give us food… and others not so much."

"They don't want anyone to know where we are," I try to answer her question without sounding simplistic about it.

"The least they could do is let us change into street clothes," Annie is feeling self-conscious about still being in our bedclothes.

"This gives them an advantage…" I point out.

"I would think we would stand out more this way," Annie is not thinking like them.

"They aren't concerned about us standing out since they are keeping us locked up most of the time in places like this and transporting us mostly at night when fewer people will see us. If they were to let us get dressed, we might be more likely to try to escape, thinking we could blend into crowds, if we could find any."

Annie sighs, apparently understanding the situation better now. "Are you getting hungry?"

"No… I'm past hunger…" I respond. "Don't think I would want to eat what they have been offering us. Likely give us stomach problems from bacteria we really don't want in our guts."

"Why hasn't that been a problem in the camp?" Annie's voice is rising now above a whisper and I am sure the men know we are talking. Just not sure if they know what we are saying.

"Everything is fresh in the camps. Washed, dried, cooked to make sure any bad bacteria are killed before it gets into our body. They have had the English here forever, so they know what weak stomachs we tend to have. They know how to feed us so we don't get sick at the camp… but I'm not sure these guys know that."

"No talk," comes from a voice behind me. He apparently heard Annie and probably listened to my response before telling us to shut up.

If we are in a building somewhere and we are mostly whispering, what difference does it make? No one is going to walk by and hear us. No one is going to peek inside and see us sitting here with our hands zip-tied behind our back and hoods over our heads. I realize it is getting hotter here than the other places we have been so far. What does that mean? A change in the weather or someplace where we are more exposed to the heat of the sun and less air movement? A city maybe? They tend to be hotter and that would explain why they sat on me and left the gags in until we were in a place where no one could hear us even if we shouted. Would not make any difference anyway, since whoever heard us would likely not have any idea what we were shouting.

I suddenly realize the one guy who understands some English is the one who is here and just yelled at us. “Bathroom?” I ask expecting he will not respond.

To my surprise a few words are exchanged with someone who is closer. I feel a hand under my left arm, pulling me up to my feet and pushing me in a direction. When he stops me, the hood comes off and I see I am standing in front of a western style bathroom. An actual toilet and sink. The zip tie is cut and I am pushed into the room, and the door closed behind me.

Down come my pants and I park myself on the toilet, pushing hard to empty what remains in my bowels, which is not much, since it has been a while now since either of us ate anything. I likewise empty my bladder. Just as I am finishing, the door opens and Annie is standing there, hood off, blinking at me with a masked man holding her left arm. Finding actual toilet paper, I wipe and pull up my pants as I pass Annie who is now coming in. Did they even give me a full minute to do my business? Not much more. The door slams behind me, zip tie to my wrists, and the hood back over my head.

It is not long before I hear them bring Annie back and push her down to sit beside me.

CHAPTER THIRTEEN:

LILA THOMPSON

The FBI agent is gone, but we still do not have any answers. "We should be talking to somebody more senior, somebody who knows what is going on."

"I talked to the Director… Agent Plainsman is one of their best investigators." Angelica informs us.

"But is that what we need here? Someone who investigates rather than riding herd on those Kenyans?" I am just not comfortable with the situation.

"He is more likely to ask the right questions of those in the field…" Beau responds unhelpfully.

"But an Indian…" I begin again.

"Native American…" Howard corrects me. He would… Mr. Politically Correct.

"You have to cow-tow to all those minorities… because you need their votes… but Indians have a reputation…"

"Native Americans are as hardworking as you or I," Howard refutes me again. Have not seen this side of him before, but then again, we have not had this discussion before.

"Indians are lazy drunks… and I don't want him as the guy trying to find the kids…" I am not going to let this go.

"Hold on Lila," Beau puts his arm around me. I know he is trying to calm me down, but I wriggle free and stand back from him waiting for him to try that again.

“I have several Native American engineers at the Tucson testing facility,” Beau continues to watch me closely. “They are some of my best spatial thinkers. They see things differently, but that ends up being an advantage in a lot of the things we do.”

I nod to Angelica, “You said you already talked to the Director… you can call him again and tell him we want someone else. Someone we can have confidence in.”

“And who is that?” Angelica is letting me know she is not in favor of doing as I am asking.

“I don’t know… a Deputy Director or someone who can call up those Kenyans and tell them what they need to do. Someone who will go over there and lead the thing… right there… on the ground.”

“Agent Plainsman said we have someone there on the ground with the Kenyan officials.” Beau must think I am embarrassing him because he is taking their side. He never does that. What is he doing?

“I want Charles home! And I don’t believe this Indian is able to do that… bring him home… alive.”

“We are absolutely going to give him a chance to do his job,” Beau continues. “Angelica already talked to the Director so he knows the importance of having his best team working this.”

“But he was disrespectful to you…” I respond to Angelica. “Telling you to stay out of the investigation. Who is he to tell you anything?”

“He’s right,” Angelica responds calmly. “I have to walk a fine line. I can’t deploy Pentagon assets to find them as it would absolutely be a conflict of interest and would likely cause me to be replaced. But the intelligence agencies can ask for assistance from NSA and the various defense intelligence agencies without the need for my involvement. I have to expect that is what they are doing. Particularly since Agent Plainsman brought it up.”

"You are not going to change my mind on this… he needs to be replaced with someone who can get the job done. And if you won't make the request, I will… through Danny Wilson."

"Our Senator…" Howard shakes his head. "The minute you go to Danny, the media will be all over it and we clearly don't want that."

"Why?"

"What if…" Beau starts and stops to make sure I am listening. "Let's say someone does have the kids. What if they don't know who they are? They think they just hit the jackpot by capturing a couple Americans. And anyone who is staying in those camps has to be rich almost by definition. They're trying to figure out how to make their ransom demands and all of a sudden, the media blows up with who they have. Realizing they are out of their league they kill the kids and walk away to hide."

"Or they go to the Russians, Chinese or the Iranians and say 'let's make a deal'." Angelica inserts into the discussion. "That is absolutely the last thing we would want to happen."

"Wouldn't they return them to us?" I am not following what she wants me to know.

"More likely they would put them in a prison as spies without a trial. We have no insight as to who they are holding because they don't make any records public. We would never know what happened to them, because they would likely die in prison." Angelica explains to me.

"What if…" Howard inserts to get our attention. "What if we are all thinking just from our own frames of reference. I understand why Angelica is thinking the worst. She has to do that all day. But what if they haven't been kidnapped? What if they went out on a safari and their vehicle broke down and they've been stranded out somewhere? That would explain why their phones and clothes were still in the Kisumu camp. There are other explanations. We have to recognize this may all turn out differently than we are fearing. The kids are likely fine, either way. We just need to let the authorities have the time and support they need to get the job done. Stay out of their way. Don't slow things down. Too much supervision from above means they have to do extra reporting rather than extra investigating."

"Howard has a point," Beau looks directly at me.

"I hope he is right," I stare Beau down. We are going to have a frank discussion when we get home because I am not happy with his lack of support right now. "But that Indian has to go."

"Would you feel the same way if the agent was a woman?" Angelica asks me with a curious expression.

"A young woman? Yes." I shake my head. "A woman who has been leading major investigations for a while and bringing in the bad guys… I would be comfortable with that. But what's the record of this Indian? Who has he brought in? Who has he brought home? I just don't have any confidence in someone who is clearly in over his head."

"Would it help you to know that Agent Dakota Plainsman has three Director's Commendations?" Angelica tries to make me think I am being unreasonable.

"For what? Showing up? That's their reputation. They get drunk and don't show up sometimes for days on end. Everyone knows Indians can't hold their liquor."

"Do you know where that comes from?" Howard steps into the discussion.

I shrug because it is just common knowledge.

"When the US Army rounded up the various tribal nations out west after the civil war. They would bribe the tribal leaders with alcohol… get them drunk for days and days and then take them off to reservations. Usually, marginal lands where they couldn't grow much of anything. They made the tribes dependent on the government. Kept them from growing outside the reservations. Put the kids in special schools where they tried to brain wash them into not being what they were. It was a shameful time in our history. But it wasn't the tribal members who were lazy drunks, it was us, who took away their freedoms and made them dependent on us to live."

"That's so woke…" I dismiss Howard's narrative.

"Do the research… not on Fox News, not in the blogs or social media… go out to the states with tribal nations. Go to the court houses. Read the actual documents. Go to the reservations and talk with those who still live there. Do the hard work of finding out the truth for yourself rather than taking the easy way out by living in your jar of prejudice." Howard is not backing down either.

"Not worth my time… after all… there aren't that many of them left. We killed most of them, didn't we?"

I see Howard shudder, "Listen to yourself. 'We killed most of them, didn't we?' You just acknowledged what I said about it being us and not them that is the problem here. And that many? There are six or seven million Native Americans living today on hundreds of tribal lands in like fifteen or so states. Not all of them are in the west, either. Some of them are not so far from here."

"That's bullshit, Howard," I push back now. "There are like three tribes left… all out in Oklahoma as that is the one state no one really wanted… why there's not much else there."

"Do the work, Lila… find out for yourself. We don't live in a simplistic world. There is no room for ignorance or prejudice. You're a doctor… would you join a practice where the other docs refused to use antibiotics to help treat patients?"

"That's settled science…" I respond to not answer his question.

Beau puts his arm around me, not to restrain me, but to make contact so I cannot ignore him. "I don't know about you, but I plan to help Agent Plainsman find them. I have some connections that might help us. He didn't say anything about not getting involved, and it will be a whole lot better than just sitting around waiting for news. And I can do things independently that will keep you out of trouble, Angelica, and yet hopefully get the kids home sooner."

CHAPTER FOURTEEN:

ANNIE THOMPSON

I am so thirsty. No idea how many days it has been… probably a lot. Is that part of what they are trying to do to us? Keep the hoods on so we have no idea if it is day or night? One day or thirty? What Mom would call psychological warfare. Disorient the enemy so they do not know what to expect next. Then they are relatively easy to defeat. But that does not make any sense since these men already have us as prisoners. There is nothing for them to defeat. They are not asking us any questions, seeking a confession for something someone else likely did. They have not put us in a prison. So, I do not know what they expect of us.

It was painful to pee, because there is so little left in there. What happens when you have not had any food or water in a while? I could ask Charles, but they got mad when we were talking. I do not want to get them angry with us. Would they beat us? Waterboard us? What would they do? Since we have no idea who they are, or what they want, it is impossible to know.

I decide to ask, "What do you want?" I call out.

"Know soon." It is that same voice. Only one of them answers or ever speaks English.

"Why can't you tell us now? We're not going anywhere." I respond.

"We are probably better off not knowing," Charles responds.

"How do we maintain hope when we don't know what we are up against?" I know I am losing it.

"Hope is all we have, babe. We aren't in control of anything that will affect the outcome, so we have to be patient and take each thing as it comes at us." Charles sounds more resolute than I feel.

"How do you do that? Oh, that's right. You're a doc and docs always have to be optimistic about the outcome of every procedure you perform. It's in your DNA." I certainly do not feel that way. Even though as a lawyer I have to be optimistic about the outcome of every case I take to trial. But optimism for both of us comes from preparation and we certainly were not prepared to be taken hostage on our honeymoon. No way we could prepare for what has happened.

"What did your mother tell me that one time?" Charles asks to see if I am following him.

"No one walks on the moon without leaving footprints?" I guess he is telling me that people are trying to find us. Even though we cannot see where we are or where we have been, the vans we are riding in are leaving footprints. That people who know what to look for will figure out who took us and likely why. And then they will be able to find us and set us free.

I hear a door open and footsteps coming toward us. A short discussion again in that same sing-songy language I cannot fathom. My hood is lifted up, the gag tied in place and the hood goes back down. In that brief moment I see a fifth man. He does not have a mask up, but I have never seen his face before. He could be anyone. He was watching me and somehow, I do not think that was a good thing. Could mean he intends to rape me at some point. Or maybe he is seeing me as the golden meal ticket to a big payday when he contacts Mom and Dad. Only they have not asked us who to contact and that has me worried. How would they know unless they ask us? The longer this goes on without them asking us anything, the more I think they do know who we are. Are they negotiating with the State Department? If this were any part of the world other than Africa, I would have a better idea of what to expect. But this part of the world is just such an unknown to almost all Americans. Who comes here except the rich who want to see big animals? Who else, besides businessmen who want to buy local goods and oil and those who want to sell everything from cars to crypto. No wonder the people here think we are all rich. Those are the only Americans they ever see.

Hand under my arm and they are pushing us out the door. Is this the place that had the five steps? Hand under my arm again, leading me down the steps and then across the dirt to the road where the van had been. But if I am remembering correctly, the van left as soon as we got out. Does that mean we are going to be in a different vehicle this time? I try to move the hood around so I can see down and out. Is it day or night? Seems to be night. Still warmer than most of the nights until now. Makes me think we are in a city, and the noises of a city are here, but distant. Probably means we are on the fringe of a city, but not in the downtown area. Suburb maybe? And if a suburb, which city? As I remember looking at the map, there are not many cities in this part of Africa.

The door to the van is open, the same rough hands turn me around, push me back until I sit down on the floor of the van, lift my legs and push me in, where I end up lying on my back, with hands behind me. Rough hands again push me towards the side of the van and as I slide, I feel something sharp run into my left hand. I pull it out and feel blood in the palm of my hand. Not a lot. But something sharp!

The back door slams shut and I hear the engine start up. Engine sounds different, this is a new vehicle… not brand new or anything, but new to us, new to moving us around. So, if anyone spotted the other van we were in, they will not be able to track us in this one, unless they were watching the place we were staying. And if they were watching, why did they not come in and get us out? Have to assume no one is watching.

The van shakes back and forth as it gathers speed on the rough dirt road I walked out on. Then there is a bump as we apparently have come up on a paved road. The ride suddenly becomes smoother. Definitely on a paved road.

The men up front engage in a short conversation. I am not sure if there is anyone here in the back with us or not. I suspect the answer is yes, given what they apparently did to Charles. I could hear them tying him up. Maybe there are two of them back here. Need to be very cautious about the sharp point I found. It is right here behind me somewhere. Prick! Found it. My fingers feel the sharp protrusion. I try to rub the zip tie against it but end up cutting my wrists almost as much as the zip tie. If I can get my hands free, there may be a way to get away from these men. Surprise them somehow. Have to rely on Charles for most of that, since no one is going to be afraid of me. Maybe a hundred pounds soaking wet.

I am not going to let the bleeding stop me from getting free! I keep rubbing the zip tie against the sharp point. Feel the deeper cut on my wrist but I am making progress. Just have to keep the cut away from the veins, but I do not know how to do that when I cannot see what I am doing.

The van takes a curve and I roll further into the side, which causes me to stop my exuberant sawing on the zip tie until we straighten out again. Wish I could see where we are, but even if I could I would have absolutely no idea where I am or where they are taking us. Nor could I communicate with anyone about our plight.

Back to sawing. I pull apart with my wrists and feel the zip tie giving a little. At least I have weakened it to the point it should not take much more sawing to be free. I slow the rate of movement, trying to pull apart more, which will hopefully weaken it and cause it to saw quicker. And then I feel the SNAP! I can move my wrists apart, but not too much. Do not want anyone back here with us to know what I just did. I rub the cuts in hopes of stopping the bleeding. In the meantime, I try to stay still so the men in the back with us will not suspect any change.

Now the question is can I get Charles over here to saw his zip ties? How do I do that without being obvious? Even though my hands are fee, I would need a sharp object to cut Charles ties. Cannot just undo them with my hands. I wiggle at the sharp point, but it seems to be a part of the frame of the van. I am not breaking it free, even though that would be the ideal situation. Use it as a knife, rather than a sharp point on the van chassis.

The van slows and ultimately pulls over to the side of the road. Are we meeting someone here? And if so, why here? Wherever here is. Is this where I die? I got my hands free. The first step in regaining freedom, but almost immediately we pull over. Did one of the men in the back here with us see what I was doing? Did he leave me alone because he knew we were stopping soon? Or did he signal the driver that it is time to dump this load? Dead by the side of the road. Is that not how most stories end? In sight of your goal the road ends and that is all she wrote about you. Why did I ever marry Charles? If I had just let it be. Live together. Be happy. Have kids even… but not get married. Marriage is an ancient tradition, but it is only a tradition. There is nothing that makes it a requirement for anything other than paying group taxes. You and your spouse. Married, filing singly… you can do that, so why can you not declare yourself single, filing married? If you are committed to each other, have been living together for the whole year, sharing expenses. Why not?

If we had just kept on doing what we were doing, we would not be here… in Africa. He would not have gotten that stupid long focal point lens for his damn camera. He would not have thought the perfect place to use it was Africa. He would have kept on with his residency and we would be that much closer to private practice and an income that would permit us to do whatever we wanted long after Mom left her current position. Long after anyone would care who we are. Anonymity. Is that bliss? I do not have any idea about anonymity having grown up in a family that was on the front page of the local and then national papers almost daily. How did a homebody like me ever end up with Howard and Angelica as parents? Must have been the mail man. That is all I can think of. Or maybe I was adopted and they just have never gotten around to telling me. That must be it. Adopted from a family where the father worked for garbage collection and the wife cleans houses. Both in sanitation. At least that would explain why I tend to get obsessive about wearing clean clothes. And if not sanitation, maybe they were both social workers who tried to help the poorest live a decent life, even without the means to do so. That would explain why I decided I needed to marry a freaking doctor.

CHAPTER FIFTEEN:
HOWARD MYERS

Frank Ibrahim comes to the door of my Capitol office. As head of security for the State of Virginia he has a lot of connections, not only with various law enforcement agencies across the country, but also within the federal government where he once worked.

I get up from my desk and come around to the two comfortable chairs to the right side about half way towards the door. There is a low table in front of the chairs where I have a coffee table book on the history of the State of Virginia, with some great pictures I often look at to get ideas of where to go on vacation where I will also be able to mingle with constituents.

Frank waits for me to sit before he does. I notice the earpiece and bulge of his sidepiece in the shoulder holster. I have wondered if he ever got angry with me if he would be the one to take me out. He would have the easiest time doing so, since he is the only armed individual allowed in my offices.

"We are not getting a warm feeling about the kids…" I begin since Frank was going to check with friends in the CIA, where he previously worked. He advised against the trip, but I do not always listen to his advice. This is now one of those times where I wish I had. But it is hard to say no to Charles, particularly now that he is an adult and a doctor at that.

"How long since you last heard from them?" Frank goes right to the main point.

"Sunday… when they left Nairobi. Took a picture of the two of them from the balcony of their hotel room. City in the background."

"And they were supposed to have left on…"

"Tuesday to drive to Tanzania and visit the Serengeti… the main attraction of the whole trip."

"So, they should be on their way home now?" Frank is trying to time line this whole thing.

"Tomorrow," I correct him.

"They never arrived at the Tanzanian camp… you confirmed that?" Frank wants to be precise and so far, I have not given him much precision.

"FBI did for us," I let him know the Bureau is involved in the case now.

"If the Bureau has it, what can I do for you, sir?" Frank takes a step back to show his deference for the feds.

"We… the four of us, parents… want to make sure we are doing everything we can… legally and ethically… to help the Bureau find them and bring them home."

"Why do you think the Bureau isn't covering all the bases?"

"It's Africa, Frank…"

I watch him process that statement and finally a single nod. "The Bureau has to work through the police in that country. Which one did you say they went missing in?"

"Kenya. Kisumu Safari Camp on Lake Victoria." I answer the specifics and watch him close a single eye trying to picture that part of Kenya.

"Lake Victoria… that's all the way the hell over on the other side of the country from Nairobi, isn't it?" Frank is trying to picture it but has a lot of gaps to fill.

"It is," I realize what he is pointing out. Long way from the central government. And in Africa, distance is freedom to do what you want.

"My Sudan contacts tell me that part of the world is tough from a law enforcement point of view. Pretty wild, not a lot of people out there, probably a day or more just to drive out from the capital and they don't go out unless someone has already done something to someone. And generally, from what I remember, the someone is a rhino because of the horn's erotic value. Or elephant for Ivory."

"You clearly know more about it than I do, Frank."

"Can't do anything about the fact they are there… that means we need to figure out how to find them and get them safely back home, with the least muss and fuss… am I correct in that assumption?" Frank is up to speed.

"As usual, you have gone right to the heart of the matter," I note as we have talked about this in the past.

"I have some friends in the Bureau and can ask some questions… unofficially… probably over some beers where there is no trail of official anything." Frank frames it just right.

"That would be appreciated," I confirm my acceptance of his approach that will keep me from any criticism for using state employees to address a personal issue. All on his own time and at his initiative.

"Let me ask a question… what is Angelica doing? Don't want to get tangled up with the big boys."

"Nothing," I confirm. "She can't. She's waiting for the FBI to ask for assistance, but if they don't there is nothing she can do." I summarize for him.

"No wonder she is all over you…" Frank now sees another dimension to the problem I am trying to address.

"Not all over me, but she is just feeling frustrated that she sees over the most powerful military force the world has ever known and she can't employ it to help find her daughter."

"No one fears the State of Virginia… at least since the Civil War… but we still have resources at our disposal to help our citizens. They may be getting other people to do things at our behest, but we are long in relationships if not in resources." Frank summarizes.

"Speaking of relationships…" I raise another opportunity for Frank to consider.

"My CIA contacts in Sudan…"

"You remember I have a complicated history with the Agency…" Frank is reluctant. "They still think I screwed up and are not about to forgive and forget. But the guys in Sudan… they say things are pretty quiet in Kenya. Were surprised to hear about Americans going missing. Hadn't heard anything."

"Thanks for trying. Angelica will call the Director and have a conversation at that level…"

"Which will not give you any answers or offers of help. The Director doesn't know and can't be seen as doing any favors for a cabinet member. Waste of a call, but for protocol's sake she might just want to give the Director a head's up. Brenda Wolfson is as good an international lawyer as you'll find… but that still leaves a lot to be desired when you are talking about special operations under her purview."

"What about Smitty?" I throw a suggestion at Frank.

Frank physically reacts to that name. "Smitty… now there is a name I was not expecting to hear from you, sir."

"She is in the right place to know what might be going on in that part of the world." I point out.

"Smitty…" Frank has to think about my comment before commenting back. Smitty is a senior intelligence officer at the NSA, which means she listens in on communications all over the world, except in the US where such listening is illegal… at least everyone agrees it is illegal… except it is still a source of intelligence when needed. "Smitty… would have more insight than anyone I can think of."

"Do you think FBI would consider using her?" I have to ask for an opinion here since neither of us really have any idea if they would.

"Hard for me to know, sir," Frank is hard at work solving this problem now, which is more than I could ask of him.

"When was the last time you took her to dinner?" Smitty and Frank were an item at one point… a long time ago, before NSA had one of their frequent personnel reviews to make sure there were no foreign intelligence officers who had penetrated them. And since Frank's last name is Ibrahim, that was a problem for Smitty, who is Midwest pure American.

"I'm not sure she will accept a dinner after all this time." Frank is weighing what happened and clearly is not happy about the way it ended. Likely neither is Smitty, as she has never married, to my knowledge.

"What else can I do for you, Frank?" I decide I have given him all the insights I can at this point. Hopefully he will be able to find something that will be of use in finding the kids.

"Double my budget every year for the next five years and I might just be able to do all the things you put in my job description."

"Unfortunately, you know I don't have the power of the purse in State government. I can recommend it, but the House formulates the budget from my recommendations and we start from there."

"I know, sir. But I had to ask. And just a final question, and you can tell me to mind my own business, but how is Angelica really handling this whole thing?"

CHAPTER SIXTEEN:

FBI ANGENT DAKOTA PLAINSMAN

Juma Kamau stares back at me on the Webex. As the Kenyan Director of State Security, the shiny dark faced man, with close cropped graying hair, is primarily responsible for protecting the senior government officials. "The problem is, everyone in government thinks they are senior, even if they joined the government yesterday," Juma points out, with a bite that tells me he does not laugh at the situation but wants everyone else to.

Since he is the most senior law enforcement official in the Kenyan government, he also gets the opportunity to talk to people like me, from around the world, when something goes wrong for one or more of our citizens. Lucky Juma. But Lucky for me, Juma speaks excellent English and has travelled to the US. He understands our country better than many of the others he must respond to. That makes my job so much easier in finding out what is really going on.

"We have the opposite situation here. Most of our senior people don't want our protection," I reflect. "Until it is too late."

"I hear you," Juma nods knowingly. "Is that what happened in this case?"

"State Department was given a courtesy notice after they were already in country, but no specifics as to an itinerary," I give him the facts as they were given to me.

"Important people all think the same. If no one knows, no one can cause them harm," Juma displays his knowledge of how such people think. "What they do not realize is that today, no one goes unnoticed by those who have the means."

"And more and more people now have the means," I reflect on the increasing difficulty we are having keeping people safe when cell cameras are everywhere, and there are a million places to post pictures that not everyone in them want out there.

"Indeed," Juma responds as if he has already gone on to his next thought. "We may be faced with just such a situation. Your State Department informed us that Dr. and Mrs. Thompson were married just what? A few days ago?"

"Yes," I know he understands the situation, but wants me to understand there are as many cameras in airports and train stations in Kenya as there are in the US. Only in Kenya, people who operate such systems are very poor and easily corrupted.

"We have reason to believe that many of our border guards regularly provide photos of interest to several governments that we would prefer they did not." Juma admits as way of explaining how a young couple, travelling incognito, could still be identified by more than one group that might want to do them harm.

"Such people live in every country, Director Kamau," I hope to ease any tension between us by confirming that I do not blame him or Kenya for what may have happened.

"Even yours, I have been told," Juma grimaces.

"Even my country has such people in sensitive positions of trust," I confirm.

Juma looks away from the camera on his computer. Apparently, he was hoping I would deny that such could be the case. Probably hoping there was some place in this world where corruption and foreign surveillance do not exist as in Kenya. I understand his desire, having had to fight for equal access in everything I have ever tried to do in the country regarded as the bastion of freedom.

"My people are in the camp at Kisumu as we speak," Juma confirms they did not just go out, find the phones and luggage and return. They are investigating and looking for any indication that would tell him what happened to Dr. Thompson and Mrs. Thompson. "What they have informed me is there is no indication of a struggle. There is no indication of harm coming to anyone. There is no indication that anyone forcefully entered the camp."

"What about the camp staff? Have you interviewed everyone?"

I hear a sucking sound as Juma inhales, not wanting to answer this question. "At this time, we have not. And you wish to know why."

"I do… wish to know why," I try to sound agreeable, but also fulfilling my responsibility.

"Have you ever gone on safari, Agent Plainsman?" Juma decides he needs to put this answer into context.

"I have not had the opportunity to visit your beautiful country, although I hope to remedy that… but hopefully not now." I try to make a point.

"Safari camps are not hotels as you think of them in your country," Juma begins his explanation. "They are far from any city, or even settlement, as we think of them here. Everything is trucked in. Food, water, fuel for the generators that power the lights and cook stoves and refrigeration."

"What about communications… I understand their cell phones were found in the camp. Why would they have left them behind?"

"I have asked this very question," Juma responds apparently anticipating me. "What I am told is most visitors wish to take pictures with their phone cameras. Even if, as in this case, they bring special cameras to take pictures of animals from far away. Something about how quickly they can get a photo with the cell camera. With the long lenses and special readings for light and all, the others take so long to set up that the animals are often gone."

"That is not what I have been told…" I inform him. "Our people said they likely left the phones at the camp when they went out to see the animals so as not to lose them."

"A common misconception," Juma informs me. Apparently, he has heard this often. "Until now I thought that to be the case. But I asked the camp director personally."

"You have been out there?" I am surprised.

"I have. This is a high-profile case. My president does not wish to deliver bad news to your president. I have been told to use every means available to return them to you as quickly as possible."

"I am grateful your government has engaged to such a degree. So, the fact that the phones were found at the camp at Kisumu is unusual?"

"Highly," Juma responds immediately. "My investigators have not found any evidence of a forcible removal from the site, but we are operating under the assumption that is likely the case."

"Who?" I go to first.

"Not why?" Juma wants to clear the air such that the other questions will not be a dance to not admit who the young couple is.

"She is Annie Myers Thompson, daughter of the sitting Secretary of Defense," I put out there so there is no ambiguity.

"Your State Department did not wish to share that information," Juma has realized that I am not going to make his job harder. "But the fact that the call came from a senior State Department official to our Foreign Minister alerted us to the fact this was not just a young couple on their honeymoon."

I am going to like working with Juma. He tells it like it is and can see through the bureaucratic bullshit we all deal with all day long in situations like this. "Thank you for reading ahead…" I do not know any other way to express this without sounding disrespectful of my own government.

"One possibility… that is very hard for us to verify…" Juma does not want to raise this, but apparently thinks that because I do not really understand Kenya, I need to be aware. "There have been instances where hungry animals have come into the camps in the middle of the night."

I am stunned. He is suggesting what? That Dr. Thompson and his wife may have been… "How is that possible? Do the camps not provide any kind of security?" I demand to know.

"Actually… they do not. The camp staff is asleep until around four am, when they begin to prepare the morning meal. Every night there is a five, to six-hour window when animals may enter the camp."

"Animals… like lions…" I try to fathom what he is suggesting.

"There are many animals quite capable of killing and eating men and women. What my team has seen has not ruled out such a possibility." Juma wants me to know that he has not ruled it out. That is not what he thinks happened. However, he does not want me to accuse him of not having informed me of that possibility. Particularly if their bones are found not so far from the camp.

"Thank you for the morbid scenario… but back to the ones where we might actually return these young people to their families, homes and professions…" I try to turn Juma back to the questions at hand.

"I had to inform you of the possibility, as much as I do not believe that is what we are dealing with."

"Who, then?" I repeat my earlier question.

CHAPTER SEVENTEEN:

BEAU THOMPSON

"Can you bring the drone down lower?" I ask Joe Alvarez who is flying a small drone in widening circles around the Kisumu camp. Looking for any indication of what may have happened to Charles and Annie.

"Sure boss," Joe responds. I do not know why he calls me boss, but he has since the first day he went to work for my company. Short and pugnacious, Joe loves to fly the drone, loves to parse through the video it sends back for any clue to the mystery we are trying to solve that day. Joe is the best I have ever seen at picking clues out of video feeds. He must not miss a thing. And that is what I am counting on as the days continue to march away from us. Still there is no indication of where Charles and Annie may be or why they are not on a flight home today.

I have never been to this part of Africa. No reason to in my line of work. Safari was never high on my list of must go do things. But the images coming back from the little drone that is half way around the world are beautiful in an austere kind of way. Not lush and green… it is a dry climate and it seems I remember that is one of the threats to this region. Drought. The waters are evaporating. More animals must drink and bathe in a whole lot less. Rivers are running dry. Rivers that animals from all over would follow in migrating because that was where they could always find water and plant life to eat… when not feasting on each other.

Not a lot of wildlife this close to the camp, but I am seeing monkeys in the trees and smaller animals that must come to the camp area expecting the larger predators will not come this close to the humans who have been known to kill the bigger species that roam this area. From what Charles said, Victoria is relatively light on herds. The masses of the animals of interest are in Tanzania in the Serengeti. That was why Charles wanted to do Kenya first. Learn how to see what he wanted to first before going out to the migrating herds that are now so stressed by the water and plant-life shortage.

"How is this, boss?" Joe checks back now that he has brought the drone down several hundred feet. I was looking towards the horizon at the higher altitude, but now I look almost straight down. Looking for something that might have dropped from them as they may have walked off into the bush, or been forced to walk away from the camp by someone who took them, but did not want to be heard or seen. Th*at makes sense, doesn't it?* But truthfully, assumptions may be the shortcoming of this whole search effort. I am assuming they did not go willingly from the camp. I am assuming they are still alive, somewhere. But if that is the case, why hasn't anyone contacted us about them? From what Angelica has said, it seems the entire Kenyan Army is now engaged in looking for them. Not that she asked them to do so. Since we do not know when they went missing, we also do not know how far away they might be. You can fly half-way around the world in eighteen hours. They've been gone a lot longer than that.

"Boss?" Joe interrupts my thoughts.

"You find something?" I instantly jump to what I hope is the case.

"In my experience… if we have not seen anything at this distance from the camp… I don't think they walked out." Joe just lays it out there for me. One of the things I like about him is that he tells me exactly what he thinks, and it is usually informed by a depth of experience I do not have.

"What do you recommend, Joe?" I really do not want to hear what he is about to tell me.

"I want to go over to their tent and trace everything I can from there," Joe keeps the drone flying in the expanding circles in case I do not agree. "If you want to keep flying the bird, you can do so from there. Just if it goes down, you'll need to call me."

"Probably a good idea…" I am feeling defeated, but need to keep pursuing everything until something clearly narrows the range of possibilities. So far, nothing has eliminated any other explanation.

"Soon as I see you've taken control…" Joe waits for me to do so.

"Got it…" I am now flying the bird, as Joe refers to the drone. A small quadcopter, it has four rotating propellers on top and a sixteen-megapixel camera hanging below. It is simply amazing how much high-resolution imagery can be captured and transmitted from such a small device. And since the battery is good for about an hour of flight, it can cover a lot of ground in a short time. *I need to watch the battery... need to be able to get back to the camp before it runs out.*

The landscape moves quickly below. I see absolutely nothing that seems out of the ordinary. And I am sure I am not seeing everything Joe was. The question is whether I would see anything out of the ordinary that might suggest Charles and Annie went this way. Or that someone… not from the camp was going in to take them away.

Lila walks into my office, "Hey babe..." I greet her without looking around. I know her step and catch her trying to sneak up on me all the time. It has gotten to the point she is never surprised anymore.

"Is that the camp where they were?" she asks as she comes up right behind me and looks over my shoulder.

I do not answer her question directly, deciding to skip on ahead in this conversation. "Joe doesn't think they walked out, so I'm continuing the aerial search while he does a more targeted investigation at the camp itself."

Lila seems fascinated by the fast-moving image before us, does not ask a follow up question having apparently gotten all the information she wanted. Suddenly she puts her right hand on my shoulder, "What's that?"

"Where?" I bring the drone to a halt, hovering, waiting for the next instruction from my console.

"It was on the right, movement that caught my eye…" Lila leans over me now, trying to get closer to the image we are both studying.

I move the drone back along the same path it has been flying, but I do not see what she did. I bring the drone up a hundred feet to see if it would find whatever she saw. Nothing comes into view so I retrace the flight path a little further and then Lila points to a tree.

"That's what I saw… what is that?"

I watch as a monkey moves through the branches of the tree Lila pointed out. Suddenly the monkey leaps from one tree to another, catching branches and swinging itself up to a perch where it can surveil the area around it for a predator that is likely hungry and more than willing to settle for a monkey snack.

Lila pulls back from the screen, "Oh… is that…"

I bring the drone down so she can see the monkey more clearly and as I do so, I notice movement on the ground, which looks to be some kind of very large cat. Probably a very hungry large cat. Also, likely what the monkey is watching and trying to ensure cannot get to it.

"Would the kids have climbed a tree to avoid a cat?" Lila asks, contemplating what she has just observed.

"They should have been with an experienced guide," I point out to my wife. "And I doubt they would still be up in a tree after all this time, even if they had resorted to seeking safety like that."

Lila exhales deeply. I did not realize she had been holding her breath.

"I'm going to keep circling the camp now…" Need to let her know we are done here. I engage the drone to continue the concentric search and glance up at Lila, since we have already gone over this area. She looks so worried, still clinging to the hope the kids are alive and fighting off the fear they may not be.

My phone rings… "Hey boss… I may have something here," Joe does not sound excited, apparently not wanting me to get my hopes up, but something important enough that he thinks I need to know about it.

"Something?" I echo.

"I found tire tracks very close to the tent where they were staying. Didn't think much about it until I checked the other tents. No tire tracks in front of them. So, I asked the camp director if they pick up the guests at their tents and he confirmed they do not. Then I checked the tire tracks against those of the Range Rovers they use to go out on safari. Not the same. I'm sending you a text with the picture of the tread. Might be something we can use if it is not a common tire…"

"The tracks look relatively fresh?" I have to ask. If they are old then we are wasting our time, but I have never known Joe to waste my time.

"Still clear, so no one else has been here since then. No one walking through or animals walking across. Yeah… I think they are fresh enough to be of concern."

The image pops up on my sat phone. I look at the tracks and agree they appear to be recent. I forward on to Agent Plainsman at the FBI with a note, <Agent… tire tracks from the Kenya Camp, outside Charles and Annie's tent. Can you identify?>

Lila puts her hand on my shoulder again as I bring the drone back to camp. "Joe… could you use the drone to follow those tire tracks? Probably needs a new battery."

"I'm on it, boss," and he hangs up.

CHAPTER EIGHTEEN:
CHARLES THOMPSON

This time they are taking us a long way from where we have been. Another country, maybe. The distances here are not that far, from country to country. The other men in the vehicle have not said a word in a long time. Nor has the speed varied much since we left that last place. But still… they are keeping the hoods on, gags in, and hands bound.

Are they afraid we will be able to identify them if we are set free? That is the only thing that makes sense to me. Why we have hoods and they have masks on. Right now, I could walk past any of these men on a street and have no idea it is the same person. The only clue I have is the voice of the one who has spoken a few times to us now. If I heard that voice, I might recognize it. But even then, I likely would not be entirely sure. He has spoken so few words.

I have to assume they are holding us for ransom. Only thing that makes sense. But why is it taking so long? That part does not make sense to me. But then again, I really do not know anything about kidnappings and ransoms. And in this part of the world… who knows how it all works? But these men seem to know what they are doing. Keeping us on the move… can only mean they are afraid that someone might see something suspicious and turn them in. No more than a day in any one place. Even the vans they are moving us about in seem to change every day or two.

I am finally no longer hungry all the time. Guess that means my body has finally decided I am not going to be getting much nutrition soon, and is starting to adjust. Annie has a lot less fat than I do. Makes me worried that she may get weak a whole lot quicker than I will. And if she is weak that could mean her body is doing real damage to her organs. Not a pleasant thought. I have to find some way to get her something to eat, something to get our bodies back into balance.

I feel Annie move. It seems she wants to change her position. Must be getting sore lying on one side all this time. But then I feel my hood move up just a tad. I look down and see Annie peering up at me. She has her hood back and her hands are… free!?? What does this mean? I listen since I can still only see very little, mostly just her eyes. A deep breath and then I listen carefully. No change in the speed of the vehicle, no talking among the men in the van. How did she get free?

Annie moves her head as if she wants me to move, but quietly. I know the men are still in the van because it has not stopped for them to get out. I try to scootch in the direction Annie seems to want me to go. I keep scootching, quietly, until I come to the wall. Now I feel Annie's hands pushing me back, towards what I think are the back doors. I could be wrong about that, although I have tried to remember everything.

She pushes me a little more and I suddenly feel a sharp something… *what is this?* I realize it is part of the frame of the van. A sharp piece of metal protruding… apparently just enough that Annie was able to cut the zip tie.

I hook my zip tie over the protrusion and start to saw away at it, but I instantly feel the sharp cut into my wrists. Got to slow down here. Don't be in such a hurry. I do not know when Annie found this, but we have been driving for hours. I have to be patient, although we could arrive somewhere at any minute. I try to slowly saw at the zip tie. As much pressure on the cutting surface as possible. But the problem with this approach is that it cuts me deeper at the end of the stoke. Do not think I have cut a vein yet, but I am feeling blood on my fingers, so I have not escaped with just a minor cut, and wrists are no place to play with sharp objects.

Deep breath, slow hard sawing. Single strokes in each direction. Cut the plastic as much as possible on each stroke. And although it worked for Annie, I cannot tell how much progress I am making. Cannot tell if I am half way through or just beginning. And even if I get my hands free… what am I going to do with four armed men? Absolutely they will not be expecting us to have our hands free. Element of surprise and all that. Yeah… but even if I disarm one… there are three more who will put a bullet through me before I even figure out where the safety might be on whatever kind of weapon they have.

Are we better now having our hands free and just continuing to go along with whatever this plot is? If we take any action against them will that end our lives at that point? More likely than that we will get away. And get away to where? Never mind worrying about that part. Keep sawing… if we have options that cannot be a bad thing.

The van begins to slow… Oh, shit. We must be close to where we are going. I try to speed up the sawing. Hope to get it to break, but no matter how much I put pressure on the tie, it holds. Now the van slows more and begins a turn to the left. This road is very bumpy, in comparison to the paved road we had been on for what seems like hours. Good news is that we are almost somewhere. The bad news is I no longer have much time to finish cutting this zip tie.

The two men in the front start a conversation. Again, it is in a language I cannot decipher. Sometimes I can guess what people are saying in a language I do not understand by the tone of voice and how they raise or lower the end of the words. This language just seems beyond me. There are clicks and other sounds that have no meaning in western languages. They could be talking about their kids playing street soccer, or how they are going to kill us this time because they did not get the ransom they were expecting. Not a pleasant thought, but a realistic part of our situation. I cannot assume that just because they have not harmed us yet, they will not. We have no visibility into what is going on out there or back home.

The road is very rough and the van has slowed even more. Hard for me to keep sawing away at this zip-tie because it keeps coming out from the sharp edge and I keep cutting my wrist more each and every time it comes out and away. I try to push the wrists apart… put as much pressure as possible on that weakened zip-tie, but it continues to hold. I should stop trying to saw at it because the van is just getting tossed all around. But I have no choice. We are likely almost to where we are going. It is either cut it now or lose the opportunity. There is no reason to believe they will take us from this location to the next in this same van. In fact, it is more likely they will not, based on their pattern to this point.

Annie touches me, apparently also worried as to whether I have been able to cut through. My lack of response to her touch should answer her question.

After hooking the tie around the sharp edge, I try using very short stokes to my sawing, hoping this will stay on the blade side even with the bumps. This approach seems to be working better. But it is also likely cutting a whole lot less plastic away. No choice. Got to keep at it as long as possible. But then a thought occurs to me. What if they spot that Annie's hands are free? Or that Annie tries to surprise them somehow? I cannot talk to her to coordinate a response. I just need to hope she plays it as if she were still tied. I do not know if they check our ties or not. We cannot see. But I have to assume… and that is always a bad thing to do… but I must assume they do not check our ties expecting we have nothing that would make them any less secure.

A big pot hole or something tosses us up into the air. I do not come back down in the same place. Now I have to search around to see if I can find that cutting surface. Scootch… but in which direction? I roll and find the wall first. Okay. I was right up against the wall when I was cutting away. I decide I probably landed more towards the back door, just given the forward movement of the van when we were tossed up. Scootch up a little and feel for the sharp point. Not here. Scootch again. An inch or less at a time because I cannot use my hands to help me. It is all my feet and legs.

I feel around, but still, this is not the same place. Nothing that can help me cut through the tie. Another scootch. I feel what might be where it attaches to the frame of the van. Another scootch and yes. This is it. Hook over the zip tie. Try to saw away with those same mini-strokes as we are being thrown around in the back of this van. Is anyone else back here with us? If they are I cannot believe they are asleep or anything. They must be watching us. Does that mean they are simply waiting for me to cut through as well, and then they will put another tie around our wrists? Is all this for nothing? Cannot think about that. Keep sawing… keep cutting away the tie that binds me. Give us options as I do not want Annie to feel she has to do something more to save us from whatever these men have planned for us.

The van comes to a stop. Now I have a moment to put as much pressure on the tie and as long a stoke as possible. Until the back door opens. Stroke… stroke… stroke, pull apart as hard as I can… stroke, pull… it has to happen… now.

I hear the front doors open and feel the van rock as the two men get out and then slam their doors shut. I hear the footsteps as they come around to open the back doors. But they stop. I keep sawing, pulling, trying to break the tie. I listen to the sing-song voices, but the exchange only lasts a minute or less. Then the footsteps and I hear the back door open before the light tells me it is day time. They are unloading us in the day… that must mean we are out somewhere that no one is going to see them taking us out and walking us into another building.

I feel the strong hands on my feet, pulling me away from my cutting edge… it did not cut through. Shit, I failed to get free and may not get another chance to finish the job. Now we find out if Annie plays it right or this is the end of the line for us. I am apparently the first one out the back. Someone stands me up and turns me to my left before stopping me. I hope they are waiting to get Annie out. Do not even realize I have stopped breathing until I hear her feet touch down on the dirt. At least they did not bring us out on a gravel road with sharp pointed stones that cut our feet. Dirt is better.

They march us to another door, another building, only this time they knock and wait for someone to answer. Is this someone's home?

CHAPTER NINETEEN:

ANGELICA MYERS

She is back, at least I think it is a she. The tiny owl that sits in the tree just outside my Georgetown home. Howard is at the mansion because he still has a state to run. But we keep this apartment in the district for me and us on some weekends, when Howard comes up. Sometimes when he is here on state business, he will stay over with me rather than head back down. If only Richmond was a little closer. But then if it were, there would have been no Civil War. Not enough distance to keep armies from marching in and taking over the other. I am actually amazed at how close they are.

The owl looks at me with those piercing big eyes, the tufts of hair that look like ears and a face that humans have ascribed to wisdom, for ages. What does she know that I do not? Does she think it folly I try to keep America safe from so many who would do us harm? Why am I the most qualified or the right person to be sitting in this seat at this particular moment in history? Or am I? Is this the test that will determine if I am the person I think I am? The person who puts nation ahead of family and personal travails? Or will I prove to be the same self-centered egoist who has been in this seat for most of the history of our nation. Who was it said you cannot get to this place without being a ruthless person capable of the most horrific acts? Sentencing people all around the world to suffer the devastation of war and the resulting famines and plagues that always follow. That is my job. My job. But if I were not sitting in this chair… it would be occupied by someone… likely a man, since all my predecessors have been… who do not find war so horrifying. Men who have tried to take death and mutilation of our troops out of the equation, while at the same time imposing all that and more on those who would take up arms against us. And there are likely more who are willing to oppose our will than support our imposing it on them. Thus, the Ugly American. Is that who I am? Someone who blindly goes through the world and life without seeing or experiencing the harm we do to others?

I told the Senate in my confirmation hearings that I will not be as eager to go to war as some who have been here before me. I am an advocate for diplomacy. Find common ground, use restraint, seek peaceful means to resolving conflict. But for some reason, those politicians, my husband included, seem to feel that if you have the strongest military in the world, it needs to be exercised from time to time, just to prove out doctrine and weapon systems and logistic support. Determine whether it is the tiger in the jungle or a Potemkin Village?

Restraint… when provoked. That is what I said I would use. And now I have been given an unexpected test of my core beliefs. Will I walk my words, or will I find another way, as I did so many times when that was my job. And having found that other way so easy… I became horrified at what I had become, and broke with what everyone said was going to be a bright future… to become something quite the opposite, where that was not to be expected.

The wall screen in my office illuminates telling me that one of my generals wants my attention. His name comes up first, "General Tsetse…"

"Madam Secretary…" is the reply I hear before his image appears. He is in his office at the Pentagon wearing combat fatigues. Not a good sign. "You asked me to share all of the intelligence we have been requested to supply the FBI."

"I see that coming in. Do you have Cliff Notes for me?" I ask to use the name of the very old summaries of books students used to use before the internet. I do not know why the Department of Defense uses such old references, but somehow, they persist… likely because everyone who works there now has heard them since the day they started.

"All our imagery and signals intercepts for forty-eight hours before and after." General Tsetse responds as if it were a simple request. I know it is not because we have so much collected data from those two sources that we have to automate our searches to find anything in it.

"And is there anything of value in what you provided?" I push him now, not liking how the game is played between the civilian and military intelligence organizations even though they are supposed to be integrated in operations.

"The area in question is not one we generally pay attention to, so assets are not continuously surveilling."

"Is that your way of saying it was basically useless and you would have been happy to tell them that if they had simply asked?"

"It is their operation; we are merely assisting…" General Tsetse thinks anyone not under his command is an idiot. Generally, that would include me.

"Did you discuss their request with them? Provide insights that may have shaped their request to be more targeted?"

General Tsetse turns his head to look at me. I have seen him do this in the past when he thinks he is being asked a question or being requested to do something that is a total waste of time… for him. "The request did not come to me… it came to NSA. Their analysts pulled what was requested, gave us the parameters and retrieved our analysis."

"Standard procedure… for a very non-routine set of events," I remind him.

"I am being very sensitive to protecting you, Madam Secretary. Should I do anything more than is the standard response, you could be subject to criticism and possible censure, for exceeding your authority."

"Thank you for being concerned about me, General. But that is not the question I asked."

"AfriCom is my responsibility, Madam Secretary. I know I was nominated to this role by your predecessor, but none-the-less, you have not deemed it necessary to replace me in this role, or appropriate to promote me to another. Given any other orders, I am and will continue to command my forces as appropriate to protect our nation's interests in that part of the world. And if I were to treat one set of circumstances differently than another, that might give you cause to remove me, and justification for the Senate to agree."

"Why is it General, that you and I always seem to be sparring?" I respond without looking at him, but rather at the owl that continues to sit in the tree outside my window reminding me that I need to have wisdom to do this job.

"Sparring?" The general knows what I am saying, but has chosen to dispute my choice of words.

"If your son decided to sail around the world in a small sailboat…" I begin and he knows where I am going.

"My son would never…"

"Besides the point for a hypothetical…" I shut down his response. "If your son chose to sail around the world in a sailboat and went missing in the South Pacific. Would you expect Admiral Nelson to only conduct his search as he would if the missing individual was the son of an elevator operator in Manhattan?"

"They got rid of all the elevator operators in Manhattan years ago." General Tsetse tries to show that my illustration is impossible and therefore not relevant.

"A retired elevator operator, from New York, now living in Florida in a retirement home. Is that better?"

"A more plausible hypothetical… but still not relevant to my actions to date."

"Or lack of actions to date," I correct him.

"Madam Secretary… you may replace me at any time you feel I

am not doing my job. But absent this one instance where you have a conflict of interests, when have I not done my job?"

"General… you seem to have forgotten that we are all part of the same team here. There is a reason our government chose to have the military directed by a civilian. And I know it is particularly difficult for you to take orders from someone who never served in the military. So… I am going to solve the problem. You are hereby relieved of your command. Effective immediately you will report to Fort Belvoir with a travel kit until such time as you receive new orders, which will come from Army Personnel. Those orders could come in the next twenty-four hours or in the next twenty-four months. The needs of the Army will dictate."

"As you wish…" General Tsetse ends the video call abruptly.

I call up the Commanding General of Special Operations Command, "General Hatfield," I greet him as his familiar image appears on my screen. There is a moment of delay before he responds, "Madam Secretary. How can I help?" The confidence in his voice is quite the contrast to General Tsetse who always seemed to feel he was under attack and therefore had to circle the wagons when we spoke.

"I am unhappy…"

General Hatfield nods as if he were intuiting what I am thinking. "I take it the FBI is struggling and could use a hand?"

"If you were to contact Agent Dakota Plainsman, that would make me much happier."

"Understood," General Hatfield is thinking this through. "Is there specific assistance they need?"

"Your insights would be invaluable to their investigations…" I conclude the call.

CHAPTER TWENTY:
FBI AGENT DAKOTA PLAINSMAN

"General Hatfield, I am giving you access to our casefiles and the intelligence provided by NSA. What would really help me right now is your ability to fill in any gaps. What aren't we looking at that we need to? Information about who is active in that region that might have been involved. We asked NSA for that and their response was it was not part of their remit to assess that kind of information."

"NSA said that?" General Hatfield seems genuinely surprised. "They do tend to defer to CIA. Maybe that is what you walked into. Depends on who you are talking with."

"That's helpful… who would you suggest I talk with over there?" I decide might be the quickest way to get what I really need.

"Agent Plainsman… that is your name?"

"Dak… short for Dakota," I respond hoping I can break through barriers here.

"Dak… I'm Kemal Hatfield, by the way… my mother is Iranian and father was a Kentucky moonshine runner, when he wasn't working for AT&T. Don't ask how they got together… way too long a story."

"Over a beer sometime… I'll buy," I respond hoping that will get us back to the question on the table of who I should be working with at NSA.

"Look… your bureau and my command have very different relationships over across the Potomac. I could give you my guys… but they are used to our kind of missions and we have a trust relationship built that… quite frankly… you guys just don't have. Not easily transferrable. My guys can get whatever you need. We can do a SOCOM analysis and figure out how we would use that information to run an op. But from what little I know… an op may not be what you need." General Hatfield is giving it to me straight… which is exactly what I need.

"And if I need you to do an op to get them out?"

"Channels for that exist… need to use them."

"Okay… what would you suggest?" He is not making this easy for me, but then I prefer that. Do not want SOCOM coming in and shooting things up if that is not warranted, and so far, I do not know enough to know whether it is or not.

"Call this guy at CIA I know… Yuri Tereshkova is his name. He's a legend over there and he is well connected."

"A Russian?" I almost fall out of my chair.

"Yuri was born there… granted. But he's been an American almost as long as I have."

"What does that mean?" I am not sure what he is saying.

"Yuri's family was sent to the gulags for having independent thought. A curse they visited upon him. And when he put Russia up against USA… he decided we may not be perfect… we may not always be good… but no matter how you slice it, we are better than what he had known. And he would like nothing better than to bring down the government that sent his family to their early death."

"You trust him?" I seek a confirmation.

"What is more important is the people who trust him," I find that an odd endorsement but I will take it thinking he must be talking about the President or CIA Director or somebody well above my paygrade. "I'll make a few calls… get folks lined up to feed you whatever we have. Now I have to warn you… that may not be what you need… but likely the best we can give you." General Hatfield is gone.

Yuri Tereshkova… holy shit. He's asking me to trust a Russian about a probable kidnapping in Kenya… which may not even be that, given the high profile of the parents involved here. The last thing I want to do is get CIA into this case. They fuck up two car funerals for sport.

The safer thing is to call Beau Thompson, which I do. "Mr. Thompson… Agent Plainsman here."

"Did you get the tire tread photo?" he asks without even saying hello."

"I did… thank you very much for that," I respond to try to get this conversation into a conversation and not a heated dumping fest.

"Well…" he wants to know about the tire tread.

"Hankook 215/75R15. The most common van size in the world." I read from the email response from our technical team.

"Hankook… is that Korean?" Beau asks.

"Yes… but they are one of the primary tire sellers in most of Africa and that is the most common van size for mud and snow, which is what they tend to use for vehicles in that part of the world. You don't always have a paved road, so, they buy those tires to keep from getting stuck. Aggressive tread."

"Short hand… no smoking gun. Every freaking van we find in Kenya is likely running those tires," Beau is not happy… apparently expecting he had narrowed the list of possible kidnappers only to find we are no closer than before he found this clue.

"I don't know if you can consider this good news… but it means it is more likely they were kidnapped. That means we are more likely in a position to get them back… and hopefully alive. What is confusing to me is why we have not heard from whoever took them."

"This long is not normal… for kidnappings…" Beau asks almost looking for a reason they are likely dead.

"No… it is not what we normally see in kidnappings… but that could have a couple different meanings."

"What do you mean?" Beau is only partially listening.

"Could mean they just figured out who they have and had an 'oh shit' moment. That is paralyzing their response because they don't know what to expect from us." I give him the first of the whole list I have created.

"Or?"

"Charles and Annie died when they were taken and the captors are trying to keep as much distance between us and them and they can. The problem with that is what happened to the bodies?"

Beau almost goes vertical with that explanation because it fits what we know. "I refuse to accept that outcome," Beau responds. "There is no evidence that happened at the camp. And if it did not happen at the camp… I don't think it happened."

"I am just giving you the hypotheticals… likely one of them, and our problem at the moment is figuring out which one it is." I respond to his dismissal, hoping he will at least consider it.

"You said two possibilities. I cannot accept either one." Beau is still processing the second scenario.

"There are more… it could be they ran into someone they knew in Kenya… med school or law school for her and they decided to join their safari. That happens from time to time. When it does… we lose sight of people for a week or two. Suddenly they are landing and coming through immigration in New York or Chicago and no one had any idea. That is the optimistic scenario."

"But not one you think likely," Beau pushes me.

"I am not a fan of coincidence…" I respond honestly. "Rarely explains the cases I have worked in my career here."

“Then what do you think is the situation we are facing?”

“Amateurs…” I give him a plausible scenario I have seen before. Not sure I really believe this now, but it might explain some of the things we are seeing.

“Either they know who Dr. and Mrs. Thompson are… or they don’t. If they know… it could be they are negotiating with whoever sponsors them… turn them over to the sponsor who will have to deal with the US Government, or not… try to negotiate directly… but they don’t know how. If they don’t know who they have… it could be they are trying to figure out who will pay a ransom for them. Do they go directly to the family or do they work through the Embassy since that is the representative of the US government in their county. Amateurs are so unpredictable because they don’t know what the usual way of doing this is. Does that make sense to you?”

Beau looks at me as if trying to decide whether I have any idea what I am doing and whether I am the person to lead this investigation. “Your experience is all domestic… is that right?” Beau asks.

“It is…” I do not deny what he has just accused me of.

“Then why should I pay any attention to your theories that are not informed by experience in that part of the world?”

“Because I have brought home every person the bureau has asked me to bring home.”

CHAPTER TWENTY-ONE:
HOWARD MYERS

I am in the district for meetings with the Federal Highway Administration about funding for interstate highway maintenance. Historically this has never been a contentious discussion, but for some reason the feds have decided this is the time to ask us to fund more than in the past, even though the funding ratios are set in law. All bullshit as far as I am concerned, and I have already talked to our congressional delegation about it. But still they wanted all the governors to appear, and beat us up, to show who controls the purse strings. Why I ever decided to run for governor now eludes me. This is not the kind of leadership I hoped to provide. But for some reason, when certain people get a little power, they want to change all the rules, even when the law says they cannot.

When I arrive at the apartment, I find Angelica in her office in a heated conversation. That is not unusual. It seems every time I come home, she is in a heated argument with someone who disagrees at one level or another about anything she wants to accomplish. She talks strategy. They talk tactics. And it is as if one is speaking Greek and the other Turkish… two languages that will never lead to understanding.

I trundle down the hallway to the office I use when here. It was a bedroom where we set up a desk and computer I can log into. Not an ideal situation, but it works for us. I'm not about to spend a whole lot more money for me to have the convenience of working from where ever I am. I also am not here all that much, although it seems I am here more than before, because this ends up being where Angelica is. Never realized how all-consuming the Secretary of Defense job can be. Particularly for someone who is not from the defense establishment. And Angelica convinced the President she would bring a different set of eyes on a bureaucracy that is infamous for resisting change. I think

Angelica underestimated the task she was taking on. She has been home to Richmond fewer and fewer days the longer she has been in this chair. And I miss her terribly…

I have just logged on when Angelica wanders into my office. She walks right up to the desk, leans across and kisses me as if she has been waiting all day for that opportunity. I know I have, so I try to communicate that in my response.

"It's been a good day… relieved one of my combatant commanders and won a budget debacle with congress that threatened the whole transition I'm pushing. How about you?" Angelica drops herself into the one chair in the room not behind the desk.

"No accomplishments to compare with your successes," I respond with a grin.

"Yeah… I'll trade you any day." She responds, but I know she is not serious since she does not even know what I accomplished today.

I decide to go right to what I know she wants to talk about, "What have you heard? About Annie?"

"They are still officially missing… which I guess is better than being officially dead… although that has been known to not be true as well… but all in all… there seemed to be no movement today and that is why I have a new commandant of AfriCom."

"Sorry you had to make the change…" I know how stressful it is to relieve someone since certain congressmen seem to think it their job to question everything she does.

"It was overdue…" she tosses aside as if it were no big thing, even though I know it was.

"Who are you putting in there?" I ask as she apparently needs a few minutes to readjust.

"I don't know yet," she answers honestly, but surprisingly, as she usually has these moves all planned out well in advance.

"Why is that?" I pursue her reluctance to explain fully.

"I have to see how Annie and Charles gets worked out…" she looks at me since she is telling me she is basing a government decision solely on a personal event, which she has always said she would never do.

"Did you talk to Agent Plainsman today?" I pursue her.

"No… did you?" she looks as if she had not thought about this.

"I did… he had apparently just gotten off the phone with Beau…"

"Nice to know we are all keeping him from doing his work," Angelica sounds annoyed with Beau and I have never heard her be critical of him in the past.

"Not the case… he is fully engaged in bringing them home quickly," I inform her. "He did explain to Beau why he got this case…" I dangle out there knowing she will bite on that one.

"Lila certainly doesn't want him," Angelica remembers the discussion after the first meeting with Agent Plainsman.

"Still doesn't… but Beau told me that Agent Plainsman has never not found the missing person or persons. When you have a perfect record, I guess the FBI decides it is time to really challenge you."

Angelica looks at me curiously… "But this is the fucking African Veldt… not Peoria."

"I hear you, but the truth of the matter is, the FBI works through law enforcement in other countries. It will ultimately be worked out by someone other than an American FBI agent. They call them liaison agents for a reason," I inform her.

"Howard… maybe we should just take a trip ourselves… stop in Kenya on the way to Las Vegas… see the sites, kick some butt and bring the kids home… what do you think?" Angelica sounds like she is beginning to look back and not ahead.

"You know what Agent Plainsman told me?" I decide to change the subject.

Angelica shakes her head, too tired to try to play guessing games.

"That the site was so pristine, the Kenyans thought maybe the kids were abducted by aliens."

Angelica nods, "Makes sense…" she looks at me and I see her mind is going back to earlier discussions. "When you don't have a fucking clue, you just attribute it to something else you don't understand. But then again, in Kenya, there are probably a lot more things that happen there they don't understand than here."

"Not necessarily…" I try to bring her back to this discussion.

"Oh?" Angelica asks me to explain.

"What do the Kenyans know better than anyone?" I start down my thesis.

"Life in the bush?" Angelica leaps forward and lands in the neighborhood of where I was going.

"Have you been reading about the drought? In Kenya and most of Africa?"

"Sounds familiar, but where are you going? We're not blaming their disappearance on Climate Change, are we?" Angelica is not going to be patient with me on this one.

"The animals are stressed this year…" I point out.

"I'm stressed every day… where are you going?"

"The animals… the big cats and all the herds are finding their water supply is almost exhausted. Plant life is disappearing. That is their only source of food other than killing other animals."

"The cycle of life… what else am I supposed to know about this, Simba?"

"This is not the Lion King… this is serious and it's for real. I did some research. There have been more attacks on humans this year than any prior recorded year."

"If there had been an attack on Charles and Annie, the camp personnel would have reported it."

Angelica seems to want to dismiss this theory… but it also fits the facts since the tire tracks seem to have led nowhere. "The camp personnel scattered to their homes when the last of the visitors were no longer there for them to feed and guide."

"Are you done? This has not been a helpful conversation," Angelica does this to me every time I tell her something she does not want to hear.

"No, and I'm not saying their bones are scattered across the African Veldt… but we have to realize there is a different explanation we cannot dismiss… particularly since there has been no contact from a kidnapper. That is what does not make sense. Why keep them all this time when you could have your money by now and be out spending it?"

"I am not giving up hope…" Angelica nearly shouts at me.

"Neither am I. But we have to prepare ourselves that the outcome may not be what we want and hope for."

Angelica looks at me. I have seen that look before. She is telling me she needs a hug and I need to give it to her right now. I do as her eyes command, come around the desk and kneel before her, pulling her towards me and embracing her tightly. We hold each other for a while. Neither of us are ready to let go. Neither wants to confront the current situation. Acknowledge that we are powerless to do anything to bring them back home one day sooner, even though we have spent most of our adult lives accumulating the power that should safeguard not only our families, but our state and nation.

"Take me to bed…" Angelica asks and we both know it has been too long since the last time.

CHAPTER TWENTY-TWO:

ANNIE THOMPSON

Someone is cooking. The distinct odors of the spices they use in this part of the world greet my nose and make me aware. I feel the heat from whatever it is they are using to cook with. Could it be a fire? In this part of the world, it is almost impossible to tell what people might be using. The place we are in… it seems smaller somehow. No echoes like the other places. A house maybe? It seems like there is not as much air above us as before. And the cooking and small space make me believe we are in someone's home, as I doubt they are cooking just for us…

If this is a house, that would mean they are changing tactics. Why would they do that? Could it be they are afraid someone has seen something and reported it? Afraid that if they keep moving us from warehouse to warehouse the pattern will be spotted and the authorities will know where to look next? Or maybe this is all part of the original plan. Keep moving to new locations, regardless of what they are. Just keep moving us. But every time they do, I would think that would make it more likely someone will spot us. But the distances between stops has probably ensured no one who might have seen something would have any idea where we have gone.

The more I think about what they have been doing, the less hope I have that anyone will find us soon. Find us eventually… yes. But the question is whether it will before we become a liability and not an asset? That is how father would look at it. Always financial frame of reference. Guess that is how he got to be governor. You have to have a lot of assets to even consider a run, and a lot of favors owed to you to motivate supporters. And that means you spend most of your life doing favors for others and keeping the chit for when you need it. Better to be the daughter of parents who have a lot of chits to call upon. Charles and

I have no chits. Will that make us bad parents?

Luckily our captors have pushed us up against a wall so they cannot see my wrists. See that I have been able to cut through the zip tie. I am holding it in my hand to make sure they do not find it and realize one of us is free. I cannot tell if Charles was successful or not. The only thing I can do is assume he was not and hope if something happens, I will find out he was. In the meantime, I have to keep pressing my wrists together so our guards will not realize what I have done.

Apparently, the hoods are staying on here. Even more reason to believe we are being held in someone's home. They want to make sure we cannot identify people or places where we were held, which is the good news. Means they do not intend to kill us. But I need to be prepared that could change at a moment's notice. Particularly, if the authorities find us. That becomes a very dangerous moment. While I would be elated that this nightmare is finally coming to an end, if these men think they will be killed in the process of the rescue, they might just kill us. Two weeks ago, I was only thinking of the life Charles and I have before us, and now I realize that life together may last only a few days, if things go terribly wrong. And so far, on this trip, that is exactly how they have gone.

I am getting thirsty, but I have to be careful… If I drink too much I will have to go to the bathroom. Then they will discover my wrists are free. How do I balance this? I hate to ask for water because I assume it will be local water and full of all kinds of unfriendly bacteria. I could end up sicker by drinking the water I need than not. Guess I will not ask for any. They laughed when I asked for bottled water… when was that? Seems like a month ago.

"Charles?" I ask softly, hoping to not call attention to us, but we have exchanged only a few words all this time.

"I'm here…" he bumps against me with what I assume is his shoulder, although I could be wrong. He is also responding as quietly as I am talking.

“Are you okay?” I try to keep this plain vanilla because while we know at least one of the guards can speak English, for all we know they could all speak better English than we do.

“Depends on how you define okay…” Charles is always the literal one.

“You’re still with me…” I decide is what I really want to know.

“I am… married to you, even…”

I have to smile at his expressed emotion, even though I know he cannot see it. “As I am married to you. But you know… in our vows we didn’t include anything more than in sickness and in health…”

“Yeah, well… kidnapping tends not to be an everyday event… at least not for most people,” Charles sounds like himself… not too stressed out. That is good. But I dare not even hint about his zip tie because if they were not listening to us before, I am sure they are now.

“What should we be doing about water?” I decide is the right question to ask. “Will it make us sicker to drink their water or continue to dehydrate?”

“I don’t think we have any choice… we have to hydrate or we could end up in shock…” Charles answers clinically, which tells me he has been thinking the same question I have.

I shake my head to myself. Charles is right. Digestive distress or shock… which would I rather not have? I speak up, “Could we have some water over here?”

No immediate response. But rather than repeating myself I wait.

“Water?” Charles repeats my request.

Someone approaches and I hear something placed on the ground in front of me. The hood is raised, but only just above my mouth and a ladle or dipper of some kind touches my lower lip. I open my mouth and water is poured into it and all down my chin and throat. I shudder as the water rolls down my chest. The ladle is refilled from what I can barely make out is apparently a bucket. Well water for sure. All the bacteria I can swallow all at once. Diarrhea here I come. More of the water washes down me than reaches my mouth this time. I wonder if the guard is doing that on purpose. Do I smell that badly after I do not even know how many days I have been rolling around in the back of vans and sitting like a potted plant in one warehouse or another. Or maybe he just wants to see what I would look like in a wet t-shirt contest.

All I have seen in the brief moments my hood was slightly raised confirms we are likely in a house. Dirt floor, but it seems there was a chair or some kind of furniture not so far from where we are sitting. The bucket was plastic with a metal wire to carry it with. The ladle was also plastic and I have to assume everyone here has been drinking from it without sanitation between users.

"Food?" a voice asks as I hear Charles receiving his requested water. Cannot tell if he is any more successful at getting the water into his mouth. The voice is the same one we had heard before. The one who definitely speaks English but has been minimizing what he says. Likely trying to make sure we cannot identify the voice.

"Bread?" I ask in return, trying to think of what is the least likely to give me food poisoning. Fruit or vegetables would likely be washed in this same water. They might be okay to eat if cooked, but bread is baked and least likely to be full of the nastiest bacteria. Then I realize this man may come back and cut the zip ties so we can eat the bread and he would find my free hands. I am backed into a corner now. What do I do? Nothing I can do now except wait. But the lesson learned is to not ask for anything. Let Charles do that. They may also take the request better coming from him. I can hope they do not have any bread… more likely this guy was thinking about the food they are cooking. Also, more likely to be something they will free our hands to allow us to feed ourselves.

However, I realize they are keeping the hoods on us. They do not want us to see this place. And if they cut us loose, the first thing we will do is to raise the hood to see what we are eating. I do not think they want us to do that. I take a deep breath knowing the next few minutes may determine whether today is our last day on this earth or whether we are finally going to be lucky about something.

The guard walks away. “Well water…” I say softly to Charles.

“Better than total dehydration…” Charles responds.

“They didn’t give us much…” I put out there to see how Charles responds.

“I noticed… could have several meanings, so don’t read too much into it.”

“Any thoughts on why this is taking so long?” I am trying to see where his mind is at. He sounds good… focused… thoughtful. Even though we are both dehydrated to a major extent.

“Is it? Taking a long time? I don’t have a frame of reference…” Again, Charles is telling me not to read too much into the situation. It will take as long as it takes. We do not know what these men are asking for. Whether they are even talking with our parents, or are they only talking with the local government people, who may or may not even know who we are. But I am sure, by this time, a whole bunch of people must know we are missing and are working hard to find us. We just happen to be somewhere it is not easy to find anyone.

One of the men returns. My heart skips a beat and then begins to race as we are now either going to be found out, fed, or moved one more time. But we just got here. Do not think they are moving us again quite so soon. I realize I have stopped breathing and force an exhale before resuming normal breaths. The man stops in front of me, apparently looking down. He just stands there. Why is he doing that? Is he looking at my wrists behind my back? Maybe he is reading something on his cell phone. I do not know what to expect, but I have to believe it is not going to be pleasant, whatever it turns out to be.

I hear someone helping Charles to his feet, although it is clear Charles was not expecting to get up. They take Charles away. I listen carefully to try to understand where he is going…

CHAPTER TWENTY-THREE:
LILA THOMPSON

I ring the doorbell of the Myer's Georgetown townhouse. I had sent a text earlier to Angelica and she responded that Howard was here with her, rather than in Richmond. I am not sure if the man who answers the door is his security or hers. They all look the same. "Dr. Thompson," he greets me. "They are in the study waiting for you." The security men always used to wear grey suits, but now they apparently try to make them blend in. This one is wearing a Georgetown University sweatshirt and jeans with hiking boots. The boots seem out of place for an urban home. His longish graying hair also does not seem to fit the mold, but what is the mold these days.

The townhouse seems small to me, but that is probably because usually only Angelica is here. With the long hours she puts in at the Pentagon, she is not here all that many hours in any given day. With the price of real estate in this area a smaller townhouse probably makes sense.

"Lila," Howard greets me first as I enter the study, which is decorated in neocolonial style, which I have never cared for, but it is true to the character of the townhouse. When people decorate for the time period of the structure like they have, that tells me they think of the house as more of a museum than a home. Also probably makes sense as I would assume Angelica entertains here periodically. The house is decorated more for the guests than her own taste.

I nod to Howard and acknowledge Angelica with a weak smile, "Have you heard anything?" I come right out with the reason for my unscheduled visit.

Angelica shakes her head to lower my expectations without giving me a long explanation. Howard motions for me to come over and sit on the love seat across from theirs. I do as Howard has indicated for me and sit down as they do.

"I'm really sorry to be a pest…" I begin.

"Lila," Howard shakes his head, "We are all in this together…"

"I know… but I'm having chest pains, and that is causing me to have trouble breathing, and I can't sleep not knowing what has happened to Charles… to Annie. I know I'm the weak link here. The two of you and Beau… all such strong people. But I'm not like you…I don't do well with stress… with not knowing they are safe."

"You are not the weak link, Lila," Angelica responds to how I see myself. "Charles chose medicine over invention because of you. Annie fell in love with Charles because he is a lot like you. Don't underestimate yourself or your importance to the kids returning home safely."

"But the time… since they went missing…"

"We don't know what that means, and because we don't know who is behind their disappearance, we are simply not in a position to understand what to expect," Howard responds this time. "This is hard on all of us."

"The police always say the first forty-eight hours is the most important. That is when the clues are fresh. That is when the police figure out most crimes. Forty-eight hours came and went before we even knew something had happened… and now it is over a week. This can't be good news. I'm afraid… that something went wrong on the first day and that is why we haven't heard anything…" I am trying to express myself, but I know this is all coming out in a convoluted mess.

"Don't set your expectations from the movies you have watched," Howard continues to respond to me although I can see Angelica is ready to jump in if he does not. "Movies are never a reflection of reality. They have to amp things up to get your attention. They focus on the extremes and not on the real sources of conflict. Not what you or we should expect. And this is all happening in a part of the world that is so different from what we experience every day. We need to keep an open mind, let the professionals do their job. We need to be ready to help them when they return. And that is one place where you have all the experience we do not. Every day you help people cope with trauma, stress, frailty, and uncertain futures. When they return, you will be the most important of all of us, because you have the experience and knowledge of how to help them put, whatever this has been, behind them."

"You sound optimistic this will all be over soon…" I respond to Howard.

"Not soon enough," Angelica notes looking at her husband in an unfathomable way. I cannot tell if she is agreeing with him or not. Angelica looks towards me, then settles her attention on my eyes. "We aren't sleeping either." She lets that sink in for a moment before continuing. "Someone wants something. We don't know yet, what that is. When they finally contact their government, our government, the Red Cross, Tree Huggers Anonymous… whoever… when they finally contact someone, then the game begins. Until that happens people follow clues… but clues seldom lead you to the perpetrator. People do. The clues just tell us who the people are who we need to talk to."

"How can you be so calm about the situation?" I want to scream.

"Believe me… we are not calm…" Howard responds, glancing at Angelica. "We are briefed the moment any new information comes in. The problem has been there is very little new information. In fact, that is what is driving both of us crazy. Just how little information these highly regarded professionals have been able to provide to us."

"All the more reason to think something awful has already happened to them…" I drop on them like a bomb.

"On the contrary," Angelica responds steely. "If something had happened as you are projecting… likely by now we would have found some clue or indication of that fact. We have nothing that would support such a conclusion. The only thing that makes sense is someone is holding them until the time is right. What dictates the right time, I can't even begin to imagine. But then again, I can't imagine anyone kidnapping them in the first place."

"What are your security experts saying?" I press them both, knowing Angelica has the whole US military at her disposal.

"To be patient." Angelica states flatly.

"How can you be when it's Charles and Annie out there… somewhere… God knows where."

"Our whole lives we are telling our kids to be patient," Howard turns the conversation. "When they get a little older… they will be able to do something they are not prepared to do today. They need to be patient while their brains form better reasoning skills, or more coordination, or better judgement. Whatever it is, they need to be patient. Charles needed to be patient to get through Med school before he could start practicing his specialty. Annie needed to get through law school so she could take the bar exam and then practice. They had to be patient to find the right person with whom to spend their lives. If they had not been patient, they would not be together today. If you and Beau had not been patient would either of you been doing what you are doing today? Patience is not so much to ask."

I let Howard's lecture sink in. They give me the space to do so. But then Angelica rises and looks at a cell phone. "Excuse me for just a minute. This is something totally unrelated, but I must respond to it immediately." Angelica does not look up but answers the call as she walks toward her office. "What are you recommending?"

"What is Beau saying?" Howard asks me.

"He is in constant communications with all of his contacts in that part of the world. Flying drones, listening in on private conversations, talking with government officials and private individuals. He is not leaving any stone unturned. This is all he is doing. Focusing all his energies on finding and bringing them home safely."

"There are things Beau can do we cannot," Howard reminds me.

"And he is… but you gather more intelligence than all the other governments in the world. Somebody must have seen something, heard someone say something, talked to a neighbor who noticed someone in the neighborhood, someone who doesn't belong. Something."

"We can second guess the guys in the field… but they know much better than we do what is real and what has no bearing on our case. There is so much information out there, the problem is not gathering the reports, but simply sifting through it all and being able to decide what has relevance and what does not. There is a lot more chaff than wheat when you're trying to make flour." Howard is trying to be patient, but I can tell he does not want to continue this conversation much longer.

Angelica returns, sits beside Howard, and places her phone before her as if she may get another call shortly that she will also have to answer. "What did I miss?"

"Sifting…" I respond so Howard will not try to revisit the whole conversation.

Angelica nods and glances at Howard, "We could go through all the theories that have been floated, but frankly it would be a waste of your time. There are so many and yet the facts do not fit very many of them, and some where they fit well… just defy credulity."

"Like what?" I respond, unsure where she is going.

"The Kisumu Camp site was so pristine that one Kenyan official seriously suggested an alien abduction." Howard responds.

"I hadn't considered that," I respond earnestly.

CHAPTER TWENTY-FOUR:
AGENT DAKOTA PLAINSMAN

Yuri Tereshkova does not look like a Russian. Probably because he has lived in the US almost his entire adult life. Taken from his family when a mere teenager, he was trained by the KBG and placed in the US when he was in his mid-twenties. But after only a few years spying on America, he had a change of heart and defected, only to join the CIA where he has had a distinguished career. Yuri is not a big man. In fact, he barely stands as tall as myself. Black hair and deep dark eyes that seem to deflect any attempt to understand what he might be thinking. He is athletically built and trained to be a gymnast for a while before being selected for spying over tumbling. All these years later he seems to have placed a premium on staying in shape.

Yuri does not look up as I slide into a chair across from him at the CIA cafeteria at Langley. He is studying a map, although looking at it from above I could not tell anyone what country or area he is looking at. “I do not know how I can help you,” Yuri still does not look up.

“The Kenyans have come to a dead end,” I explain how he might.

He now glances up for a quick look and then back to his map, “Could have saved you time if you’d have come asked us first.”

“Protocol,” I respond and I know he will understand what that means.

“Their country, their investigation…” Yuri responds to confirm he does.

“What does CIA know?” I decide to be direct since he was with me.

"We know that whoever is involved, it is not the usual players..." Yuri pronounces before finally looking up and engaging me with an ironic smile. "But then... you know that too."

"What does that mean to you?" I decide to test how much he has put into this case.

"Amateurs... at least as far as kidnapping is concerned. Might be smugglers... there are a lot of them in that area. Bringing in contraband and making a living off the risk premium."

"Risk premium..." I wonder what he means.

"The extra amount they charge to risk getting caught and going to jail... although I would not be surprised one or more of those involved have already served time for one thing or another."

"What would they be smuggling?" I wonder how much information he is willing to share.

"Diamonds, guns, slaves, drugs, whatever you want but aren't allowed to have."

"Slavery... do you think..." I pick up on one he tried to bury.

"Unlikely... could see that if they only took the woman... but to take both? That seems to me they are looking for something bigger than a single sale," Yuri looks beyond me as if remembering something.

"Single sale..." I push for more explanation.

"This part of Africa... they kidnap a... mostly young women... and sell them to someone who ships them to another continent and is going to make money on a continuing basis. For the ones who kidnap her... it is a single sale and move on to the next one. They aren't in this business for the long haul. One transaction and move on."

"One theory..." I begin to look for his reaction, but he cuts me off.

"I really don't care about the theories the Kenyans have come up with."

I sit back realizing he really does not have a high regard for the Kenyan authorities. I wonder what is behind that. "What's yours?"

"Did the Kenyans ever discuss smugglers?" Yuri pushes back on me.

"No," I admit.

"Because they don't want to admit the smugglers have infiltrated the government and police. They all share in the profits. And that is why so many things there remain illegal."

"You think the government may have had a hand in kidnapping the Thompsons?" I push harder on Yuri now.

"I didn't say that…" Yuri ducks my accusation.

"Then what are you saying?"

"They will not suggest an explanation when they know for a fact there has been no formal involvement of a particular group or faction. Not from investigating, but because they are part of that revenue stream."

"Revenue stream… you seem to think this is all about money…" I seek clarification.

"Everything is about money…" Yuri seems surprised at my question. "If they are not looking for a direct payoff, they are looking for an indirect payoff… and that might explain why you still have not heard from the kidnappers."

"What do you mean?" I need more.

"You sure you work for the FBI? You seem to be taking longer on the uptake here than most agents I've worked with in the past." Yuri almost insults me. No, he did insult me.

"If you have this all figured out, why don't you call up Mrs.

Thompson's mother and tell her where she is?" I push back, daring him, knowing he doesn't have it all figured out.

Yuri looks at me strangely, apparently trying to figure out something I have alluded to but not been explicit enough about. "You have no idea about this part of the world, do you?"

"What does that mean?"

"This is a part of the world where the Russians, the Chinese, the Indians and the Iranians are all trying to buy influence. The French are on the fringes here with troops trying to quell civil wars. We are there too… but without nearly as much money or influence as all the others. There was a time when ideology was king. In those days you could appeal to people's hearts and minds. Today it is all money. Who is going to give me something I want. Of course, I will have to give them something they want… either access to rare minerals, or markets for their products or soldiers who will go fight in their proxy wars. Everyone wants something different than the others. Some just want to keep the US in turmoil. That's Somalia… where the Iranians give pirates fast boats and arms to disrupt shipping. Where the Russians arm guerilla groups that blow up shopping malls, where the Chinese provide loans to build railroads and bridges and hydropower dams so the local people will buy Chinese consumer goods and vote against the US in the UN.

"What about India?" I notice he mentioned them but gave no further explanation.

"They just want to sell Mahindra trucks and equipment and software to run everything that has a computer chip in it." Yuri summarizes his experience with India in this part of the world.

"Are you suggesting that one of those countries may have been involved in this disappearance?"

"Would not be surprised to find this kidnapping was shopped to all of them and went to the highest bidder." Yuri watches me try to digest that thought.

The dissonance from his competing scenarios has me confused, "You just said you thought this looked like it was done by amateurs… people who don't do this kind of thing for a living. And now you're saying they went out and got the backing of a government hostile to America?"

"That makes more sense to me than your half-baked theories, handed to you on a platter by a group of Kenyan officials who are merely looking for the quickest way to get this hot potato out of their hands and into someone else's."

"Why are you so hard on the Kenyan's?" I finally have to ask.

"I spent six months there learning the trade with my Russian colleagues as part of my training to come to this county. I know first-hand how corrupt and incompetent they are, when it comes to situations like this. They also murdered my best friend, who stayed on there after I left. He discovered the true extent of how much they had been penetrated by the different intelligence agencies… selling what they knew to the highest bidder. They are not only corrupt and incompetent, but also cruel and vengeful, even though they bring the situations on themselves."

"You're saying they would as quickly plunge the knife in my back as protect it?"

"That's my experience." Yuri glances back down at the map he was studying when I first arrived.

"But in this case, you don't think they are involved? Why?" I push him again.

"Tourism is too important to Kenya… They have to overcome the third world impression most tourists have to begin with. Tourists have to feel safe or they will simply stop coming. The only good thing as far as the Kenyans are concerned is this hasn't gotten out into the mainstream media. And they are hoping it stays that way. But they also have no idea how to resolve it. That is clearly evident. Which brings me back to who is aiding those amateurs involved? Russia, Iran, China or someone else?"

"You are sticking with your amateur theory…" I am still not sure I buy that explanation, but he certainly has caused me to think about this case differently. And since he has worked this part of the world and I have not, I need to consider his insights.

"At the moment… it is the only thing that makes sense to me."

CHAPTER TWENTY-FIVE:

ANGELICA MYERS

Edmund Jackson's rugged dark face appears on my Webex screen. He is not wearing his congressional suit. Must mean he does not have to go defend an action or budget item to the intelligence oversight committee today. He has a lot of gray sprinkled through his short dark hair and I would venture to guess, since I get to run the same gauntlet on capitol hill, that each gray hair represents a single unpleasant encounter with that group of people. It is one thing to provide insight, but everything having to do with the trillions of dollars the US government spends in any given fiscal year, has become a struggle for ideology. Whose ideology is winning today and let us make sure that ideology is getting the funding from our agencies whether that makes any sense or not.

"You sure you want to have this conversation?" Edmund Jackson asks me.

"Have you found them?" I respond, hearing the dread in his voice.

"We have not…" He responds immediately knowing what I am thinking. "But I can't tell you if that is a good thing or not."

"What does CIA know, that you can tell me?" I try to give him room to maneuver.

"Madam Secretary, as you know, this is a courtesy call and I cannot discuss things with you that I have not informed the oversight committee of in advance."

"I know the rules, Mr. Director." He used my formal title so I return the favor.

"I have the file up on my computer, and despite what you might think, I have read every word in it. I have also called in those who performed these assessments and questioned them directly. Now you and I both know this is well beyond what I do for almost any case we are pursuing. I just wanted you to know we are doing everything in our power to find them and ensure they are properly returned to you safely."

"But…" I voice what I hear in my head having been on that end of the call way too many times.

"Not even a thank you?" Edmund protests.

"You know I only thank someone for the results they have gotten, not the effort in getting there," I remind Edmund of something he is well aware of.

Edmund nods just once to acknowledge, "We have no credible evidence of who has them, or where they are. No communication means we also do not know specifically what they want."

"Isn't it obvious?" I blurt out. "They want me to resign because I've ramped up our preparedness and prepositioned forces and supplies that are interdicting the various groups trying to wrestle control from the elected governments."

"The President's 'ensuring democracy' initiative…" Edmund gives voice to what I just described.

"The President believes that prosperity in Africa, which has the fastest growing populations in the world, can only result from free and fair elections. Not tribes marching on the capital city and throwing out whoever the people chose last time."

"The French tried that in Mali and got their asses handed to them…" Edmund observes.

"They did, but that was because they did not defend a popularly elected government, but rather those who were in power and were friendly to France," I give him my shorthand understanding of the events in that country. "They did not understand the grievances against that incumbent and underestimated the will of those who sought change. We have both seen what a powerful thing change is in the minds of an electorate. If things aren't benefiting me right now, let's change and bring in someone new who might do a better job of scratching my itches."

"You always bring an interesting turn of phrase to every conversation." Edmund seems to be remembering something I must have said.

We both sit there for a moment in silence now that I have voiced my theory of what is happening to my daughter and her husband. "Do you agree with my assessment?" I finally restart the conversation.

"Not entirely…" he surprises me. "That program is associated with the President. You are merely the person who is putting the pieces into place. You really have not had an impact in that area yet, as your troops are just beginning to arrive. And until there has been a decisive encounter, where Americans in the mix change the outcome for a country… why does anyone care how many Americans have put themselves into harm's way?"

"Then why Annie?" I am almost crying now, having blamed myself and now seeing that maybe I am not the reason this has happened. Or if I am, it is for something other than what I am focused on at the moment at work.

"Target of opportunity," Edmund responds. "Now this is not based on any reports I have been given and why this is not something I have discussed with the Intelligence Committee. This is Edmund Jackson answering a question with a considered opinion, and that is all it is. Do not go have a press conference saying the CIA thinks your daughter was a target of opportunity."

"You know I am not talking to anyone about what we discuss and continue to hope and pray the media does not pick up on what has happened, because it will only make things worse."

"Glad to see we are on the same page," Edmund muses further.

"As I have thought about it, we gave the Nairobi Airport facial recognition software to go hunt terrorists… when was that? Maybe a year ago. That software would have access to passport photos and can cross check national terrorist databases. What if… the Kenyans have added other photo databases… public photo databases like all the social media platforms out there with the help of the Chinese? And what if… someone in the airport security team set some kind of alerts so when high value people come through the airport… they sell that information off to persons of interest, as we would refer to them."

"Meaning the intelligence teams from the different countries active in Nairobi and Kenya." I complete the thought.

"Who then go find locals willing to kidnap these high value people and hold them until their sponsors can make use of them." Edmund continues a different theory than I was expecting. "All speculation. No reports confirming any of this, and no discussions with oversight."

"Which is probably the only reason it hasn't leaked into the media…" I point out.

"At this point the only member of the committee who is aware we are looking for Annie and Charles is the Chair and she would not talk to the press if they were waterboarding her." Edmund displays a curious smile in thinking of his committee chairperson. Not a look I have seen before.

"An interesting theory, but if it were true, how do we find them when someone has evidently gone to great lengths to make sure we cannot." I go right to the heart of my lingering concern.

"I have others, and in fact, if I were to literally read the reports in this file, it is not the one I would jump to. But call it a gut feeling or whatever you want… the official information we are getting does not square with the insights our people are bringing back. That means there has to be something else going on here. And while we have not seen other instances of such kidnappings in this region, everything about this case is different than other high value people who might come through."

"You said we gave the airport the software and system about a year ago?" I pick up on a thread.

Edmund consults his screen before his response. "Yes."

"If the Chinese were to have enhanced the system that would have taken six months to a year. And in that case, Annie and Charles may be the first to have been picked up and renditioned in some fashion."

"Just like we have been doing with terrorists for decades, even using some of the same tools." Edmund now seems glum about his theory.

"I'm coming back to the fundamental question, Edmund… how do we get them back?"

"If this is the first of what may become technology enabled kidnappings of high value people, then the world becomes like Brazil where ransoms are almost considered wages. And if that is the case, then we have to develop an approach to make sure these kinds of kidnappings can't happen. And that may mean a gruesome end to the kidnappers in this case. I mean literally atomizing them so there is absolutely no trace, no grave, no indication they ever existed."

I hear the ruthlessness in his voice that I remember when he was my superior at the agency. I feel better about this conversation because I know it has become personal for Edmund Jackson. Not just because he knows Annie. Not just because he is doing this for me. But because he truly sees that a global threat may be emerging. One he has to get in front of and stop before his agency is overwhelmed. There will be similar cases of high-profile people who are known to senior people in the administration. Edmund has to find Annie's captors, but I am not sure the oversight committee will be happy with the atomization of them.

CHAPTER TWENTY-SIX:
CHARLES THOMPSON

The hood comes off… oh, oh. Is this where they discover Annie has freed her hands? My heart skips a beat as my eyes adjust to the total darkness of this place. I cannot even see the man who took my hood off. Although I feel his presence, hear his breathing and the movement of him. It seems he is standing over me. Crazy how dark it is here. No light at all. How did this guy see enough to pull my hood off? Know where I am? But then I realize he has had more time to adjust to the dark. More time to decide what to do with us. Us? Where is Annie? I do not hear her? Did they not bring her here when they moved me?

I try to call her name, but the gag is still in and it comes out a muffled, "Ahhh…nuh!"

Fingers touch the back of my head, are they going to take the gag out? No. Whichever one this is simply is making sure the gag is tied tight. Why are they afraid I will say something now? Because Annie and I were talking before? Maybe. Is that why they apparently separated us? But why remove the hood in a room where I cannot see anything? I do not understand why they are doing what they do, other than they may simply be wanting to keep us off-balance. Confused. Not see any patterns to what they are doing. If we do not know what they are going to do next, it is hard to plan anything that might permit our escape. But even if we found some means of escape. What then? I have no idea where we are. Not even what country. I am sure of one thing… since we have not been on an airplane, it is unlikely that if we did escape, we would be able to talk to anyone. I doubt many people speak English wherever we are. And most would likely not know what to do with us since we are still in our bedclothes. What's wrong with this picture? And if we did escape… these men would be tracking us down. There is nowhere to go, nowhere to hide.

We also cannot just sit here waiting to be rescued. That would be the easy way… but with all the movement from place to place and random times of movement, it must be very hard to find someone. Particularly when those who have you do not want to be found. I am sure they have not been moving us in the same vehicle. Would help if we did not have the hoods on next time they move us, but they have not been willing to do that in a while. Not likely they will now.

I try to pull my wrists apart, hoping that all the sawing I did in the van weakened the zip tie enough it will break. But as much as I strain to break it, the zip tie holds. Just not enough time. I do not even know if I cut the tie a little or a lot. If I keep trying to pull it apart, will it eventually break, or will I be wasting my time and strength? And since they have not been feeding us, I am sure my strength is not what it was.

A door closes somewhere. I get the impression this is a house and not the kind of building where they had been keeping us before. Does that mean whoever lives here came home? Does that person know we are here? What if…our captors have brought us somewhere the owner was not expecting us? Would they do that to make themselves even less predictable? It is just so hard to figure out what they are doing.

Are there more of them now? I think there were four. Have they joined others here? That would make it even more difficult to escape, if there are more of them. Or is this a changing of the guard? New people taking over, taking us somewhere else. Be even less predictable. That would make sense.

Where is Annie? What are they doing to her? Did they bring me here so I would not know what they are doing to her? Not have to listen. Not have to endure the knowledge of what they are doing to her? Or listen to her struggle against them. There is nothing I can do. Not only am I unable to help, I do not even know where she is, or where I am for that matter. Probably in a house, somewhere in Africa.

How long has it been? How long since they took us from the Kisumu camp? Not being able to see the sun, I have to admit I have no idea. It seems like a month and yet it also all blends into a couple of days. I really do not know and have no way of figuring it out. And not knowing makes it hard to decide if we should be rescued soon or is it still early in the process of trying to find us. Knowing Annie's Mom, I am sure she is doing everything she can to find us. And Dad? He probably has every listening device known to man being scanned for any indication of where we might be. I do not know if the people who captured us know what Dad can do, but they seem to be doing the right things… at least as best I can figure it out… to make sure he cannot pick up on a conversation that would tell him where we are. I do not really even hear them talk to each other, let alone on a phone or radio.

And while I am thinking about it, why are they not talking more? What is going on? People tend to talk when they are together. Why are these men so quiet? I wonder if they even know each other. People who do tend to have conversations when together. It is the silences one hears when people who are not sure what to talk about, who have no shared experiences or common acquaintances are together.

The door to this room opens and light temporarily blinds me. I hear, more than see, someone come into the room. Now my eyes are adjusting more to the light. I see furniture in the room… looks like wicker chairs and a table like I have seen in rustic settings. Then I see shadows in the doorway. They come into the room and the door closes behind them. Someone pushes someone down next to me.
"Ahhh…nuh?" I again try to call her name, hoping for some kind of response.

"Churs…" is her gagged response. It is her. She does not sound like someone who has just been raped… dazed… unable to focus. Thank God for that. I let out a deep breath, not having realized I must have stopped breathing there for a moment. I lean into her so she knows where I am, and instantly feel hands pulling me away from her.

"Ohhh…kuh?" I ask as the rough hands let go of me.

"Esss," she responds as if from deep in her throat.

The door opens again. A figure moves into the room as if carrying something. The door closes and we are in the dark once more, unable to see anything.

It sounds like two metal plates have been put on the floor in front of us. Is this where they cut my zip tie and find Annie is free? I do not know how many more times I will have to wonder if this is the end of the road. I almost wish she had not cut through. Then there would be no retribution threat out there. We would be docile captives. Doing exactly what they want us to do, rather than trying to find a way to resist. Get away.

The door opens again. And still another man enters the room. Does this mean all four of them are in here with us? Or is this the person who lives here? Maybe. The new person says something to the man who put the plates down. Same sing-songy language. Not sure what they are discussing. Probably something to do with us. Is he telling this guy not to bother feeding us as we will not be around long enough to bother with? Or is he telling him to cut our zip ties so we can feed ourselves? Or maybe he is telling him that we are going to move before dawn and he needs to get some sleep before the sun rises. Who knows what they are discussing, but whatever it is, I am sure, it has something to do with us.

Then the one thought I have been suppressing pops into my mind. What if someone has spotted us? What if someone is coming to rescue us? What if these men have been tipped off by someone that we have been seen and help is on the way. I instantly reject this thought. The reaction of the men in the room would be entirely different. They would be bracing for an attack on us. Nothing they are doing indicates that is what they are reacting to.

One of the men who has been in the room with us, goes to the door and steps out, closing it behind him. Why do they keep closing the door? Why are they trying to keep us literally in the dark? Make it even harder for us to identify them? That makes sense. If we have mostly seen shadows, it is very hard to confirm this shadow is that of the men who have us when asked to testify in a court of law.

The aroma of the food in the dish finally greets me. Spices I do not recognize. Definitely cooked as the sweet aroma of a cooked vegetable is in there somewhere. But what vegetable? I would guess a potato, but I am not sure they even grow in Africa. Could be a plant similar to a potato, but not a potato.

Would I eat a cooked potato? Most likely that would not upset my digestive track as much as the water we drank earlier most likely will. And I am sure that upset will occur at the worst possible time. Nothing I can do about that. But this makes me wonder if we need more water to stave off dehydration.

With that thought the man who left a moment ago, returns with the bucket and ladle. He approaches me first, ladles water over my head. I taste the wetness in my gag, but the man does not remove it. I get moisture, but not water. The water is cold and I shiver.

The bucket man moves over to Annie, ladles water over her next. The men start chattering in that other language. Apparently, they can see what I cannot. Annie in a silky nightgown, water causing it to cling to her body. I struggle more trying to pull the zip tie apart, but it does not give. If they harm her now… Is that what separating us was all about? They wanted to heighten my concern for Annie, then introduce her back to me, showing she was unharmed. And now, they are putting on a show for each other and intend to rape her before me in a room where I cannot even see what is happening but can only hear. Let my mind fill in the blanks. Make it even worse. Why these psychological games? Are they trying to break us? No… they have not asked a single question. It is as if they do not care what we know or think. We are just the pawns in a much larger game we cannot see nor understand with the little information they are giving us.

I hear Annie shiver and the sing-songy voices react to her. Another attempt to pull the zip tie apart and still I am bound. Unable to intervene. Unable to help the woman I love. The man pours the rest of the water in the bucket over Annie. She shrieks with the cold water, but it is muffled.

CHAPTER TWENTY-SEVEN:
BEAU THOMPSON

Joe Alvarez is my imagery guy. Just back from Kenya. He knows pixels better than anyone I have ever met. Joe does not look like an intel guy. Started out doing photography as a hobby as a kid and got really good at manipulating the pixels to completely change the nature of the pictures he was taking. From what they said about him, he got a number of awards in art shows for the innovative way he manipulated photos to create art from just another picture.

Joe is also a short guy. Maybe five foot two inches. Long stringy blonde hair and patchy beard. He looks like a refugee from a commune somewhere. A casual observer might also think he has a chip on his shoulder from being pushed around all the time. He never would have made the offensive line on even the worst high school football team. But he was quick and became a star on the high school soccer team. From what he said in his interview. The bigger defenders could never keep up with him because he was down much closer to the ball than they were. His soccer career ended, however, when he was kicked in the head by another player, who was supposedly going for the ball. Joe never bought that story as it resulted in a concussion. He has never wanted to play a competitive sport since. Joe knew that his eyes and his mind were the keys to his future. He was not going to give anyone a chance to take the keys away.

A quick study, when Joe joined our team, he was playing with drone footage for use in movies. He was expert at making a poor shot turn into a million-dollar vista and the studios loved what he did. But Joe got bored. And that is what I have been fighting the whole time he has been with us. My toughest job is to find something that will be a challenge for Joe. If he is not learning something new or inventing a new process or procedure, he is not happy. Joe needs to find himself in unexplored territory or it is just another job. As he told me in that interview, if he was looking for just another job, he would have gone to just another company and not mine.

"I have automated the search as much as I possibly can, but the general shape of their bodies and facial recognition parameters in a two-step process are about as good as I can get at the moment. When it pulls up the closest matches, we can tighten the criteria. But until then…" Joe is telling me how he is conducting my imagery search for Charles and Annie. The biggest problem is the dearth of assets that were in the sky capturing imagery that may have something of interest.

"Did you go back over the prior day?" I ask knowing that others have tried to reconstruct what happened to them, but I asked Joe to go back to the day before they went missing to make sure we had a means of identifying them from the assets that are available.

"I have six hits on them," Joe confirms. "Missed breakfast and leaving the camp, but caught them shortly after sun up heading to the game preserve."

"Closed jeep… how did you positively ID them?" I push for more detail knowing he is giving me the highlights.

"Next pass… found the jeep and them taking pictures with that big honking lens you gave Charles." Joe grins knowing that was about as positive an ID as anyone would get.

I nod, knowing he was likely right, "You build a reference image for your current search?"

"For each of them… yes," Joe sets my mind at ease. He is doing what I hoped he would do. Take this search as a major time driven challenge. We have to find them as quickly as possible and need to take any shortcut that will result in a positive ID.

"What about the other hits?" I ask curious as to whether there might be an indication of what happened in the day before images.

"The rest were like the second image… setting up or tearing down that big lens. I was surprised I never caught them just taking pictures. Must be an attention thing for Charles… About an hour and he is ready to go to the next place…" Joe implies Attention Deficit Disorder.

"Not Charles. Annie is the one who gets impatient. And I understand…" I respond without having to give it any thought. "I mean… how many pictures of the same animal do you want to take? His camera can take video at up to 35 frames per second. You do that for an hour and you don't have enough time in the day to look all of the images you have captured."

"That's why I'm using automated AI assisted analysis to select the single best frame," Joe informs me. Lots of people pushing the envelope there. But I am just waiting for the dust to settle before I commit to anything other than the proven approaches at the moment. And by proven, I am talking about algorithms that have been in use for at least six months as that is just how fast this whole thing is changing. And I do not see any slowing of innovation in Artificial Intelligence on the horizon."

"How many hits have you had since they apparently left the camp?" I decide is the key question I need to have an answer to, although I think I know the answer.

"A lot of false positives… but I'm more worried about a false negative… we don't know if whoever took them has changed their appearance somehow. Rendered our bush model irrelevant." Joe seems to be really focused on that issue.

"Meaning, you want to make sure the algorithms don't ignore a person who does not fit the model a hundred percent because their appearance has changed."

"Once the model discounts an image, it goes into all the imagery that has been discounted," Joe mulls on something, but does not voice the thought. "We would have to start all over with slightly modified criteria… but the problem is getting that modified criteria. How do we know what is different? What was just enough that the algorithm says, 'not her'?"

"How are you addressing that concern?" he now has my attention.

"I did an analysis of disguises. Most have to do with hair or fake noses," Joe informs me of his approach.

"Hair I can see… but fake noses?" I am surprised by this one.

"You see actors in movies with them all the time. Makes them look totally different. The nose is often the first part of the face that you look at closely. That's why so many people have nose jobs… it completely changes how they look."

"Hawk nose versus ski slope… that what you're talking about?" I guess.

Joe takes out his phone, takes my picture, plays with it a moment, and then shows me the image of me. I have to look a second time to be sure it is me as with a hawk nose nothing else seems the same. Even with the same hair style and length. "I see your point. Is that what you think they are doing? Changing their appearance with prosthetic noses?"

"And wigs… usually longer hair than short, just because most people who aren't in their teens and twenties seem to have moved on to shorter hair." Joe informs me with another point I would not have considered.

"Now that I know what you are looking for…" I begin, but Joe is expecting my impatience.

"I train the algorithm to look for the most likely appearance enhancements in addition to the base case. It has given me several images to examine… but so far…."

"They have all been mismatches…" I interrupt him now knowing where he is going.

"Yes… so far," Joe seems reluctant to confirm the truth.

"And it takes ninety-minutes or so for the satellite to come back over the same area." I seek to confirm how often he gets opportunities from space.

"Actually, those at lower altitudes don't come back over the same spot immediately. Only the geosynchronous satellites do. And there are none parked over Africa. Middle East yes… and there is some capture in the area of interest, but so far…" Joe sounds frustrated by the satellite clusters.

"What you're telling me is, the issue is not the ability to find the needle in the haystack with your algorithms, but having enough imagery of the right places at the right time." I summarize.

"AfriCom has been pushing for a dedicated satellite… but since they aren't pumping oil…" Joe makes a comment on our national choices.

"Angelica may be able to accommodate them, when this is all over," I observe knowing that will not help us right now. Spy satellites take years to build, launch and burn in once they achieve orbit. We simply do not have that kind of time.

Joe nods in understanding, "So…" he begins to get my attention having gone off on a mental tangent. "I discovered this image on the last hit at the Kisumu camp."

"Evening," I guess. "What is it?"

Joe displays an image of something that is mostly obscured by a dense grove of trees. Using his pixel power, he begins to peel away the layers of vegetation and lets the algorithm complete the image as if looking at it directly. The more that peels away the more the hidden image appears to show a white colored van sitting under the tree with internal lights on, but no external lights.

"You think someone might have been in this van… waiting for them," I surmise.

CHAPTER TWENTY-EIGHT:

AGENT DAKOTA PLAINSMAN

The Thompson house is quite different from the Virginia State Executive Mansion where Howard and Angelica live. Smaller... at least on the ground footprint, but I suspect there is more to his house than meets the eye when you drive by or even enter. Modern style... grey stone and concrete exterior. Metal fence surrounds the property with security cameras mounted at strategic positions not accessible from the outside of the fencing. That way no one can disable the surveillance and get into the premises. Smart. But Beau Thompson is legendary in the security business.

I roll up to the gate and reach out to push the button, but do not get a chance to perform that task before the gate begins to open. Somehow the system he has for his home, identified me without any direct involvement of the traditional Identification and information exchange. I pull into the compound and drive up in front of the garage. Only a moment later a black Tahoe enters the gate and pulls up beside me. A secret service agent jumps out, opens the door and Angelica and Howard Myers exit the vehicle.

"Agent Plainsman..." The Secretary of Defense greets me and I nod to her. Howard comes around from the other side, shakes my hand.

"Governor," I greet him.

"I hope you have good news for us, Agent," the governor responds and I follow them into the house with secret service agents on both sides of me, who kind of glare, apparently wondering why a guy in a Subaru Forrester is attending this meeting.

Beau Thompson greets us at the door. He even knows the secret service agents by name and shakes their hand as well. Impressive. How many people take the time to get to know security detail members since they rotate so much?

Lila Thompson greets us inside and shows us the way to a media room… a huge media room with the biggest screen I have ever seen outside a movie theater. It takes up the whole wall from floor to ceiling and must easily be twenty feet or more across. The screen is currently displaying a waterfall scene from some remote jungle paradise.

Beau goes to the front of the room. "Agent Plainsman, you can fill us in from here. Any imagery or data you wish to access… I can bring it up for you."

Nothing like a little intimidation to make one feel inadequate. I am getting the impression he may be setting me up to validate the skepticism Mrs. Thompson has already voiced, from what I understand.

I decide to shift gears given this opportunity. "Could you bring up the latest imagery from the Kisumu Camp?" l request of Beau.

"Pandora…" Beau addresses his system. "Kisumu Camp, Kenya… most recent imagery."

"Your system is named Pandora?" Angelica asks Beau.

"Not a common word, and it's kind of symbolic that I never know what I am going to get from any request I make to open up the world to my inspection." Beau seems delighted to explain this to Angelica Myers.

"Latest and greatest?" Howard Myers asks Beau Thompson.

"Updated every twenty-four hours with whatever will enhance the searches we need or the information we need to display." Beau assures him of the accuracy of his assumption.

The waterfall disappears and an aerial image of the Kisumu Camp, where Charles and Annie Thompson were last seen alive. "This is the camp where they were," I begin and ask, "Could you elevate the image so we can see where it is in relations to Nairobi?"

"Pandora. Elevate and include Nairobi. What is the distance?"

A female voice… non-descript responds, "Two-hundred and fourteen miles by land. Generally, more than six hours to drive it. Similar to trying to drive from Washington to Providence, Rhode Island."

I begin the discussion. "The major difference is in Kenya there may be a few thousand people along that route rather than the tens of millions along the Washington to Providence route."

"Your point?" Howard Myers goes right for the jugular.

"In Kenya not a whole lot of people are likely to see you if anything happens."

Angelica intervenes, "You're telling us you have no idea where our kids are."

"Your jumped to conclusion is inaccurate…" I respond with a level tone of voice.

"Then where are they?" She comes right back at me.

"Most likely, somewhere in this image," I respond.

"Most likely does not win you any awards for quickly resolving this case, Agent." Howard Myers seems angry that he came here for a briefing and this is what I am giving him.

"This case… as you referred to it… is not following any of the patterns we have come to expect. When someone goes missing there is usually a claim of responsibility within twenty-four hours. In this 'situation'," I deliberately change the term he used. "There has been no contact from the kidnappers, but we believe they have been kidnapped. There is essentially no evidence of any other explanation for their disappearance."

"Weasel words," Lila Thompson accuses me. "You don't know anything and yet you expect us to trust you to return our kids home. If they are still alive… and I for one am not entirely sure of that… they are likely scarred for life. How could they not be given the circumstances? And you have no idea who might have been behind this whole event?"

"We know more than we can share at the moment…" Is my usual defense.

"What clearance do you need?" Secretary Myers challenges me. "I'm sure I have it. If you and I need to go into a Secure Compartmented Intelligence Facility I can quickly arrange it."

Before I can respond, the image behind me changes. I turn to look and see an image I have not seen before. "What is this?"

Beau Thompson responds, "This is likely the kidnappers about eight hours before they removed Charles and Annie from the camp."

Angelica looks at him surprised, "How…"

"My guy is better than your guy…" Beau responds as if this were a kindergarten argument.

"Looks like any van you might see in any US city or suburb…" Howard Myers responds still staring at the image.

"That is a significant issue…" Beau responds.

"How many are there?" Lila wonders aloud.

"One hundred and fifty-nine-thousand, one hundred and twenty-eight according to the most recent registration data." Beau responds.

"And how many are white?" Lila asks hoping the answer will narrow the number.

"White vans account for approximately sixty-seven percent of all vans or one-hundred and six-thousand, six-hundred and sixteen," Beau informs us. "Piece of cake."

I have to speak up now, "We found a tire track that would appear to have been on such a van. It was actually parked in front of the tent where Dr. and Mrs. Thompson were staying."

"How much will that narrow things?" Howard Myers seems to think I have been withholding this information.

"It is a Korean tire, Hankook, which happens to be the size of the most popular van tire in Kenya. On something like fifty-two percent of all vans in country. When we put this all together, we can narrow that list of suspect vehicles significantly. However, it is only a validation once we have found it, and not an indicator of which vehicle might have been involved. There is no database in country we can go to that will tell us what white vans have that particular tire, although likely something like fifty-thousand or more." Beau informs us.

Angelica looks to Beau, "Can you geolocate white vans in the area within a timeframe of the kidnapping and establish where they went?"

"That is in progress," Beau Thompson responds grimly. "But we have to recognize it is going to take time to eliminate suspected vehicles because there are so many and our imagery data points so far apart. And if they change vehicles at any point… particularly in the middle of the night… well… let me just be clear… I am doing the heavy lifting here, but I give it a low probability of yielding any useful results."

Angelica Myers turns to me, "And what is the Bureau doing to bring our kids home other than eliminating people who aren't involved?"

"We have a voice profile we believe is from one of the kidnappers…" I inform them.

CHAPTER TWENTY-NINE:

HOWARD MYERS

Angelica and I climb into the Secret Service Tahoe completely deflated. As I shut my door, I look at her, waiting for the Secret Service agents to pull away from Beau and Lila's home. I wait until we are past the gate and on the highway. "Is Agent Plainsman over his head?" I finally ask.

Angelica shakes her head, "I don't think this is a law enforcement matter…"

"Meaning what?" comes out sharper than I want it to.

Angelica nods to the Secret Service agents in the front seats and then shakes her head. This all means she will not say more until we are some place we will not be overheard. Even though the agents are discrete, since they have been pulled in to give testimony before Congress and also in courts of law, that assumption of discretion is no longer safe. While I do not like that we cannot have this conversation now, I at least understand it.

"My guys are giving me a different read…" I admit that I have been holding this back and see the sharp look in response. "They are going strictly on the fact there has been no communication. No demand, no claim of responsibility, nothing…"

"There are other explanations…" Angelica shoots back assuming what I am about to say.

"They think the snatch may have gone bad," I put out there for her consideration.

She does not miss a beat as she guessed, apparently correctly, where I was going. "Don't buy it. If that were the case there would have been some sign or indication at the camp rather than nothing other than a single tire track."

"That sounds more like hope talking than a realistic assessment," I respond and give her a moment before continuing. "The fuck up could have come after they left the camp. An accident, where the other party was killed and so were the kids. Could be another party was tracking them, saw the snatch and tried to grab them from the original kidnappers and they were caught in a cross fire. Could be that Charles tried to defend Annie and was killed. And that started a bigger response that she got caught up in. There are just so many possibilities of how the whole thing could have gone south." I try to get Angelica to at least be open to the possible explanations.

"If something had happened to Annie, I would know it. Feel it," Angelica shakes her head. "She's alive…" Angelica looks up and out the window. "I don't know where just yet. But whoever has her will make a mistake. And when they do…"

"Hold on…" I know what she is thinking and have to get her to put that aside.

"Howard… she is our daughter… I am not going to not do everything necessary to bring her home."

"Are you ready to resign if it comes to that?" I push her hard now, knowing this is my only chance to get her to temper her expectations.

"Why would it?" She is at least considering my point. So many times, she does not.

"We don't know what we don't know… I'm just saying… it could come to that."

Angelica looks out the window again, not wanting to confront the truth to what I am telling her, knowing it is absolutely the last thing she wants to consider, but must.

"Okay," she looks at me again, having concluded some thought.

"What are you trying to tell me?"

"In your role… you represent the establishment. You direct it, set the policy and enable others to protect the nation. Underline others."

"I know where you are going…."

"Listen… If you go rogue you can never be the establishment again. No one would follow your directions when you failed to follow the precedents, rules and expectations."

"She's our daughter… I don't see you getting on a plane to go look for her."

"I don't have the background for that… you do. If I were to go over, I would be more of a distraction than help. I know that and you should know that too." I point out the obvious.

"That's not how it would go down…" Angelica is not backing away from the option, even though I am trying to convince her it is not an option for her.

"Okay… where would you start?" I test her theory that she can make a difference herself.

"I've already started, I talked with Director Jackson this morning and got his take on things."

I should not be surprised since she worked directly for him when she went back to the agency. I know enough not to ask her more about this in the car as she will not answer me anyway. "And did he give you an approach?"

"No, but I think Yuri might be able to help me there." I remember that Yuri was her partner during her first tour and a major reason her operations went so well. I also remember that Yuri's soul is dead. He has little regard for following direction or believing anyone other than himself. Not a good starting point if you are trying to bring back someone alive.

"I thought he was working some big covert operation…" at least that was the last thing she had told me about him. But that was also a while ago, as we have had not needed to have a discussion about the agency or her time there in a very long time.

"Successfully concluded. He's riding a desk and a very unhappy agent. Practically daring the agency to give him a more important role."

"You slept with him… is that really all over?" I put out there to hopefully bring to her attention this is just not a good idea.

Angelica looks at me like she does sometimes… when I have raised a valid concern, but not one she is going to address today. "You have nothing to be concerned about… at least as far as that goes."

"Even if I were to set that aside… what is the probability that you getting directly involved will end with both you and Annie dead? I would never forgive myself if I let that happen."

"It won't," Angelica responds simply as if what I am suggesting were impossible. Except I know that is not the case.

"Promise me you won't initiate anything without discussing it with me first." I try to restrain her enthusiasm as best I can.

"We are discussing it right now…" she points out to deflate my whole gambit, essentially telling me that she has already met that stipulation.

"You want me to go…" I finally ask if this is her endgame.

"Actually… since you pointed out you have no training and would be more of a hindrance than a help… I really don't want you to get directly involved beyond what you have been doing… talking with your people and feeding ideas and insights back in to me."

"What if…" I start down the only track I can think of that might derail what I see coming. "What if… that is their plan? To lure you back into the field where they can avenge the embarrassments you and Yuri caused certain parties? Lure both of you back, knowing you would likely not go back out there without him?"

Angelica frowns as if this is something she had not considered, but could be the situation… given what she knows from talking with her old boss. I see she is uncomfortable with this thought, but also resolved she has to go bring Annie and Charles home. The conflicting emotions are written all over her face. I see her consider other information she has… probably from her various commanding officers. She is wrestling with what to do, but at least I have given her a moment's pause.

We drive on in silence, giving her space to put pieces together. After all the time we have been together I have found this to always be the best path forward with her. She needs space to expand her analysis, to consider things she does not wish to state or share with anyone, including me. But given her job that is understandable.

"Governor?" the agent who is driving asks. I know his name but I keep forgetting.

"Yes,"

"We are taking the secretary back to the Georgetown row house. Are you going to stay tonight or should I contact your detail to return you to Richmond?"

I look at Angelica, who does not look at me now. She is not ready to talk just yet, but I need to be there when she decides to. I look back at the agent, "Thanks for asking, but no… I'll be staying in Georgetown tonight."

Angelica glances at me, apparently surprised I am not running back to my job, which she has accused me of being married to more than her sometimes. I think that is just the stress of our dual careers talking, because she is often the one who stays in Georgetown rather than coming down to Richmond on weekends when something important is in progress. Her need to be near the President.

CHAPTER THIRTY:
ANNIE THOMPSON

The cold water is like a slap in the face… I do not know if I have been lulled into a semi-consciousness or what. But now it seems all my senses have been brought into focus. Even though I am in a dark room, and I am relatively sure the figure next to me is Charles, things are starting to become distinct that had not been. Light under the door situates that for me. The breathing of each of the three men still in the room tells me exactly where each is, not only in respect to me, but to each other.

The figure next to me struggles… I can only assume it is Charles and he is trying hard to break the zip tie on his wrists. That confirms for me that he was unsuccessful in breaking it in the van. Am I strong enough to help him break it? Probably not. I need something sharp or razor thin to help him. And even though I am using all my powers of observation to try to make out things in this dark room, it is way too dark to see any kind of small object. Big outlines against the thin line of light below the door I can make out. A razor blade, not so much.

My wet nightgown is clinging to me, making me feel colder than it likely is. I shiver, not for the first time. Almost uncontrollably now. But this part of Africa… I am assuming we are not so far from the camp, even though it seems we have driven for hours nearly every day… is not so dry. Not a desert like the northern parts of the continent. It is still dry enough that my clothes should lose the moisture quickly and then I will be hot again. Sweating, even though Charles seems to marvel that I do not when he does all the time. I think that is just part of living in DC… enough humidity and heat that even moderate exercise releases a torrent of sweat in most people. Not me. Only because I do not exercise and play sports like Charles. I do my fitness routines in an air-conditioned gym. At least I did. And I will again, whenever we finally get to go home.

Home… where is that? Charles' apartment in Rochester Minnesota or my condo in Washington? Clearly not the house where I grew up. In fact, it is rented out because Mom is in the district and Dad is in Richmond, living in the big executive mansion as governor. They have a tenant in the house where I grew up in Alexandria. I know the reason Mom gave for not keeping it when Dad was elected governor. Never bought that reason… that it was too big for just her since I left to go to law school at Yale, which is up in Connecticut. And she did not expect Dad to come home all that often as governor. But still, it is nearly the same distance from the Pentagon as the Georgetown townhouse she is living in now. But then again… Georgetown has more prestige than Alexandria. Is that what it all came down to? That just did not seem like her. Miss simple.

This all leads me to the conclusion I am homeless. Charles and I live apart and will even now that we are married. He has to finish his residency at the Mayo Clinic and I have to serve my Associate Justice on the Supreme Court in DC. Cannot do that from Rochester, Minnesota. And he cannot do his rounds from Washington. We knew this was going to be our life, and still we chose to commit to each other. Chose to be together when we could, knowing it will never be enough time. Deferring that home together at least until he finishes his residency and can set up his own practice or join other docs who need his specialty… or goes the Doctors Without Borders route.

I may be homeless, but coming to this country, I see that as a relative term. Home is not a house… at least not to these people. Home is a place, a lifestyle, an environment that is familiar and part of your identity. Home is where your family lives, where friends want to do things together, learn things together and make a community of like values and beliefs.

In that sense I am also homeless. I do not know if Charles can see it. He is so preoccupied with his rotations and just getting to the other side with the skills and knowledge to do his job to the best of his ability. Home is a meaningless term for him because he has deferred his whole life to some date in the future when he has finally checked all the boxes and can finally practice the profession he has spent all these years preparing for.

Our classmates from high school are well established in their careers, have kids, many of them, and mortgages to go with their suburban plots of heaven. They are knee deep in kid sports, dance, music and literacy lessons. Reading, writing and arithmetic gone wild. That was never what I hoped for. Staying home with kids. But then my role model did not do that either. And look at where she is now.

And when it comes to my mother… what she has become may have some bearing on why I am sitting here… shivering in a dark room with men with guns threatening to kill me and Charles. I doubt anyone would have wanted to take us like this if I was the daughter of Joe the Plumber and Suzie Homemaker. No money in that. No ransom likely. Mom has become a symbol, even though it was never evident to me until now. That is exactly what she has become. The face of a powerful nation, capable of sending a robot airplane to kill people half a world away. No one back home even has to see what we are doing to others. But what many people in this part of the world see and think of America.

Mom told me about a weapon system she was buying for the Army and Marines. She said the Taliban fighters used to call it the 'Finger of God'. When she told me that story, I had no idea what she was talking about. Weeks later she repeated it for someone in my presence. I asked what it meant. She explained that the Tow missile could find a person miles away and precisely track them, even if they ran and tried to hide. Once the missile locked on, there was no escape. It was like God put his finger on someone and the missile did the rest. I wonder if we are sighted, will a Tow missile lock on these men and God will have his finger on them? Will we be collateral damage? Mom never talked about that. Never mentioned the weapon was designed to take out a tank, and yet the soldiers were using it to kill snipers and soldiers who were massing for an attack. Overkill if you ask me. But will the overkill, end up being our demise?

My senses are still working at their peak. One of the men must have a cold. His breathing is shallow and more rapid than the others. I hope he stays away from us. Last thing I want to do is contract something I have no ability to fight off. And I hear my stomach rumbling more often. Probably working up to whatever drinking the local water is going to do to me… and Charles.

The door opens, blinding me with the light. I close my eyes, blink trying to get my vision back as quickly as possible. I see a figure enter the room now. See the table and chairs and shelves on the walls. What is on those shelves? It looks like cans of food… bags of grain or whatever comes in bags. This must be the pantry of this house. Maybe the dining room as well since there is a table and chairs. There must be a light in here, but they are not willing to turn it on. I am surprised the door is still open. My eyes are adjusting to the greater light. The figures in the room are clearly visible now, although I am not able to see faces as yet.

Charles is looking at me. I am not able to clearly see his eyes or his expression, but I have to think he is worried about me. I am not going to be able to communicate with him with the gag still in my mouth, so I study the now four men. That means the one who speaks English is here.

"Mumphf," I call to the men with the gag distorting what I am trying to say.

The men seem to ignore my attempt to communicate. And still the door is open. Does that mean they are feeling safe for the moment? Whatever caused them to move us into this smaller room and close the door is past? I feel the tension in the room has eased. Maybe the reason they were not talking was they were concerned someone might be listening in. I am not aware of any ability to hear into homes when people are not speaking on phones. We intercept signals, but just words? Mom has never mentioned anything we have to help us there. She talked about a through the walls radar, that can show soldiers where people are in the various rooms of a building they are attempting to breech. That is radar and not a listening device. But then again. I might just not have been around when Mom was talking about what tools they have to listen to people.

"Hehhhh!" I call to the men again.

Charles shakes his head like I should not be trying to talk with these men. But too late. One of them comes closer to me, stares at my clinging nightgown that is showing all there is to show through my silk pajamas. He reaches down and unties the gag. That permits me to take a full and deep breath for the first time in I do not know how many hours.

"Who are you?" I finally ask when my breathing settles down.

The man, heavy gold chain around his neck, still down on his one knee, looks around. He keeps his finger on the trigger of his automatic rifle. Not one of ours… must be a Russian weapon. Mom decided to take me out to a live fire exercise. I was amazed at just how loud it was. No wonder soldiers like to wear ear plugs in combat. But I also got to fire some of the rifles. That is why I would recognize one of ours. "Catch fish." The man responds hesitantly as if he is unsure of the words he is using.

"Why do fishermen carry rifles and hold me and my husband prisoner?" I respond angrily. I do not know if the anger will have any effect but I am sure if I do not show some emotion here the man will wonder if I am a spy or something. Trained to not show emotions. Like Mom. And not like Dad who can cry at any politically opportune moment.

"Fish men… cast nets," the man responds. And as I listen, I get the impression he speaks much better English than he is communicating with me. Again, he is likely trying to limit my ability to identify him after this is all over.

"Are you saying, that somehow, through no fault of your own, we got caught up in your nets?" I try deliberately to make it complex enough he will reveal his range of understanding.

"Know you," he answers, which neither confirms his ability to understand my question nor shows he did not understand my question.

"Then what happens now?" I put the simple question out there.

CHAPTER THIRTY-ONE:
DR. LILA THOMPSON

It has been a long day… too many patients. Everyone has some other ailment and only I can prescribe the magic pills that will relieve everything from hay fever to degenerative muscle weakness. They all come because the pharmas have made us their dispensary. No need to suffer, or wait for mother nature to heal. There is a magic pill for nearly everything. And every magic pill ensures the pharma will make an obscene profit because the insurance companies and employers pay for it rather than the individual who is taking the pill. I wonder how many pills would ever come to market if people had to pay the full cost of their medications. Is that the solution? Eliminate prescription drug insurance? Make people pay for the relief they are seeking? But that is not the society we live in today.

Dora, my physician's assistant sends a note about a patient she is seeing at the moment. He is not scheduled to see me, but Dora thinks I may want to talk with him. Unusual, but if Dora asks, I generally accept her advice and recommendation. I look at the patient profile. Twenty-eight-year-old male. Caucasian. Presenting symptom: venereal disease. Why would Dora recommend I talk with this patient when the treatment is standard? Must be more to this case than just what he is experiencing.

I go down the hall to treatment room six. I pick up the folder and knock. "C'min" I hear before opening the door. The patient is as described. Late twenties while male. Longish brown hair and hazel-colored eyes. Must have been blue for a long time. Was probably hoping, but now they have lightened and are not the baby blues that everyone seems to want.

"Mr…."

"Collins, Jake Collins," he responds automatically.

"May I call you Jake?"

"Nearly everyone I know does, so why not?" He seems underwhelmed by my asking without assuming. Makes me think a lot of people assume.

"I'm Dr. Thompson. Have I seen you before?"

"Long time ago. I don't get sick all that often." He responds to confirm I have seen him.

"Says here someone spread the joy."

He takes a deep breath, "Yeah… well… I was thinking your PA could just give me the pills I need to make it go away… but she kept asking me all these questions, and the next thing I know she tells me I really need to talk with you. Is there something I'm missing here? Something that will make this difficult to cure?" Jake Collins seems worried by the turn of events.

"I don't know… tell me what you told her," I am even more curious about him than before.

"Not much to tell… I work for the State Department. Picked up this little bundle of joy on official business."

"Official business… state department… what country were you visiting?" I wonder if this has something to do with Charles.

"Tanzania," I can see the tension in this young man. He is afraid this will get back to his boss and they will not send him out again.

"Just for your information, what you tell us does not go back to your employer. Your health records are protected. Just tell us what happened and your boss will never know unless you tell him or her."

"Her… Bridget Parks… she would never understand…" he is most relieved thinking his State Department career was over.

"So, what happened?"

"I checked into my hotel and found a young woman in my room. She said she was a present from the Foreign Office. She was most insistent that she had to do the deed with me or something bad was going to happen to her. What was I supposed to do? Refuse a damsel in distress? That's not how I was raised." Jake Collins is trying to make me feel better about his condition, but I think it is more a rationalization on his part than anything else.

"Where you from?"

"New Hampshire…" he responds.

I shake my head… not a southerner, who might get away with that excuse. "You helped her out, in other words," I shake my head not quite sure why Dora thought I needed to see this kid.

"I did, and that must be why I am here. Now I'm not sure if the Foreign Office was sending a message or just unaware of the girl's condition." Jake reflects.

"And of course, you were unprepared and were not carrying a condom." I surmise.

"This is not usual… I don't go out looking for…" Jake begins to explain, but I cut him off.

"Not my concern, Mr. Collins…" I respond.

"Thought you were going to call me Jake," he protests.

"I thought you were a whole lot smarter…" I respond without thinking and instantly regret my comment. "That's not fair… You're a red-blooded young man. No wife?"

Jake shakes his head.

"No steady girlfriend?" I push my luck

He shakes his head again, after a momentary delay while he thinks about my question.

“A regular girl, but not a fiancé yet,” I clarify.

“Something like that,” Jake admits.

“Was there something about this woman that you ignored all the usual warnings… like the very real prospect that she wasn’t clean?” I follow up.

“She was really attractive… I mean… if I met her in the bar… probably would have invited her up after enough drinks.” Jake admits. “This is all off the record, right? Private health information and all that?”

“Off the record… but what you are implying is you do this often… sleep with a lot of different women.”

“Red blooded… as you noted.”

I shake my head not sure why Dora asked me to talk with him, other than the Tanzania connection. “Tell me, what else did you say to Dora, my PA that you haven’t mentioned to me?”

Jake Collins has to think for a moment, “Told her the woman… she knew what she was doing. Experienced… not someone they had just recruited, if you know what I mean.”

“Knew what she was doing?” I am the one who is wondering what he is suggesting.

“She got me off quickly… I mean I doubt we were together more than twenty minutes. When you’re doing piecework…”

“Piecework?” He lost me with that analogy.

“The more men she does the more she gets paid,” Jake clarifies.

“Every thirty minutes…” I calculate.

“Two hundred dollars every thirty minutes… she’s doing all right even though she pays half to her pimp.

"Two hundred dollars an hour times ten hours is two grand a day, times three hundred and sixty days that's over seven hundred thousand dollars a year, in Africa, no less." I calculate.

"Regular entrepreneur…" Jake summarizes, but I am still wondering why Dora thought I should talk with him. None of this is really relevant to me or him. "If she were black, I'm not sure she would have had customers like me lined up."

"She was white." I realize Dora might have thought this significant. Did someone kidnap Annie to turn her to doing tricks for the western business and government officials coming through? "Dora… my PA. She gave you the prescription?" I make sure I am not overlooking something.

"She did," Jake confirms for me, and looks quizzical. "What else did you need to know?"

"Why would my PA tell me I needed to talk with you?" I just put it right out there.

Jake Collins, just back from Tanzania shrugs.

"Did you hear about missing Americans while you were there?" I grasp for the only thing I can think of.

"The mission was working on that, yes." Jake confirms.

"What were they saying?" I am thinking Dora may have asked this question.

"Just that they likely got lost and will eventually turn up… wandering about the veldt… up some tree trying to evade the lions and big cats or as someone's meal."

"It's been ten days now…" I point out and he shrugs.

CHAPTER THIRTY-TWO:

ANGELICA MYERS

Howard may be willing to let things play out… but that has never been my approach to anything in life. If I had taken his approach, we would likely still not be married, nor would we have had a daughter, who is now in danger. I love Howard, but on any given day, he drives me absolutely crazy. I am waiting for Yuri to answer my call as I sit in my Georgetown townhouse office. The one I never let Howard use.

I hear him answer. "Angel?" his unmistakable voice. He uses the nickname he always used for me. That means he has my cell phone number in his phone. After all this time I doubted he would have it. Must have gotten it from someone. His voice is raw. As if he has been talking a lot or he is having some throat issues. With Yuri I would never know anything about him, his health, his state of mind. He kept everything close and would deny any assumptions I made about him.

"Agent Tereshkova, I presume?" I respond to make him understand this is a formal call and not an attempt to resume a relationship that ended decades ago.

"Seem like yesterday." He continues his thoughts in response to my call. "We were coming into that safehouse when the bomb went off."

"I left you behind when you were clearly still alive although wounded badly," I push back on where I know this conversation is going and reviving the guilt I have carried all these years.

"I thought I was going to die and you did not need to, in order to be there when I died anyway." Yuri explains what we never talked about after he miraculously got out of that hell hole alive.

“You got the Agency valor medal… I got shit,” I remind him.

“You got your life back… had you stayed… no doubt we would have both ended up in some unmarked grave in a country neither of us had ever wanted to visit, even as a tourist.” Yuri has been sitting on these feelings for a long time. I should have had this conversation with him three decades ago.

“I did, and so did you…” I try to paint the picture this was not all one sided.

“Enough of the stroll down memory lane… why did you call this number? Call me… after all this time? As if I did not already know.” Yuri adds that last sentence to let me cut to the chase. I wonder who filled him in? Edmund Jackson? Probably. He was our immediate supervisor when we worked together and I am sure he talks to Yuri often enough.

“My daughter… Annie,” I respond.

“Who is the father?” Yuri puts out there, confusing the entire conversation since he is likely well aware I cannot say for sure who is.

“Not the issue of the moment…” I push back to get this discussion back on track. I do not have all day to work through this off-the-rails relationship.

“She’s missing in Africa… probably kidnapped, but we don’t know why.” Yuri asserts.

“I have more than one theory and they all lead back to me…” I admit.

“Don’t give yourself all the credit… could be someone mad the University of Virginia lost the basketball championship game…” Yuri reminds me I have no real insight into what is going on, although the van image and the voice mail voice have confirmed in my mind she was kidnapped and likely for political reasons. If it were just money… we would have heard something by now. At least I would have expected to have heard something.

"In Africa…" I dispute his assertion.

"Someone betting on them could have made a lot of money…" Yuri pulls my chain.

"Did you have your bet in?" I play along for a moment, but only a moment.

"I did, but naïve me… I thought the oddsmakers knew what they were talking about. I was done in the first round."

"I'm sorry you are not as clairvoyant as you would have me believe…" This conversation is so reminiscent of those we had when we were partners.

"I had you believing that… didn't I?" Yuri asks, reminding me that at one point he seemed to know exactly what the Taliban was going to do. "And obviously I did, because I'm still here, much as they thought they had me that day…"

"Yuri… you're waltzing…" I point out. That was a term we used when we were trying to get the other side to concede something and we were not ready to do what it would take if they did.

"Haven't been able to dance since I took that bullet for you in Peshawar…" he reminds me of another operation that did not turn out so well. I had to literally carry him out of Pakistan with a bullet in his hip that caused him to drag his left leg as we hobbled out of a danger zone with me doing all the hard work to get him out alive.

"What do you know about Annie and Charles?" I decide to call the question.

"Your FBI agent came by to see me…" Yuri admits and puts this all into perspective.

"Not Edmund…" I push to see if there was a subsequent discussion.

"I may have had a conversation with him… don't really

remember. I'm getting freaking old you know. Do what we used to do? Not happening. This body is just not cut out for all that bat-shit crazy stuff. I'm closer to being a freaking senior citizen than I am to being an Olympic anything." Yuri protests too much.

"And as a result of these conversations… you did your magic and came to what conclusion?" Not BS-ing him, but he always was the best scenario builder in the agency.

"Nobody on your radar…" he informs me.

"Okay… not my banker or next-door neighbor… then who?"

"I don't know…" Yuri answers unexpectedly. "My contacts are coming back with asking me if something is going on because they are hearing crickets… nada… nothing that would indicate anything had happened. And that can only mean one thing. Not someone in the networks of terrorists and so-called African Freedom Fighters. This is something different. Someone who is desperate for a different reason. Someone who just happened to find out your daughter was in their neighborhood and took advantage of lax security by design. You didn't want anyone to know they were there. Understandable. But because of your light security, a bunch of amateurs got through and took them someplace… who knows where?"

"This is your professional opinion?" I am surprised. This is not the Yuri I used to work with. He would have had a name and address by now.

"It is… Angel… you need to understand how much things have changed since you and I were bumping into bad guys in every bar and whore house in Africa. This is a whole different time. Surveillance and satellites, facial recognition, artificial intelligence… people can't do what we did back in the day. We have so much data about what people do, they simply cannot disappear the way we used to. And that does not just work in our favor. That means the other guy knows what we are doing before we even do it. This is a whole different world we live in. Where you live, you may not be seeing it. But part of the reason I'm on a desk? It's because a bunch of people a whole lot younger than me think I do not have what it takes to do field work anymore. Let me look at pictures… I might spot something the AI search algorithm doesn't. But that hasn't happened since they moved me here. It's freaking tough to get old… you know what I mean? The kids think we're senile and, in the meantime, they are building an indefensible world where the bad guy always wins."

"You telling me I should just wait and see how it all turns out?" I cannot believe what he is telling me. This is not the Yuri Tereshkova I worked with for nearly a decade.

"Come over and I'll open a bottle of vodka, like we used to. A bowl of borsch and Russian black bread? That is where all the world's problems are solved. We did that… together. You and me. And then you went off to save the world on your own. Left me behind to do the dirty work while you kept your hands clean."

"My hands aren't clean, Yuri. I signed off on more ops than you led, including a few that you did lead, although you were never to know that. I kept my eye on you. Looked out for you as much as I could from where I was. But I knew you would never be happy if you weren't on the most dangerous and consequential missions. That's why I signed off… not knowing if I had just signed your death warrant. I had more nightmares about you after we stopped working together than I did when we were. Just because I knew I had no ability to save you if things went bad."

Yuri does not respond immediately. "I did not know that…"

"That was then… right now I need to know if my daughter is alive and how we get her home." I put out there for him to react to.

Yuri is silent for a long moment. "My friends tell me your daughter is alive… but the situation is difficult… no one is sure which country is backing those who have them… so much confusion…"

CHAPTER THIRTY-THREE:
AGENT DAKOTA PLAINSMAN

Kenya was never on my list of must-see places to visit. Nairobi was much more western than I imagined, but I was only there for a few hours before the long drive out here. Half a day or so it seemed, after I got basically no sleep on the way over. And no sleep since I have been in country. Can barely keep my eyes open.

When the Range Rover pulls up, I do not respond immediately. My eyes are closed and I keep on bouncing even though the vehicle has come to a stop. Someone touches my arm, and when that does not result in my waking, the same hand pushes on me… hard. I open my eyes to see a black man staring at me. He is wearing a Kenyan Army uniform, complete with jaunty worn bush cap. When I start moving, he turns his head to look at me to see if I am truly awake or just beginning the process. He must decide on the former because he backs off and addresses me, "Agent Plainsman… welcome to Kisumu Camp."

A deep breath and I rouse myself, coming out of the Range Rover and breathing in the warm, but very dry air. It almost burns my nose with the dryness. My eyes are open and I glance around the camp, gather myself and ask, "Which tent was theirs?"

"Let me show you," the uniformed officer responds, I know he is an officer now that I see his epaulets and the rank displayed there.

The tent is not so far away… a few steps really, and I am trying to focus through the fog of a lack of sleep. I try to push my eyes wide open, but the eyelids will not cooperate. The officer opens the tent for me to enter. Inside I see a luxurious room. Large bed, bath off to the right. Permanent with the exception of the tent material closing it in. I note the full bar, but only one bottle of wine is open and two glasses seem to have been used. Surprising. This was supposed to have been a honeymoon trip.

The suitcases of the couple are still where they were left. Open and the bath is still set up for their use. They did not leave when they expected to leave. Otherwise, all of their bath supplies and clothing would have been stored in the suitcases. Their departure was clearly… in my mind… unexpected.

I approach the officer who brought me to the tent, "Excuse me, sir." The officer snaps to attention. I am not sure if I outrank him or it is the other way around. "At ease, sir. Don't want to get into all the rank stuff… let's just assume we are of equal rank. In that case…you have interviewed the staff. What did they have to say?"

The officer remains at parade rest. Arms and hands behind his back. "No one saw the guests leave the camp. Cannot tell us if it was friendly or not. Best guess is it took place before midnight, but not entirely sure. No one was active in the camp after ten and not again until about five am. If they left around midnight, they were gone a long time before anyone was up and awake. Even then they were not focused on where this couple might have been."

"Did anyone from the camp notify the authorities when they realized they had not checked out and their things were still here?" I push him now.

"This is Africa, Agent Plainsman. Westerners like yourself… you often change your mind… decide not to follow the itinerary. It would not have been unusual for this couple to have arranged another day in the bush and not notify the camp until their return. In Africa… we just go with it. No reason to question changes of plans, especially when it results in more money for the camp and staff."

I nod, thinking I understand what he is saying, but there is this fog between me and the words he is using. "Do you think I could get a few hours of sleep here before we go looking for them?"

"I'll inquire at the office." And the officer disappears. I look at the room I am standing in. A room from which the couple was likely abducted. What clue have they left for me? If only I could see what they left. See through this fog of slit and unfocused eyes.

I get down and look under the bed… a contraceptive rubber… used. I pull it out and dispose in the garbage can in the bath. I go over to the doorway and look at the floor. All kinds of footprints, all kinds of shoes, but mostly desert boots of the investigators who have explored this room. But I look through those patterns to see if there is any dust or other kinds of prints that separate from the others. One tennis shoe. I go back to the closet where his shoes were lined up. No tennis shoes. I look in her closet. No tennis shoes. That tells me someone, either from the camp or an investigator or a captor wore tennis shoes. I take a picture and send it off to Langley to see if someone can identify it. Long shot, but the only clue in this space that might have any relevance.

I exit the tent and go out to the drive in front. Beau Thompson found a tire tread out here. Are there any footprints where someone got into a van, since Beau surprised me with that little tidbit.

About four feet to the left of the tread I find the tennis shoe print and what looks like bare feet prints. Two sets of bare feet, one larger than the others. This makes me think the couple were brought out here by someone in tennis shoes and in their bare feet loaded into the van. If they were taken in the middle of the night, they may not have had a chance to change into day clothes. Are they still in their bed clothes… barefoot? Is that keeping them from resisting? I had not given this any consideration, but if that is the situation, we need to change the descriptions we have out there for them. A couple in bedclothes is going to be a lot easier to spot and report back in.

The officer returns, "Agent Plainsman…"

"Where did you lose this tire track?" I ask before he can tell me where I might sleep. I am more awake now that I have some clues and have been moving about a bit.

The officer turns and points to the entrance to the camp. "Where this road joins the highway."

"Which way did they turn?" I do not give him a chance to think about it.

"Towards Nairobi… the right," he responds looking off in that direction.

"Do you have maps of the main roads between here and there?" I push him again.

The officer nods and heads off towards a Range Rover he apparently has been driving. He quickly returns and displays the maps for me. "These are the major roads between here and Nairobi."

"Even thought they were supposed to head in the other direction… towards Tanzania."

"Correct," the officer informs me as I look at the maps. I trace out where they could have gone and realize, if they stayed on the highways, they only had a few routes they could have taken.

"Send this map to FBI Headquarters… showing the routes they could have taken from here if in fact they turned right and not left." I instruct the officer.

"What else would you like to see?" the officer asks. I show him the image Beau Thompson found and ask,

"Could you help me find this spot?"

The officer looks at the photo and tries to orient on the property. After a long moment he points in a direction, "Follow me…"

We walk what is likely a half mile or more to a spot. The officer looks around and finally says, "That tree is most likely the place you have identified."

We go to that spot and sure enough, we find tire treads that look exactly like the ones we discovered in front of the tent. I stoop down and take photos and upload them to FBI Headquarters for analysis. I notice there are no bars here for cellular reception and realize they will not receive this information until I can get to a point close to a cellular tower. And in Kenya that might be the whole trip back to Nairobi, although I do not expect to go there any time soon.

I look at his map. I follow the path to the first turn. North. I follow along and see if I stay on that road I will go towards South Sudan, but the first turn off would take me towards Somalia. “Sir: if you were planning to take someone hostage… would you go to Sudan or Somalia?”

The officer looks at me as if I am crazy, “Neither… If I were to take someone hostage it would have nothing to do with where I live or where I would take them.”

“Could you give me a little more explanation?” he has lost me.

“You are in Africa. A hostage or prisoner, or captive… whatever term you chose to describe them… It has nothing to do with where you live.”

“What does it have to do with?” I realize I have no idea what he is talking about.

“In Africa… you kill your enemy… you do not want to be responsible for them. Tells me this couple was not the enemy, but a bargaining chip.”

“I would agree… but if you had such a bargaining chip… where would you take it?” I have to peel this onion back a layer at a time.

“Not to my home… That would bring enemies to the door of my family. No. I would not go to my home. I would look for a place where no one knows me, would not ask questions about why I am there or what I am doing.”

“Is there such a place?” I ask not sure if I am asking the right question.

“Somalia…it is what you would call a failed state, with no one in charge of security or any kind of government, really.

CHAPTER THIRTY-FOUR:

BEAU THOMPSON

This data cannot be right. We have invested heavily on solving this particular problem and yet it persists. I will have to bring the technical team offsite to get them to really focus on what they apparently cannot see when they work every day in the same lab. Talking with the same people, about the same problem. That worked last time we got to this point. Hopefully it will again.

My cell rings and I glance over at the screen… Agent Plainsman. Has he found Charles? I reach instantly for the phone and punch the speaker button anxiously. "Yes…"

"Mr. Thompson…" I am not sure if he recognized my voice or is really trying to confirm he is speaking to me. Who else would answer my phone? "Agent Plainsman… I am at the Kisumu Camp."

"What have you found?" rushes out of my brain and into the cell phone.

"I am afraid that everything we thought we knew has been confirmed by being here and talking with those who are conducting the investigation on behalf of the Kenyan government.

"Confirmed… as in?" I can barely speak the words. I am dreading his response.

"The camp has been very cooperative… the tent they used is still just as they left it, even though it had been booked out subsequently." Agent Plainsman is not getting to the point. Why?

"That will hopefully assist your investigation…" I try to be polite, even though I am feeling far from it at the moment. But he is there and

I am not, so I have to make the best of the situation.

"What puzzles me is there are no signs of resistance, of being forcibly removed from the camp. It almost seems they were either cooperating or were completely surprised. What I see here does not provide any insight as to which it might have been." I can tell the agent is trying to probe what I might not have told him earlier, if I had any knowledge of things he is now seeing for himself.

"Why would they have cooperated?" I let him know I do not agree with that assessment.

"They might have known one or more of the people who removed them from the camp," Agent Plainsman lets me know there are new possible explanations we have not considered.

"They had no plans to meet anyone they knew…" I am emphatic. "They wanted to be alone, which was one of the attractions to that particular camp. They did not know anyone who had ever been there or had even heard of it for that matter."

"Are you sure of that?" Agent Plainsman challenges me.

"Quite…" I throw back at him, trying to suppress my anger that he will not simply take me at my word.

"Then you must not be aware of Dr. Thompson's work with Doctors Without Borders, an organization that has teams deployed in Kenya." Agent Plainsman makes the implications clear.

"Charles has never been to Kenya before… and if he has had any involvement with Doctors Without Borders, he has not mentioned it to me." Although he has me wondering what else do I not know about my son.

"He has explored joining them for a year after completing his residency, rather than going directly into private practice," Agent Plainsman seems to realize I had never had this conversation with Charles. I wonder how serious it was.

"He still has two years of his residency…" I point out. "How serious was this 'discussion'?"

"The recruiter thought he was very serious," Agent Plainsman adds more detail to the situation.

"Odd that he would not have even mentioned it," I reflect on conversations Charles has had with us about his post Residency plans. It was always more about what city to live in than anything else, given Annie's job in DC. It was looking likely that was going to be where they ended up. Maybe Charles was having a change of heart about DC, at least right after he finishes.

"He also met with a Doctor Hamid Chatterjee in Nairobi, the day after their arrival. Dr. Chatterjee informed me that Mrs. Thompson was present for their discussion." Agent Plainsman is informing me of something Charles apparently was not ready to share with us and Annie knew. Even so, she was willing to go ahead with the wedding. Knowing they would be apart for another year. Surprising.

"What else don't I know about my son?" I respond now showing my anger, but not at the FBI agent, but myself for not having spent more time talking with Charles.

"I am hardly qualified to answer that question," Agent Plainsman responds, reminding me I am being too hard on him, when I am the reason for my own ignorance.

"I apologize… I should not be venting my frustrations on you."

"But there is more to the story…" the FBI agent lets me know there is likely more I do not know about Charles and Annie that may bear on the situation.

"Like what?" I snip back at him and instantly regret it.

"Mrs. Thompson has been taking intensive language lessons…"

"Seems to me she is fluent in more than one already," I am trying to remember which languages… French and Spanish I am positive about… but was she also studying Italian?

"Arabic and Chinese at the same time." Agent Plainsman watches my reaction.

I know I must have a curious expression as I try to puzzle that out. "Why would the Supreme…"

"She is taking those lessons on her own time."

"She has never expressed interest…" I admit before I wonder if like mother like daughter. "Is she working for the agency?"

"They are preparing her for a covert assignment… in conjunction with a Doctors Without Borders placement." Agent Plainsman is revealing a whole side of the kids I had no inkling about, although it is clear why I would not. Charles must know about Annie. Maybe he sees it as romantic, or that he would get great experience. But the thing is about the agency. They would not be looking for Annie to do this for just a year… does that mean that Charles was planning to make such assignments into his career, rather than private practice in some major US city?

"Why are you telling me this now?" I push on the agent as it must be that he wants me to know there is more to this story than what we have been given so far… or at least, that is what he is concluding. But why just me and not the four parents all at the same time?

"I need your help with something…"

"My help? You're the FBI…" I respond without thinking.

"And like every bureaucracy, some things take longer than they should, and longer than someone not part of that bureaucracy can get information."

"You need me to help you get information…" I wonder what he has in mind.

"One of the staff here, at the camp, has not returned after her last leave. She left the morning the Thompsons disappeared. I am wondering if she disappeared at the same time for a reason."

"You think she may have been the inside person…" I realize what he is dealing with now. "And the Kenyan officials have not been able to find her."

"Correct," the agent is direct.

"You think I might be able to locate her faster than going through the official channels, since they have not come up with anything yet."

"I am looking for any means of expediting leads and clues, because frankly… there are damn few of them."

"Send me what you have on her and I'll see what I can do." I offer.

"She was the head cook. Been here just a few months. Odd that she would not return without notice."

"Are you thinking she may have left the camp with the kidnappers?" I wonder aloud.

"I am not ruling out anything at this point." Agent Plainsman informs me.

As I nod in understanding I inform him, "You have given me much to think about. And you think they may have been pulled into something having to do with these new roles they were preparing for? Why they may have been cooperative with whoever took them from the camp?"

"A plausible explanation when you have the other facts we just discussed."

"Doesn't make sense to me… if what you suggest happened, I have to think Angelica would have been informed."

"When you get into compartmentalized operations, even the Secretary of Defense might have been excluded from need to know," the agent informs me of something else I did not understand.

"And you need something on this cook by when?" I start considering the task he has asked me to take on.

"In the next hour would be great…" the agent informs me I am wasting time talking now.

CHAPTER THIRTY-FIVE:
HOWARD THOMPSON

Angelica was able to set up a private briefing with State Department experts on the countries in the Horn of Africa, which are those thought to be most likely where Charles and Annie are being held. Lila and Angelica are here, but Beau said he had to find information for the FBI team working our case and could not join. I try not to question Beau too much, as he is always doing one thing or another for all of the various intelligence agencies. And without a scorecard it is impossible to know which agency Beau is working for on any given day.

Absco Otieno is a petite young woman, well dressed and braided long hair. She seems to look through you, rather than engage your eyes. She speaks with hesitation as if she is unsure of whether she will need to change tact if she encounters any resistance. "I understand you are looking for an overview of the situation in the Horn…" she begins the formal briefing after pleasantries.

Angelica does not give her a chance to finish her sentence, "We are most interested in knowing what terrorist groups are operating there and who is backing them."

"Such a briefing would likely be classified and would generally be given by CIA staffers…" Absco is very clear about the limitations of what she can provide.

"We already have the CIA assessment… what we want to know is what does State know and what are they doing to bring our kids home?" Angelica continues being very direct.

"I am not sure I can add all that much that would be relevant…" Absco is looking for a way not to get crosswise with CIA.

"Just give us what you have… we will worry about the rest," Angelica is almost done with this staffer who is not giving her what she wants.

Absco nods, although her expression confirms she is not wild about doing this briefing. "You indicated that Kenya is the primary country of interest…"

"Yes… that is where Dr. Charles and Annie Thompson were last seen." I try to shift the focus from Angelica so maybe she will listen instead of talking.

"Kenya is one of the more stable countries in the region. Prosperous by African standards. Modern by western standards in Nairobi, but not so much in the rest of the country. Wide income disparity, many dissident factions, which can co-exist with the authorities because it is a relatively open society."

"Who is trying to destabilize the government?" Angelica drills the poor young woman.

"Destabilization comes from many different sectors. Those who stand to benefit are the usual characters… Russia, foremost, but also China and Iran are doing everything they can to cause the government to fall and set the country on the road to chaos. Those three countries are in a struggle for influence. Competing though local factions they support in a variety of ways, quite frankly." Absco recites from memory.

"Which is the most influential at the moment?" Angelica continues to direct the questions.

"From what we see, the better question is which faction and their benefactor, is best positioned to oust the government." Absco puts the question into terms she is more comfortable answering.

"If that was the question I wanted you to answer, I would have asked it," Angelica drills her.

Absco looks at the Secretary of Defense as if no one had ever talked to her this way before. Tries to figure out how to respond. She takes a deep breath and then rattles off her canned response. "The factions allied with Russia, seek destabilization without offering an alternative program. All of their rhetoric focuses on how badly the government is doing in meeting the needs of the people. They do not offer alternatives… only seeking discontent. The factions allied with Iran simply seek the end of western influence. They call attention to the discontent and dysfunction of western governments, the hypocrisy of unlimited arms for Ukraine while countries in Africa starve. The Chinese simply want commercial arrangements that favor China at the expense of the local states. You want a new railroad… happy to lend you the money to build it, as long as you use primarily Chinese labor. And those laborers stay after the project is concluded to seek to develop influence and additional commercial ties. Very mercantile."

"You are saying that any of the factions are likely to be anti-western because of their relationships with one of those three sponsors." Angelica summarizes what she wanted to know.

"There are many more allied with them than with us or any of our allies," Absco responds with a cautious smile.

"Why is that?" I ask to see if I can change the focus from Angelica's drilling of the poor young woman.

"Why has the west lost Africa?" Absco rephrases my question.

"Have we?" I follow up.

"It is the considered opinion of the State Department that our nation has underinvested in Africa, whether in terms of financial support, health and immunization, or in diplomatic relationship building. Just look at ambassadors… we have a long list of those willing to represent us in Rome or London. Not so many who want to go to Beijing or Moscow. Virtually none who want to go to any African nation. So, it ends up a career diplomat, who generally has little pull either with the career team at state or the appointed secretary. And if you want to get to the President or VP, well, those rich donors, who are sitting in London, Paris, and Rome… they always have direct access."

“How would you change that situation?” Lila asks, surprising me.

“I am not sure you can… but those other nations we mentioned? They send ambassadors who are charged with specific objectives and teams of operatives to implement them. Most of our African missions are understaffed and under-resourced, and quite frankly, more interested in furthering the business interests of Americans who come over, than assisting the nation with infusions of capital and technology to modernize their societies.”

“Isn’t that what the countries of Africa have come to expect from America?” Lila surprises me at her knowledge of how we treat other nations. “That we are just another rich nation willing to give them money to buy things from us? How is that any different from what the Russians, Iranians and Chinese are doing?”

“We have just been doing it longer, and now are reducing the amount of aid we are providing while those other nations are increasing their aid.” Absco explains evidencing some frustration in her voice.

There is a moment of silence after that response as it is likely a realization that we are getting a nice overview of the situation there from a macropolitical perspective, but very little that would give us any insight as to who might have been behind the kidnapping of our kids.

“Is the Kenyan government angry with America?” Angelica asks a question she apparently has been sitting on through this entire discussion.

Absco looks to a Deputy Secretary who has been monitoring this discussion. I have seen her before but do not remember her name. Must be the Deputy Secretary for this part of the world. The woman nods to Absco who then attempts to answer the question. “The Kenyan government tries to maximize aid to the country, maximize tourist dollars coming into their economy, and tries to not get anyone upset with them. That has been a very difficult task.”

“Why?” Angelica presses her again.

“The Chinese give the most aid, we provide the tourist dollars, and the Russians and Iranians don't give them much, but they have well established communities in country that can cause the government considerable trouble if they take positions unpopular with their benefactors."

"With your knowledge of the area… if someone were to kidnap Americans… where would they be most likely to take them?" Angelica goes to an unfair question, but what she really wants to know. "I take you don't think they would keep them in Kenya."

"The Kenyan government is the one that would be most likely to cooperate fully with the US." Absco responds as a way to stall and give her more time to consider the answer she is about to give.

"You agree with my assessment, then." Angelica continues to push.

"I do, but as to which country would they take Americans? That is not a general question I can easily answer. The reason is all of the countries in that area have minimal relationships with the US. Yes, we have embassies. Yes, we have people on the ground. But we have little in the way of influence because of the way we have ignored their fundamental needs. We have made it clear that countries with oil are of much greater interest than those who have starving populations."

"But President Bush's Aids initiative made a real impact on a health crisis throughout this region," I have to assert.

"It did, and those who were directly impacted by it will be forever grateful. But one and done does not engender long standing loyalty. We horded the COVID vaccines when so many in Africa were dying. Had we simply shared equally… you might have a valid point of people in this part of the world seeing America as a partner and friend. Both the Russians and Chinese made their vaccines available immediately. Even thought they were not as effective as ours, they made the effort."

CHAPTER THIRTY-SIX:

CHARLES THOMPSON

One more mind-numbing trip in the back of a van, hood on, gag in, and hands still zip-tied behind my back. I really do not know how to estimate time, anymore. For a while I would try counting to myself. But that got old when the minutes turned into hours and more hours and more hours. Just too much to count. So, I have tried to pass the time thinking about what we would do if we ever escaped, knowing that after all this time, escape is now as likely as rescue. If the authorities had any idea where we are, I am sure they would have come and freed us long ago. Why is it so hard to find us? The US has the best intelligence agencies in the world. It must be different here for some reason. Annie would have a better idea about all that than I do. I am sure we will look back on this time at some point and she will tell me all the things she knew but could not tell me about what is going on.

It seems we have been travelling for hours now. Hours since we left that house. And all this time I keep trying to flex and pull against the zip tie on my wrists. It amazes me that Annie has not been discovered. That her zip tie is cut and she can get her hands free. Amazed that they have been moving us about but apparently not looked close enough at her to realize the zip tie is no longer binding her. At some point that is either going to work to our advantage or will cause them to take some action against us. I am hopeful that if the latter, they will simply put another zip tie on her. But since they have provided so little information about why they are holding us, why they continually move us from place to place, it is hard to know anything.

Twist, pull, twist, pull… I just keep working on the zip tie. Hope to weaken it such that it will simply snap with a harder pull, but so far it has proven to be remarkably resistant to my efforts even though I am sure I made a reasonable cut into it in that one van. This appears to be a different vehicle. As I have not been able to find the sharp edge I worked against… when was that? How many different places ago?

Annie touches me with her feet, just making contact… letting me know she is still here with me. Letting me know we are still in this together… regardless of what happens now. I have to think she is becoming discouraged that it has been so many days… so many long hours without any indication that this may soon end. If only the guy who speaks English would give us more information about what they are doing… what they expect to happen. What are their demands? Why has the United States not met those demands to bring us home?

I think of that basketball player… who was arrested on drug charges when she tried to leave Russia a while back. That was different. In that case everyone knew where she was. Occasionally saw pictures of her when she was taken to court for yet another mock trial… they were not real trials since the outcome was given to the court before the hearing even took place. At least that is what Annie told me. I have to believe she got her information from her mother. And she should certainly know about those things. But she was held for something like ten months… almost a whole year. Other Americans have been held in prisons for nearly a decade. Is that our fate? That we will be held so long no one will recognize us when and if they ever let us go?

I cannot think like that… this is not going to go on and on and on like those cases. We are not being lawfully held under the laws of a country. We have been kidnapped. Taken against our will, even though we have not done anything against even the local laws.

Someone I read said that hope is the defining need of someone in any adverse situation. You always have to have hope to survive your ordeal. I am still hopeful. I expect we will find a way to return home. This is not the end of anything… and in fact, it is the beginning of Annie and my life adventures together. Will we ever be able to laugh about any part of this? Not likely. There has been absolutely nothing funny or humorous or even mildly amusing so far. Nothing I will want to remember and laugh about some day. All I will want to do is put this behind us and look to a better future. One that is more predictable, more positive in every way.

I touch Annie with my bare feet… both together to make as much contact as possible. Make a definite statement to her that I am still hopeful, still positive… still here with her.

Flex, pull, flex, pull… I continue working on the zip tie, but it does not seem to be getting any looser. Does not seem to be in any way less restrictive on me. Still… I have to continue to try. I get absolutely nothing out of stopping. Keeping on gives me something to hope for.

For some reason I wonder how I would ever describe what has happened to us to someone who I do not know. Someone who might be interviewing me for a partnership in a medical practice, or someone interviewing me for a different medical role, like the discussion with Dr. Chatterjee in Nairobi. How would I describe this since if I did practice overseas, in the places Annie would expect us to go, we would be subject to being kidnapped all over again. Obviously, if it can happen in Kenya, where things are relatively safe, what happens in other countries of this region? Same in parts of Asia. Even in the US people are kidnapped and held for ransom or worse. There have been cases where young women are held as sex slaves for years and decades. Have children by their captors… forced to raise those kids alone, with no help, no schools, no modern medicine to help them avoid childhood diseases. Will we ever feel safe again? Anywhere? Or will we end up like so many… security cameras everywhere. Afraid to go out alone at night. Afraid to attend events where there are large crowds. Afraid for our lives even if this comes out all right? What does an experience like this really do to your psyche? I am a doctor and even I only have a vague idea of what the long-term effects of this will be on me. On Annie. On our relationship together. After this… will we even stay together, or will just my presence become a continual reminder that I was unable to keep her safe. Is that not one of the chief requirements of a husband? To keep the wife and family safe? Have I already flunked the primary test of a good marriage? That she will never have complete trust in me… ever again?

Just the thought that I may have lost her forever, because I was not able to stand up to our captors when they came into our tent, seems to take the wind out of me. No… I am not going to let that happen. Not going to let her ever feel insecure again. I do not care what it takes, but I will make it possible for her to trust me, even if I have to spend every dime I make in my practice ensuring that. Does that mean we hire a private bodyguard? Someone who can ensure no one ever does this to us again? Or does it mean we never travel abroad again? That would be really hard, at least for me, as there are so many places I want to see, things and moments and experiences I want to share with Annie. That is what this trip was really all about. To begin to experience the wider world. To come to understand different cultures, different priorities, different ways of looking at the world we live in. We live such a sheltered life in comparison to so many parts of the world. I want to embrace all of it… the good and the bad. And unfortunately, we are getting more than our share of the bad at the moment.

This is all just so frustrating… I twist twice and pull twice now with as much strength as I have left, given we have had so little food and water for so many days. I am almost light-headed. And then I feel the SNAP. Did it really just break? I gingerly try to move my wrists apart and they go further than they have since they put this last zip tie on. Quickly I pull my wrists back together and feel the zip tie which now hangs from the little finger on my right hand. Using both hands I try to pull it back up so that if anyone looks it will seem to still be there.

The van begins slowing down. What does this mean? That they will be moving us out of the van in a minute? That they will find I am now free? Will all this work have been for nothing? A moment of freedom that I cannot use to help us escape these men? I have no idea where we are or what language people speak here, or whether Americans are even seen as friends. Shit.

The van comes to a stop. It sounds like a window is opening. As if the driver is at a police road block. Or maybe a traffic cop has pulled them over. This might be an opportunity. I need to take it. The man who I think is the driver starts to talk to someone, I suspect through the open window. Only one way of finding out if this is our one chance to get away.

I reach up and pull off the hood, look around and see the driver talking with someone, leaving the gag in, I touch Annie so she knows I am free and launch myself at the driver from behind. I grab him around the neck and pull his head back, trying to get him in a headlock as I used to do when I was wrestling in high school and college.

The driver punches the gas and the van lurches forward. I continue to hold the driver and only his seat belt keeps me from pulling him into the back with me. The other man unbuckles and climbs between the seats, launching himself at me. At first, I keep holding the driver, but now have to release him so I can ward off this second man. He tries to pull me away and down on the van floor, but I am quickly able to reverse on him and have him pinned down. But now what do I do? In wrestling I only need to hold him for a three count. That will not do anything for us with this guy.

The van picks up speed since the driver knows I am loose and his companion is not going to be any help in subduing me. The only thing I can think of to disable this guy is to break an arm. That should put him into enough pain that I can go after the driver. I unwind and pull his left arm up behind his back and push beyond the point of maximum muscular resistance and hear the crack, knowing this man is now in considerable pain. But at that moment I see Annie fly by. Her hood is off and she grabs the driver from behind, just as I had. Now the van is swerving from side to side. Just as I push away on the man with the broken arm, the van careens and flips over onto the side, tossing us about the back, as the van slides to a halt.

The two guards climb out as we try to make our way to the front. They run off. Now what?

CHAPTER THIRTY-SEVEN:
ANGELICA THOMPSON

The non-stop flight from DC to Addis Ababa, Ethiopia, is a little over thirteen hours. Time to do a little work for the Pentagon and a little time to get some rest. I never sleep on flights. Never truly go to sleep and wake up somewhere else. It was also hard to get out of the district without my usual entourage of Pentagon paper pushers. The uniformed men and women who enable me to do my day-to-day job of keeping the free world safe for democracy. However, this trip has nothing to do with my job. This trip is to bring my little girl home, safe and sound. Oh… and her new husband, too. I do not know how long it is going to take me to get used to the fact that she has a husband. Their arrangement of living separately just seems to perpetuate the illusion that they are only living together… sort of. Not in reality since they only see each other infrequently. But in fact, they are now husband and wife who have chosen to live a thousand miles apart so they can keep their careers going. I do not blame Annie. I made the same choice, and it worked out. Only Howard and I never had to live a thousand miles apart to keep advancing in our careers. Richmond to the district is about as far as it has ever been. I generally see him for at least one day on the weekends, although recently that has been honored more in the breech than the observance.

I wanted to sit in the back in the cattle car on this flight so as not to be recognized. Howard told me I was crazy to consider such a long flight cramped in a space only a little over two feet wide and two feet deep. He suggested I wear bush clothes, including boots and keep the round bush hat on most of the way. No makeup and my hair tied back would make me nearly unrecognizable. To seal the deal, he showed me a picture he had taken of me early one morning before showering. He made his point. Even I did not recognize me.

As I come off the jetway at the airport I see Yuri Tereshkova and Agent Plainsman standing with another short and thin man I do not recognize. His hair is short cropped and has a touch of gray. His teeth are bright white as he smiles almost continuously. He is wearing a police uniform, officer rank. Must be the police liaison. I walk past them as if I did not know them to see if either recognizes me. Yuri gives me a second glance, but turns back to look for me. I circle around behind them and politely ask, "Where do I get a taxi to the US Embassy?"

The Ethiopian police officer points off to his right, but Yuri recognizes my voice and gives me a hug. The police officer asks, "You know this woman?"

"She is the package," Yuri responds and glances at Agent Plainsman who is now looking at me closer, nods to himself.

I hand my diplomatic passport to the police officer and we walk through immigration without stopping since we are in the presence of the police officer. I will never officially have been in Ethiopia or any other country in Africa on this trip as this is a completely off the record event. Only the President knows for sure where I am within the government and my reporting structure. My staff thinks I am with Howard on a campaign event trip, although none could fathom why I would want to take time off while Annie and Charles are still missing.

A short ride later we are in the office of Captain Shango Desta of the National Police. The room is small with just a desk and small round table with chairs for four. Hard chairs made of a nearly black lacquered wood and very thin cushion. Almost like there is no filling in the cushion. Just two layers of cloth. I notice a layer of dust on the cushion. That either means the building is not air tight or these chairs are not used very often. I suspect that both are true. Brushing off the dirt, I sit next to the Captain and across from Agent Plainsman.

"Shango and I have shared a number of misadventures we can recollect when you have more time," Yuri begins the discussion, which I did not expect. "Shango was able to locate the cook with the information Mr. Thompson provided. She lives here in the city… has lived here all her life, according to his records. Which makes it curious that she had taken the job at the camp in Kenya. Yes, things are tight economically here. But she has worked as the lead cook in a restaurant here for decades. What made her leave, we have not been able to discern. Why she came back so soon, is also a question."

"No prior involvements?" I ask Shango, as Yuri is referring to him.

"No, ma'am. Popular restaurant, where she cooks. Four children… grown. Not living with her now." Shango provides high level details.

"Husband?" I ask since there are four kids.

"Dead," Shango shakes his head. "Decided mercenaries made more money than being a policeman."

"You knew him?" I wonder aloud.

Shango nods but does not say more.

"Has anyone spoken to her about the camp?" I follow up with another question.

Shango again shakes his head. "Yuri suggested it would be better to wait for you, although he did not tell me who you are."

"Good thing… since I am not here." I remind him. "And in that case, we should pay a call to this woman… see what she can tell us."

Agent Plainsman is the first to his feet, apparently anxious to conduct this interview and move this case along. I would bet he is under just enormous pressure to bring this to a resolution since everyone including the Director is looking for daily reports from him. Sorry about that.

The area where the woman lives is little better than what I think of as a shantytown. Buildings made of corrugated steel, with no glass in the windows, no security for the people who live there. Just a firepit and a roof over her head. Four kids in this place must have been a real challenge. And I thought bringing up Annie in a four-bedroom house was a challenge.

Shango goes to the doorway, since there is no door. He knocks on the corrugated steel and nods to a figure I can barely make out inside. A brief conversation, do not recognize the dialect, and Shango motions for us to follow him. The woman is rail thin. She has a perpetual smile, which I finally realize is a result of her skin being pulled tight against her face… likely from near starvation. And she is a cook? Wow. What do people eat here?

The woman motions for us to sit on the floor as there is no furniture, but I notice Babushka nesting dolls on a trunk in the corner. This is what they mean by dirt poor.

Shango begins the discussion in English, "Mama Bekele… you left your job and went to Kenya to cook for the white people visiting."

Mama Bekele nods, "I did."

"Why?" Shango asks, without any threat in his voice.

"Mama Bekele need money," she responds simply.

"A lot of money?" Shango follows her response with a question of his own.

"Baby… second son… sick. Need doctor. White people hospital. Only place can help him."

"How is the baby?" Shango asks with genuine interest in his voice.

"Dead," Mama Bekele responds. "Hole in heart. Took too long to make money."

"Is that why you did not return to the camp?" Shango seeks to confirm what she is suggesting.

"Pay doctor… not hospital. Not so much. Time come home. Other babies to feed."

"Who got you the job at the camp?" Shango asks the question we have all been wondering.

"Man like him…" she points to Yuri.

"Russian. What did you have to do for him?" Shango looks at Yuri.

"Call when white folks come," she responds, "Girl look like her." She points to me.

"Were you there when the white folks were taken away?"

"Asleep… not hear or see," Mama Bekele responds to Shango.

"Could you identify the Russian you called when the white folks arrived?"

Mama Bekele nods.

"I would like you to come to my office and look at pictures, maybe you can identify him for us."

Mama Bekele rises and I finally truly appreciate just how malnutritioned she is. Shango leads us out of the tin shack Mama Bekele calls home and gun fire erupts. Shango goes down and Agent Plainsman pushes Mama Bekele down as he draws a Glock to return fire at three men in an old beat-up gray Peugeot. Yuri and I crouch down and draw weapons as well. We go in opposite directions from the door. This was practiced when we were working together and even after all this time it was an immediate reaction that did not require any communication.

Agent Plainsman has to reload, so Yuri and I each commence firing at the vehicle from different directions now. The men in the vehicle figure out they will likely be captured or killed if they do not leave. The Peugeot leaps into life and speeds away, coming in my direction. I fire at the driver and am sure I hit him, although the vehicle does not stop. I get the license plate number and holster my weapon as I walk back to the house.

"Captain Desta is dead," Yuri announces. "And Mama Beleke was wounded."

CHAPTER THIRTY-EIGHT:

AGENT DAKOTA PLAINSMAN

While we wait for Mama Bekele's surgery to be finished, we gather in the waiting room at the hospital in Addis Ababa. Just Yuri Tereshkova and Angelica Thompson and myself. I reported the death of Captain Desta, but the authorities have not yet assigned someone else to work with us. That will be a big loss if it takes a while. Shango asked all of the questions of Mama Bekele. I am not so sure she would have been so forthcoming of an American asking those same questions.

"There is more to this than she told us," Angelica Thompson shares with us.

"Woman's intuition?" I ask and instantly regret it. This is the Secretary of Defense. She can have me gone in a nanosecond if she thinks I am a problem.

"Maybe a little…" she responds and I breathe a whole lot easier. "The Babushka doll… did you look around her house? That was the only thing that wasn't food or clothing. Why a Russian Babushka doll?"

"Someone gave it to her," Yuri responds as I am not going to take another chance of saying the wrong thing.

"Who and why?" Angelica muses aloud.

"The Russian who got her the job at the camp," I think is a safe guess.

"Likely… but why her? There has to be more to this than she needed money for a baby to have surgery or whatever…"

"Do you think her whole story is bogus?" Yuri asks her in a familiar way.

"I believe a Russian was somehow involved… But what Russian? Mob? Oligarchs? The FSB? Or is it some freelancer… used to work for the FSB, but saw what Prigozhin did with the Wagner Group and is trying to make his fortune through ransoms?"

"I don't buy the ransom part…" Yuri shakes his head. "If all they wanted was money… they would have contacted you a long time ago."

"You said that before…" Angelica resonates with the comment. "Which means they know who they have and are after bigger game."

"Like what?" I ask again seeing it as a safe question to ask.

"Pull the Navy out of the Persian Gulf? Move CentCom out of Qatar? Stop supplying Ukraine with advanced weapons? Could be a million things they think they can achieve." Angelica muses.

"The Russians offer to use their influence with the Ethiopian rabble to get the Americans' early release, since the rabble really have no idea who they have?" Yuri hypothesizes now.

"They obviously know we have a smoking gun in Mama Bekele," I point out. "And the Ethiopians are not going to be too happy if we can link the death of Captain Desta to them as well."

"That's your department, Agent." Angelica reminds me she is not even here.

"If I can link the death of Captain Desta…" I correct myself again. Man. I have to be so careful what I say around her.

"Better…" Yuri responds for her, as he is telling me he will not be able to help in a local Ethiopian investigation either. I really am on my own now.

"But you can help me find the shooters, just not liaison with the locals about how you did it," I push him now as I know I will need help to get that part of the final case to be made.

"Officially… I am just an observer," Yuri is telling me what has to be in the report but that does not need to be what he actually does.

The surgeon comes out of the surgical suite and approaches us in the waiting room. He is wearing scrubs and keeps his face mask on as he greets us. Average height, but much like Mama Bekele, he is a very thin man. Does not have the stretched skin around his mouth, but he could easily gain some weight and not be considered anything but slender. "You are the people who brought me Mama Bekele?"

"We are," I respond since the others are either not here or just observing. I guess I am the only one with an official role in this investigation.

"The surgery was successful and she will recover fully… but not for some time. As you have seen, she will need an extended rest period to properly heal and the wound was severe. Lucky for Mama Bekele, the bullet did not damage vital organs. But she will have a shortness of breath for quite some time."

"Looked to me as if the bullet passed through…" Yuri observes.

"It did. Not much there to stop a bullet. But the damage was extensive and most of the surgery was rebuilding tissue. That is what must heal. In the meantime, she must not do too much. If she tears the new tissue, it will take much longer to heal." The doctor summarizes for us.

"Not much cooking in her near future is what I hear you saying," Angelica summarizes. "But might we talk with her? Try to understand why someone would kill Captain Desta and try to kill her?"

"She is coming out of significant anesthesia… not sure how lucid she will be at least until tomorrow." The doctor suggests.

"If we are willing to take what she says with a grain of salt…" I offer to try to get his agreement.

“Not too long. She is in recovery now. Probably will not be awake for ten to fifteen minutes”

“Thank you doctor… for saving her life and all you are doing for your patients,” I try to ensure his continuing cooperation. If Mama Bekele is as badly wounded as he suggests it may take a while before we can get accurate information from her. Especially without Captain Desta asking the questions.

I nod toward the recovery area and both follow me.

The recovery room nurse is very short, but she strikes me as being very strong, not only physically but personality-wise. She has very short hair and big hoop earrings to compliment her white nurse uniform. “The doctor said we can talk with Mama Bekele when she awakens,” I attempt to be casual about the request, as if it were all approved, which the doctor will confirm if asked.

The nurse frowns, “You are not family.”

“We brought her into the hospital… she was shot.”

“You are the Americans who are looking for the missing Americans,” the nurse guesses.

“There are missing Americans?” I try to bluff.

“In Kenya. I hear from my sister in Nairobi. She works for police there. Investigator. You think they are in Ethiopia now?” the nurse wants to tell her sister to stop looking in Kenya.

“I’m sorry I can’t say anything at this point,” I respond so she will not get mad and not cooperate with us in talking with Mama Bekele.

The nurse is not happy she has nothing to tell her sister other than Americans looking for the missing couple in Ethiopia. “Ten minutes. I talk with doctor before he go see you.”

We approach Mama Bekele’s bed. She is keeping her eyes shut so she will not need to talk to us. I tickle her foot and she starts… wide eyed. Looks at us. "Captain?" she must remember him being shot before her.

I shake my head, "Doctor says you are going to be all right. But we have a few more questions now."

Mama Bekele does not respond, just looks at us.

"Who gave you the Babushka doll?" Angelica asks.

Mama Bekele thinks about what to say, finally says, "Netsanet, my brother."

"Why?" Angelica pushes the old woman.

"Eskander give him. Present Russian. Say I deserve."

"Who is Eskander?" Angelica is not going to back away.

"Captain… ship. Netsanet work on ship Eskander."

"Where would we find Netsanet and Eskander?"

"Berbera, keep ship."

"Somalia," Angelina notes, "What's the name of the ship?"

Mama Bekele shakes her head. Either she does not know or is unwilling to share.

"Thank you, Mama. Rest up so you can start cooking again." Angelica touches the old woman's hand. "We may come back to talk some more if necessary."

We walk out of the recovery area and I ask, "What is important about Berbera?"

"It's where the pirates sail out of, the ones that hijack container ships," Angelica responds.

CHAPTER THIRTY-NINE:

YURI TERESHKOVA

The small conference room at the US Embassy was really designed to be more of an interview room than conference room. Plenty of space for two, but we bring in a chair from a vacant office to have a three-way conversation. I am mulling the information Mama Bekele has given us as I close the door and take a seat. "Pirates?" I ask.

"Two names and a city," Angelica counters. "Can't be more than a thousand Eskanders who are captains of ships in that city."

"You're supposed to be the optimist," I remind her, since she always was when we were working together. Always optimistic that we would fulfill our missions without any issues for us or our side as a result. That was never the case, but that was the frame of mind she always went in with. She was always in charge, even when she was not. She had every mission rehearsed in her head and there was no deviating from the plan… until everything went to shit in a wheelbarrow. I have to think about that. Did every mission we were on go to shit? No. There was the rescue. That was textbook from beginning to end. But was that the only time? I am going to have to think about that for a while. Seems to me we were fighting our way out of nearly every situation we found ourselves in. Good practice for a future Secretary of Defense, who is not going to waste a single opportunity to kick somebody's butt. As far as I am concerned? Got more gray hair than she does, but someone told me she has a better hair stylist than I do.

"I am the optimist in this crowd, but that isn't saying much," she tosses off in my direction. A direct challenge to my recollection of her always charging in, even when not everything was known. Yes, I was the one who was always trying to pull her back. But she never listened to me. Probably why we never made it past that first encounter in a hotel room in… where was it? Belarus? And why the hell were we in Belarus? Too long ago and too many missions in between.

"I seem to remember…" I toss out there, never expecting to complete the sentence, but knowing Angelica will remember at least five times before she responds and she will not know which time I was referring to.

"Past life… not relevant to what we have before us," she dismisses rather than dealing with the fact she is not who she tries to convince everyone she is.

"You tell me… what do we have before us?" I throw right back as I always did. She should not expect anything different.

"A shit show… this is god-damn Somalia we are talking about. You remember the last time we were here? Trying to extract Black Hawk pilots and crew from an impossible situation. No one in control… everything just a free for all. No way we could do anything other than kill anything that moved because the alternative was, we weren't getting out alive. Never been in anything like that since." Angelica has slightly different memories… well… I guess she is entitled, given who she became and who I am now.

"Never should have been there in the first place… it was your predecessors and their genius analysts who told them there was no worries about the warlords who had moved in and pushed aside those we knew."

Angelica engages me with her bright blue eyes… those same eyes that always just froze me. Like she knew more than I ever would. "Happy to relive the past when the present isn't such a problem…"

"Not going to happen, but I've come to expect less of you over the years…" I shoot back knowing that will make her pull back. It always did.

Angelica's expression changes…memories must be flooding her mind, giving her a whole set of interpretations she can have in response to me. But then I see that old look. The one of I am done with all this bullshit. I have a mission to run and it is time to get on with it. I decide it is time to back off. We have had enough friction now to rub off the scars of so many years living different lives than the one we shared… all those years ago.

"What is the one question we need an answer to… like now?" Angelica asks, although I clearly know she already has an answer to it.

"Whether my compatriots are running this whole mission…" I toss out knowing that is what she is thinking and already having a pretty good idea of where she is going with it.

Angelica looks at Agent Plainsman… "What do you think?" She is just trying to get him bought in, regardless of how he answers it.

"Adds a different dimension… if it is not just a local snatch that exceeded anyone's expectations." Agent Plainsman is very cautious with Angelica. It is almost comical to watch him, but maybe that is because I know her as well as I do, and her title does not scare me the way it does him.

"It's not…" I assure him.

"Do you think it is your countrymen?" Agent Plainsman pushes me now, apparently seeing where Angelica is going.

"Only one way to find out… ask them," I respond and watch his expression of wondering if I am crazy.

"Good idea," Angelica saves me from myself.

Without saying another word, I rise and leave the Embassy, going down the street to the Russian counterpart. Used to know everyone here by their first name and family history. But that was yesterday. Before I switched sides. Now I am a pariah, although they still talk with me, hoping I still have some love for the mother country.

I approach the guard at the gate and show him my CIA credentials. The guard looks at my name, looks at me, clearly confused. A Russian name with CIA credentials. What is wrong with this picture.

"Asylum?" is the only word he can come up with.

I ask him in Russian for the FSB station chief. He looks at his directory and responds, "You evidently wish to speak with Comrade Dostoevsky."

"Is that his real name?" I have to have a little fun with this guy.

The guard does not answer my question, but rings a number and I find twelve… I count them, twelve armed guards coming out of the building.

"Hold on… you misunderstand me… I am not coming in. I am asking him to come out and have lunch with me… down the street. He can choose the place. Just a friendly conversation."

The guard rings a different number, repeats my request, listens, repeats my name and that I work for the US CIA. He nods in response to the instructions he has been given. Meanwhile, the twelve armed guards have lined up behind the guard shack looking as if they are about to carry my funeral pyre to the fire.

It does not take long before a familiar face comes out of the front door behind the guard as he pulls on a light jacket like the locals wear. He glances at the twelve armed guards, I see the flicker of a smile appear and is gone in an instant. He finally looks up and engages my eyes. Then I see another smile appear. This one is filled with irony, as if he has been waiting twenty-seven years for this day. Unfortunately for me… he has. He nods to the gate, comes through as soon as it is open wide enough and approaches me, now dead-pan, "Yuri Andropovich,"

"Boris Badenough," I joke since we all called him that after we saw the American Rocky and Bullwinkle cartoon show that featured a caricature of a Russian spy by the name of Boris Badenov.

"You knew I was here," Boris begins as we walk towards the café of his choice.

"Yes," I confirm, "Which is why I knew you would come out and play." Boris and I were recruits together and we were both stationed here at the same time… a very long time ago. He never left. A sign of his lack of connections back in Moscow.

"I wondered if they might send you to find the missing Americans…"

"My fame precedes me…"

"You are the only American agent who was a Russian agent here. A long time ago… but still…" Boris knows exactly how this conversation is going to go, and that is a big help to me.

"People are saying you sponsored the snatch…" I lay it out without attribution. No need to.

"Russia is always responsible for everything… even when we are not," a weak attempt to raise doubt without intending to really do so.

"Who has them?" I ask directly, knowing that even if he does know… which is likely, he will not tell me. Even for old times' sake.

"The Chinese, of course. They are the number one threat in this part of the world… or they are the number one benefactor… depends on who you talk to." Boris is having fun with this discussion. Must be really boring right now. It was boring when I was here with him.

Now that I know what I came to find out… "I understand they have excellent Polish vodka at this place around the corner," I tease Boris.

"Special Military Operation vodka… that's the only kind we true Russians drink these days…"

CHAPTER FORTY:

BEAU THOMPSON

"Boss… think we might have something," Joe Alvarez, short and pugnacious, always wearing a gray t-shirt, probably so I cannot tell how dirty it is, pokes his head into my office. Joe is my imagery analyst. He can pick more out of any three pixels than anybody I have ever met.

"What is it?" I instantly shoot back.

"Best you come look for yourself… you know how it is when you're looking for something…" Joe shakes his head, which tells me he knows exactly what he has seen, but he is not going to make it easy for me. Joe wants me to confirm what he thinks he is seeing.

As we walk down the hall to his work space in the analysis bullpen, I ask him, "When were you last home?"

"After Charles disappeared… well… if you're here, I'm here." Joe is like that. Does not say much… just gets to work. "When were you last home?"

"You'd have to ask Lila…" is my weak defense, since at this point, I have no idea when it was.

"Why the fuck did you ever let them go to Africa?" Joe is also plain spoken and direct.

"Trying to convince Charles of anything, once he has his mind made up… well, it just doesn't happen. He's a doc now. Got all the way through that gauntlet and he is nearing the end of his residency. Why would he need to listen to his father or mother, for that matter. He's his own man. And in love. And that makes it all the worse, when it comes to judgment."

"Doesn't have to be like that..." Joe differs with my take on the situation.

"You're probably right... it doesn't... but it is. Charles is the anti-Beau. Whatever I was or am, he was or is the opposite. I dropped out of engineering school because it was boring to me and I wanted to go actually build something. Charles has been in school so long..."

"I hear ya," Joe glances at me, apparently judging how I am taking this discussion. Am I done now or a I still willing to talk about things. "But sometimes... you need to share your wisdom."

"Wisdom?" I was not expecting him to think I have any since I am constantly pushing the envelope beyond what anyone could reasonably expect to accomplish. "I am certain," I laugh. "That if you asked Charles to pick one word to describe me, that would not be the one he would come up with."

Joe glances at me again, this time puzzling, "What word would he use?"

"Driven," I respond without even thinking. "Charles thought I pushed too hard... never gave him time to be a kid. Do you know what I'm saying?"

"Not the word I would have expected..." Joe bursts my thought bubble.

"Really?" is the only response I can muster.

"Charles is as driven as you are... just around a different passion." Joe is pointing out what should be obvious to me. "He is a balance of the two of you... wanting to push the envelope... which is you, but wanting to do it in medicine... which is Lila. He could never compete with you directly... never felt confident that he could live up to your expectations if he'd have been an engineer. But this way he gets to build on the best of each of you while being his own person. Why is it I clearly see that but you seem to have missed it?"

"Do you think I am not accepting of him?" I wonder aloud what I hear him saying.

"Not at all… if anything, you seem exceedingly proud… probably because you know you would never have had the patience to stay in school all those years… to wait to be what you always knew you were going to be." Joe continues to build his case that I could have had more influence over Charles decision than I seem to have made an effort to.

"But you blame me for what happened… not trying harder…" I realize what he is saying.

"No… you are not to blame… most likely even if you had been more direct with him, he would have gone anyway. At least that is how I read the situation." Joe slows as we approach his monitor.

"You're just offering advice… that I need to be more involved with Charles and not just let him go his own way." I summarize what I think he is saying to me.

"I hope the take away from all this is you have no idea how much time you are going to have with him. You assume there is no urgency to do anything… hell, he's just starting out." Joe begins to look at his monitor as he finishes his thought. "But that's not true. The time we have is not determined by us or them… and if you don't make the time, it escapes…"

"Escapes?" I am not sure what he wants me to realize.

"Meaning that once it is gone, it is not coming back. There is no do over when it comes to time. You get one shot and only one."

"What are you trying to show me?" I change the subject now that we are at his system.

Joe throws the image up on the large wall monitor and I notice the other analysts all swivel in their chairs to see the large image. "Note the time stamp."

I look at the read-out in the lower left corner. '14:37 Local Time'.

“What day was this?”

“Today… about two hours ago,” Joe responds loud enough that everyone in the bullpen can hear him.

“Zoom in on that van…” I instruct him, as I follow the image of a van that stopped as the driver spoke with someone who had been waiting for it along the road. “Where is this?” Maddening that we cannot hear the dialog between people in these systems.

Joe does as I request and we now have a clearer image of a white van, which suddenly lurches forward. “Ethiopia or Somalia, the border between them is somewhat vague.”

“What makes this van of interest?” I ask, but then watch as it careens and makes a sharp turn causing the van to roll over onto the passenger’s side. The van slides to a stop and dust rises. A moment later, the driver’s door opens up and someone climbs out. Then, another person climbs out, but needs help from the first person. Holds his arm as if it is broken or something. Both stand together, look about before they run away. I try to follow them, but quickly lose them in a maze of nearby buildings.

“This is what I wanted you to see,” Joe calls my attention back to the van.

As I watch another person gingerly climbs out of that same driver’s side door, as if looking around, apparently trying to understand where the other two had gone. This person climbs up onto the side of the van and helps another person out. Once they are both on top of the van, the first person climbs down and helps the other to do the same. At that moment the image is lost.

“You think…” I begin to ask Joe who does not wait for me to finish but simply nods. “When does the next asset get us eyes on the situation?” I know we do not have continuous view of this part of the world.

“About an hour from now…” Joe responds. “But at that point we will have no idea where they may have gone or whether the other people come back for them."

I dial Angelica, not knowing if she will answer.

"Beau… this isn't a good time…" she seems completely distracted.

"I have coordinates where they may have been two hours ago…" I drop on her to see if she has anything more recent.

"Where?" tells me she does not.

"Crossing from Ethiopia into Somalia…" I try on her, expecting her to say it cannot possibly be them. The images we saw were suggestive, but we could have easily gotten it all wrong.

"North or south in Somalia?" she seems to know something I do not.

"North nearest city is Hargeisa on the Somalia side," I look at a map Joe has inserted into the image to locate this imagery.

"They're heading for Berbera… on the coast," Angelica informs me, apparently, she has more information than I thought.

"Hold on… They may have been heading for Berbera… but something happened. Which is why we may have caught a break." I inform her.

"Are they all right?" I hear the fear in Angelica's voice.

"If what we have here is them… and I am not entirely sure… they were two hours ago. The van they were in rolled over. Four people climbed out, but that was when we lost the imagery."

"Shit… I knew I should have authorized another…" she stops herself before saying more. "What are the coordinates?"

"Coming by text… but there is one more thing you need to know… they may have escaped their captors in this roll over… or they may be back on the road to somewhere… or they may be dead."

CHAPTER FORTY-ONE:
AGENT DAKOTA THOMPSON

As we descend from the air in the Ethiopian State Security Bell Ranger helicopter, we see the van… or what is left of it, surrounded by a crowd that is making off with parts. "Guess any clues have already walked away," Yuri Tereshkova remarks. I see the tension on the face of Angelica Myers as we come in for a landing. It has taken us about two hours to make the flight after about an hour from her first request to find a way to get here. Too long. I know she is thinking that. And given the state of the carcass of the van… she is likely right.

Once we touch down, she is the first out, even though from a security point of view she should not be. No way that either Yuri or I was going to be able to stop her. She is one determined mother… Angelica wades into the crowd, looking at everything. However, at this point all the tires are gone, the seats are nowhere to be found and four men are in the process of removing the engine block. As I walk around the vehicle, I find one back door gone and the other in the process of removal.

Yuri talks with one of the men who is removing the engine block. I did not know he spoke the local language, whatever that is. But he is having an animated discussion, although the local seems to barely be paying attention since there is evidently a profitable opportunity at hand.

The ground is sandy, dusty. Probably were footprints at one point, but with all the people clustered around, most in bare feet, it is hard to make any sense of what I am seeing. Based on the description Angelica gave me of the imagery, I look around by the driver's door and find four sets of prints that apparently were the result of jumping down. Two had shoes and two were bare foot. One was heavier than the other… that could have been Charles. This would mean that they are still dressed in bedclothes, which is likely how they were dressed when captured, in the middle of the night.

“You find something?” Yuri must have noticed what I was doing.

“Not sure… but if I’m right they are still in their bedclothes.”

“Would certainly make it easier to spot them in a crowd of Somalis, although their western appearance might also contribute to that.” Yuri always has an understated response to any situation, at least that seems to be what I have observed about him.

“What did they tell you?” I ask Yuri.

“Two guys are hiding out not so far from here…”

“Not Dr. and Mrs. Thompson…” I note.

“Ethiopian… but the guy I was talking with… he’s seen them come through here a lot. Thinks they are probably working with the pirates, but that is just a guess on his part. Something about their shoes.”

“Pirates wear shoes?” I am surprised.

“Boat shoes… you know… grippier than shoes you or I would buy to help them walking around on the deck of small boats.”

“I thought the pirates went after cargo ships…” I am only half listening now, thinking I have seen where the deep tracks have gone.

“They do… but the intercept boats are small and fast to be able to catch up with the big ships.” Yuri explains to me, but I am now following the trail of the prints I have found. Hard to do with all the others than have walked across this area after them.

“Why would pirates want to kidnap a couple from a Kenyan tourist safari camp?” I toss out now that I have a direction on the footprints and continue following them, even though Yuri is trailing behind, apparently not sure if he wants to continue this discussion.

"Kind of what they do… but also different in a fundamental way," Yuri responds as if he is still thinking this through, but in a kind of neutral voice. No emotion in it, not like his ego is on the line in this discussion.

"How so?"

"You commandeer a boat… it's all impersonal. Taking money from an insurance company… only indirectly. Big bucks… millions of dollars. Now that will feed a Somali family for a lifetime. But kidnapping people. Whole different thing. It's personal. You are dealing with people. It is much more likely that you will need to kill someone and that is a very significant line to cross."

"Are you saying they may be dead?" I glance up, get an impression, that he is seriously considering all the possibilities from this event, and right back to the tracks so I do not lose them. I am following what I think are those for Charles. He weighs more than the average Somali, whereas Annie is much closer to their stature. Her prints are more likely to be indistinguishable from all those from the locals who have come to feed on the carcass of the van.

"Are you seeing any indication they may have been killed here?" Yuri asks me point blank.

"No," I confirm, "Although that doesn't mean anything. We don't know what happened, why the van flipped, why they were left behind… if that is what happened. Why the guards are still nearby and whether Dr. and Mrs. Thompson are in their custody or not."

"Then what are you seeing?" Yuri sounds frustrated with my non-answers. At least as far as he is concerned.

"An unplanned event…" I begin. "You said… or maybe it was… what am I supposed to call her?" I nod toward the secretary but do not wait for a response. "That the van stopped talked to someone here. But as the driver talked… the van sped away only to flip over here. Do we know where that person made contact with the van? I need to see if I can track that person down."

“That your claim to fame? Being a tracker?” Yuri asks annoyingly.

“Never made any claims to fame,” I respond angry that Yuri thinks I must have one.

“Then why you? On this investigation? There have to be a hundred agents who could have taken this assignment.” Yuri is expressing a lack of confidence in me. Seen this a hundred times before. Just got to ignore it. Move on. Do my job.

“I must be sleeping with the Director’s wife…” I shoot back to hopefully cause him to change the subject.

“How is she?” Yuri does not miss a beat.

“I’m not someone who kisses and tells. Now, if you would excuse me… I need to see if I can follow a trail here.”

Yuri motions for me to proceed and backs away. I see him approach Angelica out of the corner of my eye, but I focus on the footprints I have been following. They lead away from the van. Two sets. One deeper than the other, but they are walking close together. More like a couple than two people who barely know each other. The stride is short. Like they are in a hurry to get away from the van, but also like they have not been doing much walking recently. That tracks. Bare feet. Stepping cautiously because it hurts to step on anything uneven or sharp.

Now that I am out of the huddle of people stripping the van, it is easier to spot the footprints, easier to be sure. I am picking up my pace as I go and soon find I am quite a way away from the van, Angelica and Yuri. I do not know what Yuri’s game is. Why is he here? Why is he so dismissive of me? Just because I am Native American? Just because I was not a traitor who changed spying for one country to spying for another? He is the one who should not be trusted, and yet I am the one who is not. Trusted or respected for that matter.

Footsteps approach me from behind. Lighter than Yuri’s which leads me to expect Angelica. I am proven correct. Without even looking up I address her as I take pictures, “Yes, I think I may have found their tracks.”

“How can you be sure?” Angelica asks, unsure whether to believe me.

“Experience…” is the only explanation I will give her.

“Where are they going?” Angelica looks around, unsure.

“My guess is away from the van…”

Angelica looks at me, considering my response. “Not going to some place?”

“Do you have any idea where you are?” I stop long enough to confront this line of questioning.

“The border…” she responds unsure of what I am asking.

“And you know that because…” I frame it for her. “You were told that was where you were going. But Dr. and Mrs. Thompson have no idea where they are. What country. What city may be in any direction. They do not speak the language and likely will not be able to ask for help. They are truly on their own, trying to elude the people who took them hostage. They have no idea where to go, just as you do not. Believe me… they are simply trying to get away from the van and the people who took them.”

“If you are right, how do we find them?”

I stop and look up at her, “A vehicle stopped here and they got on board… their tracks stop.”

She looks frightened now, “Was it their captors or someone else?”

CHAPTER FORTY-TWO:

ANNIE THOMPSON

Our wrists are zip-tied in front of us as we sit on seats in this almost identical white van. What kind is it? Nissan, I think is what I saw on the grille as it approached us on the road. I still do not understand how they found us so quickly. I also do not understand why they are letting us sit on seats here with hoods off and no gags. What is different here? Are we someplace else that they feel safe? That we can be seen and nothing will happen to them? Does that mean we are in a country now that is not friendly with the US? I think that could be said for most of the countries in the Horn of Africa and probably through the rest of Africa and the Middle East for that matter.

I glance over my shoulder. We are in the middle row of seats. The driver and the English speaker are in the front and two others are behind us with weapons pointed at us. Neither has a broken arm. Must be two new guards. The rifles may be below the window level, but I can see them as I glance back.

Charles has his head down, apparently blaming himself for letting us get caught again. What was he going to do? Neither of us had any idea how to escape from wherever it is we are. "Not your fault," I whisper, leaning closer.

"I let you down… again," is his helpless response.

"You have not let anyone down. There was nothing you could have done differently…" I try to get him to be more positive about the situation, although I am having trouble being positive. We had one opportunity and now we will likely not get another. It is up to Mom to do something… I have no idea what. But if she does not, I have to assume this will not end well.

"I'm supposed to stand up for you… keep you safe, and all I have done is let them keep us tied up and driven all over the world, or so it seems to me," Charles has to get out of this blame funk.

"They haven't hurt either of us… so be happy about that." I try to get him to look at the more positive side of the situation.

"If we don't get to bite into a hamburger soon… there may not be anything left of us." Charles is raising an issue I have been wondering about.

"How long can we go on like this?" I ask a little louder, expecting at least the guy who speaks some English in the front seat will overhear.

"Water is more important than food. We are well below replacement levels." Charles observes.

"You think we have parasites because of what we have been drinking?" If I can just keep Charles fixated on the things he knows, maybe that will help him get out of his funk.

"Is your stomach upset?" he responds as if his is and he is just checking to see if I am experiencing the same thing he is.

I nod rather than answer. I do not want the men in the front seat to get too much information about the state of our health.

"Then the answer is likely, yes," Charles looks at me as if he is trying to figure out what he can do about the situation… medically. And there really is not much that he can do.

"Is there anything we can take, when we finally get back to a medical facility?" I try to keep the conversation going.

"I am not anticipating any long-term effects…" Charles sounds about as diagnostic as I could expect him to sound, given the circumstances.

We fall into silence again as I contemplate the long-term effects of this experience. And since I do not know how it will end, the first long term effect is that we die. That will be the longest-term effect most certainly. The second long-term effect might be a psychological one. Will I ever feel safe again? And the third, most certainly could be a heath effect. Will I have some recurring ailment? Something like jungle fever, only from the African veldt. Something no one has ever seen before? A primitive bug that lives within me, with no known means of killing it off? Charles might have a better feel for that than I do, but still… Why is it I know this experience will change both of us… and clearly not for the better.

I decide to take a different tact with Charles, "What's the first thing you're going to do when we get home?"

"That is making a rather large assumption…" Charles is having trouble coming along on this detour with me.

"Not an assumption… an expectation." I correct him.

Charles glances at me, "You go first."

I did not know how much he is struggling with this whole situation, but the fact he cannot transport himself to an alternative time and place is worrying. "Hmmm. Probably a long leisurely bath. You know I usually don't like to sit in dirty water, but just the luxury of warm water lapping at my chin as I lay back and listen to soothing music…"

"Could I join you in your hot tub?" Charles asks if this is just a fantasy for one.

"Hot tub?" I ask realizing he changed the parameters of my expectations.

"Well… we seemed to enjoy that hot tub in Mexico City…"

He is remembering a hot tub on the patio of our hotel room where we drank Champaign sans clothing before going out for dinner and drinks with a couple of his Med School classmates and their dates. A reunion of sorts for them. But a particularly sensual time for us.

"What happened to Darcy Ibrahim?" suddenly pops into my mind.

"Darcy?" I see Charles shift gears. Different time and place. Just what I was hoping to get him to do, since he seems to be struggling with the current reality. "She applied for a fellowship. Two more years of advanced study. She wants to postpone the inevitable as long as she can."

"Inevitable?" I try to draw him out more.

"Riding without the training wheels…" is how Charles decides to describe it. Interesting choice of simile.

"Is it scary for you to think about seeing patients, performing surgeries and all that without the Medical school looking over your shoulder?" I wonder.

"Maybe a little…" he admits although I can tell he really does not want to.

"What are you afraid of?" I keep him on this path of a professional rather than a personal fear.

"That I either won't know enough… or I'll make a mistake because I think I know how to do something I really don't." Charles looks at me more closely now, apparently wondering why we are talking about this now.

"But how do people learn how to do something that has never been done before?" I push him to think harder about this issue.

"What do you mean?"

"If no one has ever done a particular procedure before…, how do they decide to do it?"

Charles has to think about my question, but then responds, "When I do something I have not done before, I study… read anything on the subject I can find… talk to docs who have done the procedure and ask what is not intuitive about it. What do I have to watch out for? What is the most important thing to focus on. What do I have to be sure I do? Things like that."

"And do you practice it? Simulate it?" I ask.

"If I can."

"But a day comes when you actually must do it. How do you get prepared for what might happen versus what you expect to happen?"

"It is a lot like an airplane pilot. You rehearse and practice the procedures for the adverse situations so when they do happen, you just keep going because you automatically know what you must do to be successful in handling the situation."

"But if it is something no one has ever done, how do you get to that point?"

"Like the first heart transplant and all the organ transplants that have come after it?" Charles seems to be getting into the discussion now. Good. He is coming out of his guilt feelings.

"No talking," the English speaker in the front passenger seat calls back to us.

"Why?" I respond, without thinking. "What difference does it make?"

"No talking," he repeats.

"We didn't do anything to you, so why are you doing this to us?"

The English speaker responds, "Maybe you did not… but your Navy capture my countrymen. Send to jail. All we want is feed our families… but you Americans… you do not care about what happens in Somalia. What happens to people who starve or sick. Only what happens to big ships…"

"Big ships? What are you talking about?"

CHAPTER FORTY-THREE:

YURI TERESHKOVA

We have been all over the area where the footprints disappear, next to tire tracks which we have already identified as fitting a standard van. I have talked to as many of the plunderers as possible, but this pick up was just far enough away that no one recalls seeing anything. Vans in the area. Nothing unusual about that. People walking… nothing unusual about that either. I do not buy that no one saw anything. I think if they were talking with each other, they might be more forthright. But to tell a foreigner… that is just not going to happen. Not even one who speaks their language and lived here for way too long. But also, a long time ago.

"What do you think, Yuri?" Angelica approaches me with that same look. The one that tells me she expects me to know the answer that will inform our next actions. In this case, I wish I did, for her sake.

"Have the drones picked up anything?" I ask her.

"They just arrived," she responds as her way of saying no, not yet anyway.

"We need to know which way the van went, but once they turned onto the paved road, there was no way of knowing where they went. And they have too long a head start," I summarize.

"Hey…" Angelica is about to bring me up short. "They had a week head start and we have that down to a few hours… we just have to keep narrowing the window."

"Wasn't thinking about it that way…" I admit, "But positive thinking has never worked out real well for me, as you well know."

"We've been over that a hundred times…" Angelica apparently thinks I want to rehash the last assignment we did together.

"I'm not still angry you left me to die rather than staying with me. That happened a long time ago. You got where you wanted to go, and I'm still doing what I signed up for. My penance for not being a true believer." I try to push that aside as quickly as possible, although I know it is hanging over every encounter we have.

"Yuri…"

"No… we need to get this out of the way right now if we are going to find your daughter." I see a wince from Angelica as if she would rather not deal with our joint past when she is solely focused on finding her daughter. She evidently thinks every second needs to be focused on the task at hand.

"Just say it then." Angelica is done with this conversation.

"I still love you…" just comes out without any of the usual filters slowing the words as they come out of my mouth. Shit.

Angelica was not expecting this as she is speechless.

"Wrong… forget I said that. I had my chance with you before Howard and I blew it. Not my place to even go there." I look away from her as I do not want to see the look on her face.

"I don't know what to say to that… all these years I assumed you just hated me for giving up on you when…" She sounds more tentative than I think I have ever heard her.

"Forget it. That's all done. Gone forever. We need to… I need to get my head out of my ass and figure out where Annie is. So, you can get back to your life and I can get back to mine."

"Is that what you want?" Angelica seems to be sleepwalking through this discussion now. "To get back to your life?"

"Not the time or place for that discussion," I will not go there.

"Annie…"

"Do you really think…" she starts but again I cut her off.

"No, I do not. All I want is to help find Annie and get on to the next assignment. Without you in the middle of it." I try to sound as earnest as possible, but I am not sure she is buying it.

"Then how do we decide which way we need to go to find her?" Angelica gives me an escape from my own indiscretion talking about something I never should have.

"What does our FBI Agent have to say?"

Angelica catches his attention and waves for him to join us. When he arrives, she simply asks, "Thoughts?"

Agent Plainsman looks at me as if he is not sure how to answer the question. "They drove out of this area and headed towards Hargeisa."

"You're sure?" I have to ask since I am not confident in this guy.

"I am." He stares at me. "But what I am not confident about is whether they continued in that direction. These people have eluded us for a lot longer than the people we are used to dealing with. That means they are continuing to do unexpected things."

"If the original kidnappers picked them up," I remind him that has not been established.

"An assumption we are making as it is the worst situation," Agent Plainsman responds and looks at Angelica. "If a friendly picked them up, we should be getting a call from someone soon. And I would think that with the number of hours since the van overturned, someone should have contacted someone who would have advised us."

"You're ruling out a friendly pickup," Angelica seeks confirmation.

"I am because I have to. I must find a way of getting them back. If

I sit around and assume a good Samaritan is going to do my work for me… then if that is not the case, I will be the one explaining to you why we did not do everything possible to get them back." He looks straight at me now as if he expects I am telling Angelica that I am the reason we have not found her daughter yet.

"Then what would you have us do?" I challenge that notion without using so many words.

"Confirm my estimations." Agent Plainsman responds simply. "How long ago were they picked up, how many miles per hour, where on the major highways should we expect to find a standard van that would be carrying them?"

"Towards Berbera…" Angelica responds.

"What do you know that I don't?" Agent Plainsman asks with a tinge of anger.

"An Ethiopian ship's captain named Eskander was involved in taking them from the camp. He sails out of Berbera and I am assuming… although Yuri may have a different perspective on this… that he is taking them to where he feels safest. Where his crew and ship are located."

"Why would an Ethiopian ship's captain kidnap your daughter and her husband?" Agent Plainsman is not happy we have not given him this information before now.

"All we do know for sure is that he is a pirate, who has been boarding cargo ships and holding them for ransom. Or at least he was until our Navy started providing escort." Angelica informs him.

"Are you saying this might be personal?" Agent Plainsman responds.

"I cannot rule it out," Angelica side steps his question.

"Fifty miles an hour for five hours would put them at 250 miles. They are likely already in Berbera if that is the case, "I inform them I have been doing the requested calculations in my head.

"And if they did not go there, where would they have gone?" Agent Plainsman asks. "I cannot go with just one solution set here. I have to be working all the possibilities."

"What if they stopped in Hargeisa?" Angelica asks. "Met up with others since something happened here, they likely were not expecting."

"That would give us time to possibly interdict them before they disappear into the underworld in Berbera." I point out.

"If you knew about this captain, why didn't you share that?" Agent Plainsman remains unhappy with us. "We could have been watching the main roads going in that direction."

"They aren't taking the main roads…" I point out.

Angelica takes a call, "How many?"

I look at Agent Plainsman and shake my head to communicate I have no idea what she is talking about or to whom.

Angelica disconnects and looks at Agent Plainsman. "There are over two hundred white vans fitting the description we provided between here and Berbera, based on the drone surveillance we have started. None have rolled over to tip us off to anything." She is being sarcastic.

"Sounds to me like we need to set up a roadblock on the routes between Hargeisa and Berbera." I suggest.

"All of them?" Agent Plainsman is trying to understand exactly what we need to organize.

"How many are there?" Angelica inquires.

"Really one main road, but I'm concerned if they go off road to avoid detection." Agent Plainsman explains the dilemma.

CHAPTER FOURTY-FOUR:

LILA THOMPSON

Howard Myers comes to the door of his office in the Virginia Governor's mansion to greet me. It may be a long drive down here from the district, but I know I will get better answers from Howard than I will from Beau, even though he is my husband. I do not know if it is because it is Howard's daughter that is missing or because married to the Secretary of Defense, he is much more confident in the ability of the officials to do their job and bring the kids home. In any event, I just think I will get straight answers from him.

"Howard," I give him a kiss in the cheek. Not sure if that is the protocol for your kid's in-laws or not, but I have never been big on protocol as a doc. "Have you heard from Angelica?"

"About once an hour when she is within cell range," Howard lets me know that is not always the case without going into details I really probably do not want.

"And?"

Howard looks at his phone, apparently checking the time, "Last call was… a while ago…" I find it curious he gives me a specific interval and then immediately backs off it when he has to tell me when. "And at that point they were only about five or six hours behind them."

"What does that mean?" I have to know as I am confused.

Howard gestures for me to take a seat and as I do, he does as well. "When she called, they were investigating a van they believe the kids had been transported in. Indications are they had been in the van only five or six hours before Angelica and the team arrived."

"They are getting closer, then," I summarize my impression of what he is telling me.

"That was Angelica's impression. Much closer than we have been and Agent Plainsman believes they were the persons in the van and from the imagery collected they appeared to be moving under their own power."

"What does that mean?" I challenge the vague description even though it is a lot clearer than I could expect from Beau.

"Means they were walking without any apparent injuries." Howard summarizes.

"Apparent…" I challenge the one word that could change everything.

"All we know is what was seen by a satellite more than two hundred miles above the earth. Lots of things you can't see when the camera is that far away." Howard apologizes for his vagueness.

"Was it a good idea for Angelica to go over there?" I have to ask Howard.

He seems surprised by my question. "Good idea?"

"You know I'm in health care, and maybe things are different in all this spy and terrorist and international stuff. But in my experience, when an important person shows up…"

Howard smiles. "Like me?"

"Especially you… and Angelica."

"Her entourage is generally bigger than mine… but she left them all behind, which pissed them off unbelievably. Not even her security detail."

"Really?" I am surprised.

"She is not keeping anyone from doing their jobs being over

there, I can assure you." Howard tries to put my fears to rest.

"But… if she is calling you every hour and someone is briefing her every hour or more often… then they are spending a lot of time just reporting what they have done and what they intend to do rather than actually doing it. Do you see what I'm saying? Our people should be tracking their people down… out on the trail… following whatever vehicle they are in. Using Beau's drones to figure out which one they are in… all that stuff."

"I can assure you that is not what is happening over there," Howard responds to my fears. "The team on the ground is very small, but there are a whole host of people backing them up with technology, whether satellite imagery, drones or officers on the ground interviewing people and running down leads. It is all working very efficiently. Angelica is in the middle of it all… not as a VIP, but as one of the people actually walking the crime scenes, talking with people and crafting scenarios they need to investigate. She is hands on, not someone directing people from afar."

"I understand you and Angelica are working as hard as Beau to try to find them… I'm not trying to be at all negative. I wanted to come chat with you to make sure we are all working together as efficiently as possible to bring this whole thing to an end."

Howard looks at me like my father used to look at me when I would say something he realized was ill informed. And when I was in college, I was ill informed about a whole lot of things. Not because my teachers were trying to mislead me. But I was so deep in the sciences that every time something would happen in the world, I would ask questions that just had no bearing on the situation. Dad used to say that I would be a great spy, because no one would believe I knew so little about what was going on in the world. And likely here I am again. Wading into the deep water and trying to figure out if I can keep my head above water or whether I am about to sink to the bottom. "I'm sorry to take your time away from the very important matters you have to deal with in your job…"

"Lila… nothing is more important than getting our kids home…"

Howard gives me that politician smile I see in his ads on television.

Then something occurs to me, "You said Angelica left her security team behind?"

"She did," Howard confirms.

"Why would she do that when the kids were kidnapped? Isn't that incredibly dangerous?"

"She is with Agent Plainsman and a CIA Agent she used to work with. One of their top investigators." Howard informs me.

"Only two people when she's the Secretary of Defense?" I cannot believe they would let her do that given the circumstances.

"I am completely comfortable that she is safe and with professionals that will not let anything happen to her." Howard seems remarkably calm about it while I am a nervous wreck. Afraid I might lose my son, but at least Beau is not over there getting in harm's way. I could never survive the loss of both of them. And yet that is what Howard is faced with and it does not seem to bother him.

"She's only a bureaucrat…" I blurt out. "Not someone who is going to be able to respond to the kind of bad people who have taken Charles and Annie."

Howard smiles at me, which I find strange. "Do you know Angelica's background? How she got to be Secretary of Defense?"

"She pushed papers at CIA and got to know the President, before the President became the President. Not exactly someone who would inspire confidence dealing with terrorists. You need professionals for that kind of job. And no offense to Angelica… I have the greatest respect for her and what she has done to become the Secretary… but the two just don't go together in my mind."

Howard is smiling through my whole description of his wife. What is he possibly thinking? "Lila, that may be the impression people have of how other people get into the roles they end up in. Particularly in government, where the spoils go to the victors, and some people don't work their way up through merit. But I assure you that is not the route Angelica took to get where she is."

"I didn't mean to offend you Howard, or say anything about Angelica..."

"I know you didn't... just as you underestimated that FBI Agent, you are underestimating Angelica."

"I know she deserves to be in the job she has..."

"She does... worked damn hard to ensure she not only deserved it but was ready when asked by the President." Howard is trying to be gentle with me, but he is also being very direct. "The first thing you should probably know about Angelica that you apparently don't is, she was a field operative for the CIA almost her entire career. She only became Deputy Director for about a year before the President tapped her for Defense."

"Field operative? Like someone who did what?"

"Whatever was required as directed by the President or Director of the agency. She started out at the bottom, spent her first couple years in language schools. Did you know she is fluent in both Arabic and Chinese and can get along in Russian if pressed?"

I shake my head as I had no idea.

"She then spent the rest of her career in some of the worst places in the world, trying to enable US policy. Not an easy job with dictators and other not so nice people in charge. And in that role, she has killed people who would see our way of life changed forever. Not an enviable task, but she was good at it. So good she eventually led all the teams in the field, and all the analysts back home. Hard jobs."

CHAPTER FORTY-FIVE:

YURI TERESHKOVA

The helicopter that brought us out here is now sitting cross-wise on the road. The pilot is acting as an interpreter as we stop each vehicle and search it. So far, no one has challenged our right to do this, although I doubt the locals would support us if pressed by a constituent. We did not ask anyone. We do not have any Somali officials here, and I am very sure we are on their side of the border.

Agent Plainsman has taken on the task of searching the vehicles, opening the back door on each van we stop, but also searching trunks on the few cars. I am standing here, with an automatic rifle in my hands as the only weapon in sight. We are doing this on purpose, as we want everyone we stop to know we are serious. But at the same time, if each of us were displaying arms, it would likely raise more alarms. The agent and Angelica are wearing sidearms, but they are holstered, although visible. The pilot is unarmed, although in uniform.

"He says you are the only Americans he has ever seen here…" The pilot is interpreting what the driver of this white van says in answer to my question. The driver is bone thin and with shiny black skin. His very white teeth stand out although he is not smiling, looking at the rifle I am holding, apparently not sure if I will shoot him for no reason.

Agent Plainsman slams the back door shut and gives me a thumbs up, meaning there is nothing in the van that should be of concern to us. I look to Angelica, to make sure she is not picking up something the agent and I have not seen. She does that. Sees things I miss. Sees things everyone around her misses. I do not know how she does that. Some extra sensory perception or something. Or maybe she is just more perceptive than I am. She shakes her head, ever so slightly and looks back at the line of vehicles waiting to get through our roadblock.

"He can go," I respond to the interpreter and watch the van drive off the road to go around the helicopter. The interpreter watches as intently, apparently wanting to make sure the driver does not cause damage to his aircraft in the process.

I count the seven vans and trucks waiting, look up the road to see if more are coming, realizing there are three more I can see. The pilot asks the question we agreed upon before we started this roadblock of the next driver. I watch the driver shrug and he is clearly very nervous about the weapon I am carrying. The agent opens the back and climbs in. Must be he cannot see what is in there from the road.

"Ask him where he is going?" I suggest to the pilot.

"He is picking up used tires from a shop not so far from here." Is the interpreted response.

"Why used?" I wonder.

The pilot asks this question, and in a moment, I hear his interpreted response, "Trucking companies change tires after two-hundred thousand kilometers."

"Isn't that a lot?" I wonder as it just sounds like a big number.

Another interpreted response, "Many people cannot afford good tires. Make do. Many people want used tires from trucking companies."

Agent Plainsman comes out of the back, goes over to Angelica and asks her a question I cannot hear. Angelica shrugs and the agent nods to me.

"Okay, he can go." I instruct the pilot to tell the driver as I walk over to the FBI agent. "What did you find?"

"Two AK-47 rifles under a blanket. No ammunition clips, though. He might be selling them on the black market. If he were using them himself, I'm sure there would have been multiple clips."

"Not what we are looking for," I assume is what Angelica was thinking with her shrug. We are not going to get involved in anything other than extracting her daughter and Annie's husband. I wonder if there was a clear threat to the US that we were to uncover if she would maintain that position. Hard to tell with her. She wears too many hats.

The pilot is taking with the driver of the next vehicle. A small box truck. Must be hauling something for a real business other than these men who are driving their truck to do jobs for others or run a small trading business like the tire guy. The driver gets out of the cab to come around to the rear to open the door for Agent Plainsman, who walks over to join them. The door slides up and I notice the agent react to what he is seeing. He climbs up and into the cargo area.

Angelica is observing this whole thing, expressionlessly. When she gets in that mood, I know enough to stay away from her. Wait for her to come to me. I cannot recall a single conversation I had with her in a mood like that where I learned anything.

I decide to come around to the rear of the truck to see what has caused Agent Plainsman to climb in. As I come around the rear of the truck I instantly understand. The truck is full of barrels. The agent is knocking on each of them, apparently trying to elicit a response if someone is in one of them.

"What are they?" I ask the pilot to ask the driver.

He does not need to, apparently already having asked the question. "Fish."

"Why barrels?" I have to ask.

"Dried and salted," Agent Plainsman explains as he has clearly heard my question. "The only way to ship it in this kind of heat."

"You satisfied?" I ask in return.

"No one is kicking to get out of these," the agent responds. He knocks on three more barrels and comes to the rear before jumping down. "He can close it," is the instruction to the pilot.

I look over my shoulder at Angelica. This is not getting us anywhere. But she is calling the shots. I lock eyes with her and see her make a decision. She walks over to us and we close around her.

"What do you think? Is this a waste of time?" She goes to the heart of the matter.

"Word travel quickly, Somalia," the pilot responds.

"You think people in line are calling others so they don't have to get stopped?" Angelica looks for an explanation of how they might be avoiding us.

"Everyone have cell phone…" the pilot takes his out of his shirt pocket to show us. "Must have to do business. To arrange…"

"To buy and sell things," I fill in the blank.

"You keep checking," Angelica tells the pilot and FBI agent. "Take a walk with me, Yuri."

We walk back along the line of vehicles, looking in on the drivers, who all look much the same as the others. All rail thin. Just a strong indication that the diet of most Somalis is barely above starvation levels. What surprises me is the drivers seem to accept this intrusion as just another aspect of their daily lives. Nothing ever goes as anticipated, so there is no reason to get upset about something unexpected. It is just another day. Another trial to get through on the way to the evening meal. All of these vehicles are white vans. Different manufacturers, but almost all Japanese. Although I notice a few are types I have not seen before. I assume they are Chinese. Why Chinese? Because China is trying to establish a footprint here and the Chinese vehicles are even less expensive than the Japanese, although the Japanese have better reliability, from what I have been told.

Angelica stops me as we approach the last vehicle in line. "She's not here…"

"Should we stop searching them?" I respond surprised she is convinced.

“No, we want to keep the pressure on. Force them to make a mistake or finally contact us.” She removes her phone and dials a number. She listens and then talks to the person at the other end without even introducing herself, “Do you think you could send your drones up again? Check the other direction? Maybe they doubled back on us.”

She listens and then responds, “You’re looking at the map, what do you think?”

I watch her nod, “That makes sense… No. We aren’t finding what I hoped, but there aren’t many clues as to what they are doing or even why…yet.”

Another question from the person on the phone, and she responds, “That part still doesn’t make sense to me. The only thought that comes to mind is the kidnappers have a sponsor who encouraged them to do this, and when they did, realized there could be considerable blow-back.”

The quick response leads her to summarize, “That’s the problem… anything is still possible because we don’t know enough about what to eliminate. If you can get those drones up, that might help us understand if we are wasting time here. Thanks, Beau.” She clicks off and stares off in the direction of the approaching vehicles.

“What now?” is all I can think of to ask.

“Hargeisa is a lot bigger than Berbera and a lot easier to hide in. If their plan has gone to shit…”

“And that is why you still have not heard from them…” I surmise her reasoning.

CHAPTER FORTY-SIX:
AGENT DAKOTA PLAINSMAN

A call comes in on my cell phone. It is Beau Thompson.

"Agent Plainsman, I am running my drones back towards the border. Between you and me, I think this is a waste of time." He lets that sink in before continuing. "What's going on there that I got this request?"

"We are stopping all vehicles between Hargeisa and Berbera, hoping they stopped there long enough for us to get ahead of them." I respond.

"Hope is never a good strategy," Beau Thompson points out. "And now you are becoming convinced that your roadblock is not going to help you find them?"

"We have not been at this all that long…" I begin to explain.

"But long enough to know that word is already out and if you stay there, whoever has Charles and Annie will not drive into your checkpoint." Beau completes the thought with his own spin.

"What are you seeing with your drones?" I change the subject.

"Probably the same as what you're seeing," Beau sounds frustrated. "A bunch of traffic with no way of knowing if any of it is of interest. Lots of white vans. Any one of them could have the kids. But no way of telling."

"You want to know what you could be doing that might be of more importance?" I ask what I think is the obvious question.

“This is not a good use of my time or equipment.”

“Can your drones monitor civilian cellular communications? Text as well as voice?” I decide to see what he might be able to do that could be impactful.

“Yes, but I need to bring them back in and change out the payloads.” Beau seems to think my suggestion could be a good one.

“I’d suggest at least one keep the camera so you can get a close up look if we find something of interest by intercepting the signals,” I realize it will take some time for him to change over and we will not want to wait if we hit on something.

“I’m bringing them back into the barn. Will you pass along this change of plans? Don’t think I want to have that conversation right now.” Beau is telling me he is afraid of the Secretary.

“At the appropriate time,” I assure him. “But what else have your people found at the camp where they were kidnapped? Anything?”

“Nothing that tells us who or why. We have a clearer picture of what happened and how they got them into the apparent van they used to take them away. Most of the staff had gone into town to get provisions, which was contrary to what we had been told. Information was no new guests for three days. But in fact, guests arrived early the next morning, which was part of the reason no one noticed Charles and Annie were missing. The new guests were very demanding and had the staff running around making all these special arrangements just for them. It was a large party, that took over the whole camp except for two tents, fortunately one of the tents not assigned was the one Charles and Annie had been in. If they had assigned it, their luggage might have been discovered earlier, but the new guests would have disturbed everything and all clues would have likely been lost.”

“Why the contradictory stories?” I have to ask.

“Seems the camp owners did not want anyone knowing who was coming in.” Beau explains.

I go back to the next van in line as the pilot talks to the driver and I examine the back. As I close the back door on this van, I give the thumbs up to the pilot and glance around to see what Yuri and the Secretary are doing. They are standing down the line, next to the last vehicle and just talking. Not looking at the van, not watching to see if more vehicles are approaching. Just talking.

After I step out of the way, the next van comes up to the pilot who asks the driver the standard question. 'Have you seen two Americans?' I watch as the driver shakes his head and shrugs at the same time. That must be somehow connected. The shake of the head and shoulder shrug. Seems every driver reacts exactly the same way.

The back door is locked, I call to the pilot, "I need a key. To open the door."

"Driver says he cannot let you open it," the pilot calls back.

"Why not?" I respond, annoyed now. I am not expecting to find anything pertaining to the missing couple here. And this driver seems to not be worried about our inspection. More like he has been told not to do something and therefore he cannot.

The pilot apparently explains that the crazy Americans will kill him if he does not open the back door and reluctantly the driver gets out and comes up beside me. The driver looks at me, looks at the handgun on my belt and apparently decides the pilot is not kidding. He unlocks the door and steps back, waiting to see what I do, ready to relock it as soon as I have done whatever it is I am about to do.

I swing the door open and look inside. Cases fill the back of this van. Expensive cases, that are apparently carrying something delicate or fragile. I lean in to the most accessible and flip open the latches before opening the top. I am not expecting to find an expensive video camera. I thought since the advent of the cell camera that no one used this kind of equipment anymore. I close the top of this case and look into the next. Lights… like for a studio where they are doing a television show or something. A commercial maybe? The next case is the boom microphone. This is professional grade equipment being shipped in an unmarked van. There are several more cases, which I infer are more equipment for high quality video production.

As I come around the corner of the van, I see Yuri and the Secretary walking back towards us. I go around to the pilot, leaving the door open, so the driver will not just take off. "Ask him where he is going with his cargo?"

The driver hands the pilot a slip of paper. The pilot reads it and hands it back. "An address in Hargeisa," he reports to me.

"Do you know it?" I respond without thinking.

The pilot shakes his head.

"Where did he pick up this equipment?" I ask and listen as the question is relayed. Angelica and Yuri join us now.

"Comoros Street," the pilot responds.

"Yeka Kifle Ketema?" Yuri instantly responds. "That's Addis Ababa."

"Do you know it?" I ask surprised.

Yuri looks at Angelica before he responds, apparently choosing his words cautiously. "Yes. I used to work there."

"That's not the American Embassy," I respond having just been.

"No, it's not," Yuri is looking at Angelica who apparently recognizes the address as well. Yuri walks around to the back door of the van, looks inside the first case, sees the camera, "This is a Japanese standard broadcast production camera."

He moves some of the cases around and brings forward the largest of the cases. He opens it and looks inside. "Russian satellite uplink," he pronounces. "I have used this kind before."

"You did remote broadcasts?" I have to ask, as there was nothing he has said that would lead me to believe he has.

"Before…" Yuri responds, clearly unsettled by what he is looking at. "Where is this going?"

"Hargeisa," the pilot responds. "The driver does not know what the address is."

"Why is he coming from Berbera, if he picked up this equipment in Addis Ababa?" This route does not make sense if it pertains to the kidnapping, yet I think it must.

The pilot returns to the driver, asks the question and calls back to us, "His passenger is the camera man. He picked him up in Berbera on the way."

"Cameraman…" the Secretary repeats. "Russia is broadcasting an event in Hargeisa. Is this a coincidence?"

We all go to the cab of the truck. The first thing I notice is the passenger is clearly not Somali. Yuri asks him a question in Russian and gets an answer. I watch as Yuri and the Secretary exchange looks.

Angelica looks at me, "We need to take the driver and cameraman into custody… use the helicopter as a holding point. You need to question them, particularly the cameraman. What does he know about the event? Who will be there? That kind of thing."

The pilot talks to the driver. Yuri apparently has the same conversation with the cameraman. I follow them to the helicopter and climb in after they are inside. I slide the door closed and ask the pilot to ask the first question.

CHAPTER FORTY-SEVEN:

ANGELICA MYERS

The helicopter lifts off just before the message comes in on the display we installed in the back where I am sitting. Agent Plainsman is sitting up front with the pilot, but can hear everything through his earphones. We are also recording the message.

"We have your daughter and her husband…" The image of a man forms on the screen. He looks just like all the men, driving vans and trucks we had stopped. The accents are British English, but not heavy. As if he has watched US television somewhere along the way. As if he is trying to sound more like us. The clothes tell me very little. What I have seen on almost every Somali, Ethiopian and Kenyan man I have seen on this trip. Blue jeans and a patterned shirt or t-shirt with a message of contempt for something that is a symbol of modern society. Little do those who wear such shirts realize that someone is making money on their disdain for making money. And a heavy gold chain around his neck.

"I know…" is my simple response. Do not want to sound too confident, but also not submissive to the demands we are about to receive.

"Do you know who we are?" Eskander, the ship's captain, asks suddenly worried that my response is not what he expects.

"You are pirates…" I again respond simply.

"If I were still a pirate there would be no need for us to talk," Eskander falls back into his victimhood.

"What does your profession have to do with my daughter?" I push him now.

"The people here are dying…" Eskander begins, but I interrupt him.

"People are dying all over the world. It is not just in Ethiopia and Somalia where people struggle to live." I try to reframe his argument.

"You must withdraw your navy from the Horn of Africa and the Sea of Aden." Eskander demands.

"That is not possible… we have treaty obligations… agreements with your government and those of the other countries in this region that require our naval presence."

Eskander fires off a weapon to get my attention. "Do not tell me what you cannot do, tell me only when your navy will withdraw."

I do not respond to him, watch his frustration grow.

"Tell me when!" Eskander shouts at me again.

I do not respond.

"Why do you wish for your daughter and her husband to die?" He now plays the card I have been expecting all along.

"Why do you wish to die in a futile effort to reopen the sea lanes to piracy?" I respond.

"Capturing ships is the only opportunity for many people here to have food, water and clothing. To have hope for the future. When your navy began to shut down our efforts, many people died." Eskander wants to know that I understand the effects of my actions in this part of the world.

"Piracy was never a means of long-term security. For every ship you hijack, someone has to pay. And when that payment comes from insurance, then that is built into the cost of everything someone buys that was on that ship. It is simply unsustainable."

"I am not asking for a lecture…" Eskander is not going to listen any more. "When are you going to withdraw your navy? Because your daughter will not be released one day earlier. Nor will she be released unless I have the assurance of your president that this withdrawal will be permanent."

"A president cannot bind a future president or congress…" I point out.

"You sign treaties... they continue…"

"Who would we sign this treaty with? You?" I try to make him understand he simply has no idea what he is asking for. "And even if we signed such a treaty, we would then be in violation of treaties with every other nation in this region."

"That is not my problem… I must find a way to feed my family… the families of my crew, the people who live in my country. And all the countries here. Only ship hijacking gives us enough…"

"Have you really thought this through?" I challenge him again.

"Of course… the navy leaves we resume what we did before."

I shake my head, although I am not sure he sees it. "If our navy leaves, then the shipping will re-route… to another way to their markets. No ships will pass by the Horn of Africa, through the Sea of Aden. Then you will have no one to blame but yourselves. You will have driven the ships away. Your greed and desire to have something for nothing. If you want to make money that lasts, you need to create businesses that deliver products or services others wish to buy… not a service one is coerced to pay for."

"No lectures… you do not understand… we are desperate…" Eskander shouts again as if that is the only way he can get my attention.

"And you will kill my daughter, even though all that will do is ensure your death, that of your crew and their families, and that nothing will change."

Eskander shoots off several more rounds, "People are dying…"

"You said," I respond, enraging him. "Your wife…" I throw out there to see how he responds.

"Dead… because of no rain," he responds less hostile.

"Your mother and father…" I push further.

"Also dead because of no rain." His voice becomes sad now.

"And you became a pirate…"

"Because of no rain…" he agrees with my logic. "If crops do not grow, if animals die, if there is no work to buy what you cannot grow or raise… you die."

"How many do you know who have died?" I keep him talking, thinking about his situation and not Annie and Charles.

"Too many… everyone I grew up with in my family, where I lived."

"And that is why you came to Somalia? To be a pirate… because they were no longer starving and dying of dehydration?" I try to bring him to why he made this choice.

"What do you know of any of this? In America you do not die because of lack of rain…"

"Some people do…" I try to get him to realize the world is not how he sees it from his vantage point in Somalia.

"Liar. Americans are rich…" Eskander shakes his head.

"So are the Russians and the Chinese and even the Iranians, who come here and tell you lies about America. But some Russians and Chinese and Iranians die every year from drought, and famine and poverty. Just as here. Maybe not as many, but still too many."

"The Russians, Chinese and Iranians… they try to help…"

"How? They give you fast boats to intercept the container and oil ships that pass by? America gives your government millions of dollars every year… we send the Red Cross and others to help with food and water…"

"But not enough…" Eskander shouts again.

"But why is it just America that must save you, when Russia sells you weapons to fight each other, and China sells you railroads in exchange for minerals they need to manufacture things they sell, and the Iranians train you to fight so you will never know peace?"

"That is not true."

"A Russian man told you my daughter was going to be in the camp in Kenya, did he not?"

"Russia is our friend," Eskander shoots back. "They gave me a new boat."

"To disrupt shipping, and in return for demanding we pull our navy back so their navy can come in and operate out of your ports." I explain what he is not seeing.

"No…"

"And where is your Russian friend now that you are about to die for kidnapping my daughter? Is he going to stop us from killing you? Stop us from withdrawing aid because Somalia is no longer safe for Americans? More Somali and Ethiopians will die because you let yourself be tricked by your Russian friend. He used you and you are now going to suffer the consequences."

CHAPTER FORTY-EIGHT:

AGENT DAKOTA PLAINSMAN

As the Secretary cuts off the transmission the pilot touches down and I am ripping the headset off, opening my door, jumping down and reaching back to open her door. She is confirming the magazine for her M-16 rifle is loaded and shoves it back into latch position as I get the door open for her. She glances up and steps down holding the rifle in the ready position. We advance across the short distance to the warehouse where Yuri delivered the broadcast equipment earlier.

I know my role is to protect the Secretary first and retrieve her daughter and husband second. That is why I am leading the charge into the warehouse. The side door is unlocked and I open it just enough to throw in a smoke grenade. When I hear the explosion, I give it five seconds to spew enough smoke out to obscure the vision of those inside. Then, in I charge with my weapon on full automatic. Two shot bursts are what I have been trained to fire. Just two rounds and stop. Two rounds and stop. Anything more and I am likely to wound or kill the very people I have come to bring home.

Hard to know where I am going since I have not been in this space previously and have not been able to specifically train for it. I am moving towards the bright lights I can see through the smoke as that is where I assume they are. Assume they did not move away from the broadcast area since they are still trying to understand what happened.

Yuri comes into view first. He is standing over Dr. and Mrs. Thompson with a grease gun, at least that is what some call the compact automatic fire weapon he hid in one of the equipment cases. I continue moving towards the lights with the Secretary behind me. A movement to my left and I bring that person into my aim, see a weapon raised towards me and I fire the two-shot burst into his leg, which brings him down almost instantly. Although he fires several shots into the ceiling. He tries to bring his weapon down to shoot at me and that leaves me no choice but to put two more rounds into his shoulder. Wound if possible. Kill only if no other choice.

Another movement to my right. This one was not in the lights. I swing my weapon around but hold on firing until I can positively identify the threat. But I hear a two-shot burst from the direction of Yuri, who must have seen something I could not. That gunman also goes down. Not sure of his condition, but I go to the one I wounded, kick his weapon away, as Yuri apparently checks on the one he took down.

Still two more in here somewhere. The smoke was essential to let us maneuver here, but it makes it harder to identify friends or foe and whether they are hostile or going to surrender. As I am looking around, I hear another two-burst shot come from behind me. The Secretary has seen someone and wounded him. Moving further into the smoke I find the third man down, take the weapon from him as he is holding it next to him in a non-threatening manner. One more. Where is he?

"Don't even consider it…" I hear Yuri's voice over to my right and see the Secretary move over to where her daughter and son-in-law are seated against the wall on the floor. Yuri approaches the last man, but stops short of him. Close enough to gauge his intent without provoking him into a rash defensive move. I am not sure which one he is, wearing a long gold chain. He has his rifle in position to quickly raise and shoot. No wonder Yuri stopped short.

"Are you okay?" I hear the Secretary ask her daughter. I glance over since Yuri is watching the last armed man carefully. The Secretary seems to be checking out her daughter and son-in-law, apparently concludes they do not need immediate attention, and rises to approach the last man standing. She stops a little more than an arm-length from him.

"Who are you?" she asks, although I think she has already figured that out.

"Eskander Bekele, Captain of Sad Roger, sailing from the Port of Berbera, Somalia."

"Sad Roger?" Yuri asks.

"In Somalia, no one is Jolly… Roger."

"A pirate, then…" the Secretary concludes. "And these other men… they are your crew? Also pirates, hoping to feed their families?"

"Who are you?" Eskander Bekele suddenly wonders.

"I'm her mother. Now how would you feel if I had captured your mother and made impossible demands for her release?"

"You are not here…" Eskander is having trouble accepting that the person he was trying to extort is standing in front of him in Somalia with two men who have weapons trained on him.

"I am very much here. And very much going to take pleasure in seeing justice done."

"You will not walk out of here alive…" Eskander threatens, but somehow, I think it is an empty threat. I did not see anything that would give me cause for concern on our way in, and the helicopter pilot is waiting outside, ready to call us out and get us out of here if there is an issue.

"Apparently you were not listening… your friendly Russian is not going to come save you. He got what he wanted out of this little exercise. Deniability. Can say he had no idea you would go to this extent. But at the same time, he has sent the message that our family is not safe. Just as yours is not. The Russian is the one who will want to see you dead, make sure you cannot prove his involvement. The Russian is the one who will ensure your family dies, even though it is the result of his encouragement and enabling actions."

"Why does America hate Russia?" Eskander Bekele asks a question I have never asked myself and from the look on the face of the Secretary, apparently, she has never asked herself that question either.

She formulates an answer, "Why do you hate America?"

"You live without want… you have everything I do not."

"Why does that make you hate us, rather than want to be like us?" she asks.

"In Somalia or Ethiopia, it is not possible to have what you have, to live as you do."

"Why is that?" she pushes him.

"We are a poor country…"

"Because you do not believe in yourselves… you live a life of victimhood. Always the victim of what some other nation does to you. What have you invented that people all over the world need?"

"I do not understand your question," Eskander seems confused.

"Americans invent things… great big things… that people all over the world want. We sell those things or services and that raises the standard of living for everyone."

"Somalia cannot build things…" he offers as an excuse.

"Why not?" She remains adamant.

"Because we do not have money… or people who can make things… we are simple people. Farmers, fishermen… that is who we are."

"All I am saying is you and your countrymen can change that. Look at China. In fifty years, they went from one of the lowest standards of living to one of the highest. Not because someone gave them buckets of money. But because they trained their people to build things. They raised their standard of living. There is no reason you cannot."

"We are not China…" Eskander dismisses the argument.

"So, you would rather steal from the rich to feed the poor, than build a nation that contributes to the world."

"We know who we are…" Eskander responds flatly as he adjusts the weapon in his hands.

"All I am saying is you don't have to be that person," the Secretary glances around at her daughter and son-in-law. "Which one of you is Netsanet?"

The man lying on the ground that the Secretary shot responds to his name. "You may want to tell him that his sister was shot by your friends, but she is recovering from her wounds, because we stepped in to save her."

"My Aunt? You are lying…" Eskander responds more angrily now.

"She told us who you were and gave us insights to figure out how to find you. When your Russian friends discovered she was talking to us, they ambushed her. Tried to kill her."

"They would not harm her." Eskander dismisses the information.

"I am sure they have the same in store for you, to make sure you cannot implicate them."

Eskander thinks about the Secretary's comments. I can see he is getting more and more agitated, but does not seem to know what to do about the situation. "You are trying to convince me what we did was all for nothing. Why?"

"Because it is true. The US Navy will continue to capture pirates from Berbera or any other African ports. Until you decide not to steal from others, you will remain as you are."

Eskander squints at the Secretary, begins to turn his rifle on her. The Secretary finds a knife in her hand that had been up her sleeve, and shoves it into his throat in one quick fluid motion. She turns the blade just once. Turns away as Eskander's eyes roll back and he collapses to the ground.

CHAPTER FORTY-NINE:

ANNIE THOMPSON

This cannot be real. Mom is here. We are in a helicopter flying somewhere. Not another van. My hands are not zip tied, no bag over my head, gag in my mouth. Charles is by my side, holding my hand. Something we have not been able to do, in I do not know how long it has been.

Two men are with us. Two men I do not think I have ever seen before. How did they find us? Why did it take so long? Is this real? I still cannot believe it.

"Where is Dad?" I finally get out. If she is here, he should be too.

"Back in Virginia," Mom responds.

"You can't be here… where are all the generals and guards and drivers and all of the people who go with you everywhere?" I am completely convinced this has to be a day dream. A good one… but still a day dream.

"I wasn't going to be able to find you dragging all of them around with me…" she responds as if it were no big deal. But she is a big deal and does not go anywhere without them.

"How…" I get out the one word, but have trouble completing the thought.

"That would be a longer discussion than we have time for right now," Mom responds.

That reminds me of a question I have been asking myself, "How long has it been? They had hoods on us and kept us in dark rooms…"

"A little more than two weeks…" Mom considers as she looks at me, and shakes her head, apparently surprised she found us at all.

"Two weeks is a long time…" I reflect.

"Longer than you think when you have no idea whether someone you love is safe or even alive…" Mom answers with a strain in her voice I cannot remember hearing before.

The man sitting on Mom's right side interjects, "You have no idea how rough this has been on your mother."

"Excuse me… who are you?"

"Your mother and I were partners a long time ago," he responds and glances at Mom.

"Partners… in the law firm?" I am confused.

"In the CIA…" Mom responds quietly. "Before you were born."

"Why didn't I know you had a partner?" I ask, unhappy to be learning about it this way.

"Read my bio," Mom responds.

"You were like… an assistant director or something…" I am having trouble remembering.

"Afterwards…" is all Mom will say about that.

"You scared her to death," the same man continues. "Next time you decide on a honeymoon, try someplace safer…"

His accent is not one of the languages I have been studying… where is he from? "Are you…"

"Russian… da. But I have been an American for a long time now…"

"And as a Russian you were in the CIA? How does that work?"

"He still is in the CIA…" Mom informs me. "One of our most senior agents."

"Why are you here then? Aren't you supposed to mentor and guide the new agents or something?" This makes even less sense to me.

"I do that too. But when I learned what happened, I had to help your mother do what she does best."

"Kill people?" I respond without thinking, still in shock from that little move of hers and likely in shock from this whole incident.

"That's not the first time…" Mom whispers, or so it seems to me.

"What?" I am even less prepared for this revelation.

"Yuri and I conducted a lot of missions that involved taking out people who threatened our nation and citizens in a variety of ways."

"You were one of them…" I realize.

"As you are planning to become…" she informs me she knows what Charles and I have been doing, even though I never told her.

"You weren't supposed to know that…" I do not know what else to say to her.

"If this hadn't happened, I likely would not have discovered your plans," Mom confides. "Are you still committed to the life, or are you having second thoughts?"

I look at Charles, who is just listening to this whole discussion without saying a word. He returns my look, but I see he is also trying to take this whole change of situation in. Still trying to decide if this is real.

"Been a bit busy the last couple of weeks. Have to let it all kind of sink in. Then Charles and I will have to have a long conversation, I am sure." I reach out and touch Charles' arm. I give him a crooked smile, sure that it will have to wait. He has to get back to the Mayo Clinic when we get back to the US, and it will be a while before we have time together again.

Mom nods and turns away, apparently thinking about something she is not ready to share.

I turn to the man next to Mom, "Why is it Mom never talks about you?"

The man looks at Mom and considers my question, "Probably because we went in different directions. Do you talk about people you knew in kindergarten who went on to different schools?"

"No," I reply. "But partners… that's more than a casual acquaintance…"

Mom looks straight at me, "We live many different lives… each one shapes us, and sometimes the shaping is diametrically opposed to what we were before. We learn to adapt. We change with each life… we discover things about ourselves we never knew. But in the end, the only thing that matters is are we true to ourselves and our family?"

"Meaning did you show up when your daughter is in trouble?" I put out there to see what kind of reaction I get from her.

"That is one test… certainly. But not what I was thinking." Mom is really being opaque today.

"Then explain it to your dense little daughter."

"You are not dense," Mom reacts.

The guy, offers an explanation, "Did your parents encourage and enable you to become who you want to be?"

"Of course," I respond looking at her looking at him.

"On balance… are you happy with who you are?" is his next attempt to answer the question that Mom seems to be struggling with.

"What does it mean to be happy? I don't know how to answer your question." I push back but not really sure why. I probably should just say yes and let it go, but then again, I am a lawyer and not arguing a point would not be like me.

“Are you content to be a lawyer and a potential spy and a wife and maybe mother some day?” Mom inserts.

“That kind of fits the plan you laid out for me, with the exception of the spy part… that was all me.” I poke at her, but am not quite sure why.

“Even knowing that I did the level work you are wanting to go do?” Mom reminds me.

“Maybe I was fascinated by the fact that you succeeded in a very difficult job and look at you now. How do I compete with you? How do I ever achieve more than you have?”

“That is the question, isn’t it?” the partner asks. “Do you need to be more than your mother?”

“Every kid wants their parents to be proud of them. And isn’t achievement part of that pride? That I did more than her?” Why are we threading this needle?

“It is rare that someone who is a high achiever… someone who builds a company, for example, someone who discovers something, someone who becomes president… raises a child who does more than the parent in the same area of expertise. Many times, the child will go on to have great achievements in a wholly different field. But it is rare that a child builds upon those of a parent.” This guy seems to be as philosophical as Mom. Maybe that was why he was successful as her partner, much as Dad is successful because they do not directly compete.

“When we land, do you think I could get something to eat?” I ask.

“I’d like a shower…” Charles finally joins the conversation that is not so philosophical.

CHAPTER FIFTY:
YURI TERESHKOVA

I was not sure what to make of the invitation to lunch. Is Agent Plainsman going to be there as well? Her way of thanking us for doing our job? Will Charles' parents be there too? Could be awkward. Maybe I should just say, no. Sorry… would love to but am on my way out of the country. Only, if she called certain people, she would instantly know I am just ducking her. Lots of ways I would rather spend a few hours. But the location has piqued my interest. Why would she decide to meet at the same restaurant where she told me she was leaving the agency? The last place I had talked with her until she called about Annie going missing… all these years later. I was actually surprised it was still in business as I have not gone back. No reason to. I knew she would not be there. And besides… she had moved on. The problem was I had not. Will this finally be the nudge I have needed all this time? The events that bring home that not only is most of my life not ahead of me, but that I better figure out what it is I want to do and be in the remaining years I have. Not enough time to start over… too many entanglements from all the things I have done. Besides, who needs a broken-down old spy? As Annie alluded to, I am now a mentor and not a doer. I am the collected wisdom of my many missions. The good and the bad. Events I can feel good about and others I am trying desperately to forget. Even Angelica has no idea of the man I have become since that last meal we shared before she left me. She may have seen glimpses in the last few weeks we have been back together. But she really has no idea. And I have to assume she has no interest in learning about those experiences. No interest in having insight into what might have become of her, had she chosen a different path. Would she have been content? I have to believe she would not have been. It was inevitable that we would part ways… she had the good sense to bring it about sooner than later. She likely saved me even more sleepless nights and 'what if' day dreams. I probably should thank her for that. Thank her for making my lonely life easier than it was destined to be had I simply refused to accept her decision. Refused to let her leave when so much was about to happen. Only she could not see that and neither could I.

My sport coat beckons me, hanging from the back of my breakfast nook chair. The only chair I use as I never have company here. I did not expect to need it today, but had just not gotten around to hanging it up in the closet. It is my universal sport coat. I wear it with nearly everything because it has no pattern. Light gray. If I want to look more formal, I put a colored handkerchief in the breast pocket. I have three different colors for different types of occasions. Black for funerals, and I have been to way more than I ever wanted to, for friends who saved my life on more than one occasion. White for weddings, although, there have not been all that many of them recently. Seems only young people get married these days. Since I am no longer young, I seldom get invited, unless it is a new member of my teams. Red is the last color. What I wear if I am going out on a date. That has not happened in a long time either. Probably why I only keep the black one in the left side pocket.

Since I do not have an appropriate color for a thank you lunch, I will not wear one. But this makes me realize I will likely need one for a retirement lunch at some point. Not that I am planning on retiring any time soon, but I never know when someone higher up may think I have contributed all I can. That it is time for someone else to move into my office and run my teams. What color do you wear to your retirement? Since it is a funeral of a different kind, probably should be black… but everyone will think it should be a happy occasion… guess I need to go buy a yellow handkerchief.

As I come out of my apartment building onto the street, I find a limo waiting. I approach and look into the window. Angelica must have anticipated my reluctance and was going to come in and get me if I did not come out voluntarily. I am starting to feel like a wanted man. I knock on the window. She lowers it. "Thought we could chat on the way…"

Her body guard gets out and closes the door behind me before getting into the passenger seat up front. “You look different…” I decide to begin the conversation. “Almost like the Secretary of Defense. I saw her on television the other day.”

“I’m glad you decided to come… I wasn’t sure you would,” Angelica studies me.

“Wouldn’t miss it… how long has it…” I begin, but she cuts me off.

“Twenty-eight years,” she answers without having to think about it. Evidently, she has been revisiting the past as well.

“A lot has changed in that time… mostly you and me,” I respond.

“You’re not as optimistic…” she notes. “I’m not as fit. Too many lunches…”

“We don’t have to do this… just say thanks and I’ll walk back.”

“I never should have left you behind… I just didn’t know how to get you out. It didn’t seem you were going to live…” she begins to rattle off, but I do not want to hear this.

“I forgave you a long time ago,” I look directly into her blue-green eyes. The ones I used to get lost in. The ones I studied for any clues as to how she felt about me.

“I have not forgiven myself…” she surprises me. “When you made it back and I realized I made the wrong call… that was when I knew I had to step aside… let someone, who would make better decisions, go out with you.”

“You’re making much bigger decisions, now…” I point out, not intending to call bullshit, but to understand why she changed her mind about her judgment.

She looks out the window before answering, “What do you think of Annie?”

Her question catches me unprepared, “Reminds me a lot of you at that age…” is the weak answer I give, knowing she will not appreciate it.

“In over her head?” Angelica responds with a shy smile.

“We were all trying to figure out life, and not having the experience to know how reckless we were being.”

“You were never reckless…” she calls me on my description. She was the one who was reckless. My job was to temper her, let her gain the experience she needed, while keeping her alive in the process. Only I was the one who walked into an explosion and should have died.

“Why didn’t you come to the hospital?” I have wondered about this so many times.

“I couldn’t… see you like that. Didn’t want to remember you bandaged and broken.”

“I was that…” I acknowledge.

“You came through it all… to look at you now, I would never have known if I had not been there. Expected you to die. To be just a memory… a good memory. And now… when I needed you, there was never a question about it. As if that last mission had not gone bad and we had just parted as friends.”

“We did part as friends… more than friends, really,” I remind her as I am now hearing the story she has been telling herself these many decades.

“What was it about Howard that you knew… so quickly. It seemed to me that you were married only a few months after you left the agency.”

“It wasn’t long…” she admits. At least that part of her recollection is tracking with mine.

“Where did you meet him?” I cannot help but ask.

"Why is it men always want to know about that? About why I married someone else?"

"I want to understand… what I did wrong."

"You did nothing wrong… we just weren't right for each other, then."

"Meaning Howard enabled you in a way I could not…" I guess.

"I actually met Howard in college. We went our separate ways and when I left the agency and joined the staff of the Senate Intelligence committee, we ran into each other. Howard was staff on the Senate Budget committee. We ended up in a lot of meetings together, found out we had a lot of common interests, and that was that."

We arrive at the restaurant. Angelica looks out at the sign. I look at her. "I don't think I can do this… have lunch with you… after all this time."

"Howard and I married, because I was pregnant with Annie. And even though Howard and I tried, I never got pregnant again. We never tried to find out why, because that could have made us face something neither of us wanted to know."

"As I said… I see a lot of you in her," I decide is the best way to end this discussion.

"If she decides to go through with her plan to go undercover for the Agency…, would you look out for her?"

"Is it possible…" I start to ask, but she interrupts me again, clearly not wanting to answer this question.

"Promise me that you will look out for Annie and Charles…" she almost looks to be close to tears. "I almost lost her. Because of what I have become. She will always be a target because of me. You have to promise me." She reaches out and puts her hand on mine.

"I have never stopped loving you," I admit. "Guess I just need to make a little more room in my heart for Annie."

After stepping out of the limo, I close the door and watch her drive off.

About the Author

dhtreichler is a futurist, technologist and strategist who toured the global garden spots as a defense contractor executive for fifteen years. His assignments covered intelligence, training and battlefield systems integrating state of the art technology to keep Americans safe. His novels grew out of a need to deeply understand how our world is changing, developing scenarios and then populating them with people who must confront how increasingly sophisticated technology is transforming our lives and how men and women establish relationships in a mediated world.

Keep up with all of dhtreichler's latest work and essays at www.dhtreichler.com and www.GlobalVinoSnob.com.

Also by dhtreichler•

Finding Laughter

The Great American Ghost Cat Novel: Phantom Returns

SALVATION

HOME

LEGENDARY

BEING ALIVE

BECOMING

LUCKY

TOMORROW

TIME

LOVE

HAPPINESS

COURAGE

TRUTH

A Cat's Redemption

CHOICES

HOPE

Emergence

THE HONEYMOON

Barely Human

The Ghost in the Machine: a novel

World Without Work

The Great American Cat Novel

My Life as a Frog

Life After

Lucifer

The Tragic Flaw

Succession

The End Game

I Believe in You

Rik's

The Illustrated Bearmas Reader – Ralph's Ordeals

The First Bearmas

Made in the USA
Columbia, SC
15 July 2023

20116729R00157